"What are you afraid of, Sam?"

Nick looked at h████████████████████████Me?"

"Not you." She fel█████████████████████ wasn't a smile. "█████████████████ck, and my things are█████████████████Better to just let it go."

"Better how? Look, Sam. I know you're going back to the road as soon as the house is done, and I have no intention of leaving Widow's Grove, ever again." He lifted his hand from the passenger seat, turning it palm up. "Doesn't that make me safe?"

"Safe?" She stepped away from the car, away from him. "I don't know that word." She turned to trudge up the drive, hearing the throb of the car's engine, and feeling the familiar throb of separateness in her chest.

Dear Reader,

I can't tell you how thrilled I am. This is not only the first book I ever wrote, but my first Harlequin Superromance novel! I'm happy that a story so close to my heart found such a wonderful home.

My husband and I have ridden more than 200,000 miles together on motorcycles, and have had lots of wonderful adventures. Back when I was still riding pillion behind him, one day a dog ran in front of our bike. After a gut-clenching scare, he trotted back the way he had come, and we rode on.

But I started thinking. What if a girl, riding a motorcycle, was in an inescapable accident? Then, what if...

The idea grew into *Her Road Home*.

California's central coast—the setting for my fictional town of Widow's Grove—is one of my favorite places on the planet. I hope that the story gives you the yen to see it. If you do travel there, be sure to drop in and meet Jesse, at the Farm House Café. Then follow the road out of town. Turn in at the beautiful Victorian, sitting perched on a hill like a grande dame, holding dignified court over the tan hills.

Tell Sam and Nick I said, "Hey."

Laura Drake

P.S. I enjoy hearing from readers. Contact me through my website, www.LauraDrakeBooks.com.

Widow's Grove
Book 1 of 2

Her Road
Home

—

Laura Drake

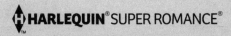

HARLEQUIN® SUPER ROMANCE®

Recycling programs
for this product may
not exist in your area.

ISBN-13: 978-0-373-71870-2

HER ROAD HOME

Copyright © 2013 by Laura Drake

Printed in U.S.A.

ABOUT THE AUTHOR

Laura Drake is a city girl who never grew out of her tomboy ways, or a serious cowboy crush. She writes both women's fiction and romance stories. She rode a hundred thousand miles on the back of her husband's motorcycle, propping a book against him and reading on the boring stretches. Then she learned to ride her own motorcycle, and now owns two—Elvis, a 1985 BMW Mystic, and Sting, a 1999 BMW R1100. She's put a hundred thousand miles of her own on them, riding the back roads, getting to know the small Western towns that are the settings for her books. Laura resides in Southern California, though she aspires to retirement in Texas. She gave up the corporate CFO gig to write full-time. In the remaining waking hours, she's a wife, grandmother and motorcycle chick.

To Mom and Nancy—the unceasing wind beneath.

Anything I'm proud of I do in your name—the blame for the rest is on me.

ACKNOWLEDGMENTS

For Al, who pulled me out of the ditch, dusted me off and set me back on the road...and who's been standing by cheering ever since.

I love you.

For Gary, who taught me what forever love is—and it isn't what I thought....

For his family, who taught me what one can look like when it's done right.

CHAPTER ONE

RUNNING AWAY FROM home at twenty-eight—that's gotta be a first.

Keeping her movements broad and slow, the motorcycle responded to Samantha Crozier's shifting weight. Waterproof gear snugged around her, repelling the worst of the weather. Through the visor of her full-faced helmet, the world flowed past in shades of gray and the water-shattered reflections of passing cars.

Sam's mind moved in broad sweeps, but unlike the bike, it didn't respond well to direction, drifting onto dangerous curves that ended in blind alleys.

I'm not running. Ohio just didn't fit me anymore. Not after Dad died. Besides, how could she become someone new while living in the same house, the same town that made her what she was to begin with?

Sam rolled her shoulders to ease the tension of the all-day rain ride. As much as she'd enjoyed her first glimpse of the Pacific, the wind had edged its icy fingers into her leathers, making her grateful to turn inland at Highway 101 past San Luis Obispo. A road sign announced Widow's Grove in five miles.

An ominous name, but it somehow fit the rainy day. The road slipped between rolling hills covered in a grass the color of a child's sun-bleached hair. Live oaks dotted the slopes, their gnarled branches spreading more horizontal than vertical. The trunks seemed to squat in the soil, as if cringing from an unseen force, their fallen branches a testament to the siege.

New scenery—new life. Who would she become, down the road? She wasn't sure. Except she did know she'd be someone who spoke her mind—who said it right out loud. Someone she could be proud of. The classic road anthem, "Turn the Page," echoed through her mind for the eight zillionth time in its tedious, endless loop.

It's impossible to outrun your thoughts—even on a motorcycle.

Imagining a hot bowl of soup and a warm, dry bed, she crested a hill. *Dammit!* A line of red taillights flashed ahead. *Too close.* Her stiff fingers scrabbled for the brake. Fueled by panic, her muscles clamped down. The front tire locked in a skid.

Instinctively, she released the lever then reapplied it slowly, downshifting to scrub off some speed. The bumper of the blue Honda ahead grew large in her face shield. She shot a glance at the shoulder drop-off. *Too fast.* Her stomach dropped. She'd end up in the steep ditch for sure.

Shit!

She put her feet out to act as outriggers. Her boots slid across the wet pavement, slower, slower. She feathered the brake, applying as much pressure as possible without locking it up.

Just when she *knew* the bike wouldn't stop in time, with a twisting, gut-clenching skid, it did.

Until the car behind slammed into her.

SOUND CAME BACK FIRST. Rain, pattering on the asphalt beside her head. A car engine idling. A man's voice yelling. A siren in the distance, getting closer.

Then the pain hit. With every indrawn breath, a white

blade of agony slashed her side. She flopped like a fish on the wet pavement, trying to suck in air turned liquid.

Small breaths. It wasn't enough. Her lungs screamed for more, but when she gave in, the blade slashed again, and she writhed. *Small breaths.*

Focused on sucking air, the sound of running feet barely registered.

"Check his neck before you take his helmet off," a deep voice ordered.

Although she liked the anonymity her helmet and leathers afforded her, she *hated* that. Why did they always assume the tall one in the biker gear was a *man?* Something tugged at her neck and she jerked, trying to fight off the threat to her meager trickle of air. Only one hand obeyed.

"Does your neck hurt?"

"No," she wheezed.

"Okay. Just relax."

Easy for him to say. He could breathe. More hands slipped beneath her neck, supporting it as they carefully pulled off her helmet. A plastic mask touched her face, covering her mouth. She opened her eyes and tried to twist away.

A baby-faced paramedic hovered over her. "This is going to help you. Don't fight it. Just breathe."

Oxygen hissed into the mask, smelling of metal. The cool ecstasy brushed her lips and her windpipe unlocked, allowing air to her starving lungs.

Greedy, she sucked the oxygen in, then froze as the knife plunged again. She tried once more, shallower. That worked. While she practiced breathing, the paramedic ran his hands over her, feeling for breaks. She shifted, cataloging pain: a tweak in her shoulder, a hot coal burning on the side of her knee and the knife hovering at her ribs, waiting to slice.

Overall, not bad, considering. She blinked rain out of her eyes and pulled at the mask. "Let me up."

The paramedic again appeared over her. He pushed the mask gently back to her face. "What hurts?"

"My ribs." Now that she could breathe, she tried lifting her arms again. An electric current shot to her collarbone. Her lips pulled back from her teeth. "And there's something wrong with my shoulder."

Zzzzip.

She didn't care that she wore only underwear beneath the one-piece leather suit. Or that the rubber-gloved fingers skimming the skin of her sides were wet and cold.

"Unhh," she grunted. He had found the spot. Poked, prodded, then moved on.

"You've broken your collarbone. Your ribs could be cracked, or just bruised. An X-ray will show for sure."

"Just help me up—I have to check out my bike."

"In a minute." He ran his fingers under her hair, at the base of her skull. "What day is it?"

"April fifth. No, wait, the sixth?"

"Where are you?"

"In the mud, on the side of the road, in California. Now can I get up?"

He frowned. "Not unless you sign a release first." He thrust a pen into her working hand and held up a clipboard with a damp form and tiny writing.

Painfully, she signed the form, and with help, sat up. She checked the burning on the outside of her knee—road rash. Blood trickled from a scraped hole in her leathers. Damn. The skin would heal, but those leathers had set her back three hundred bucks. Maybe they could be repaired.

The legally absolved paramedic helped her move slowly to her feet. As she came vertical, her shoulder protested, the heavy throb matching the beat of her heart. At the chunk-clunk sound of a diesel engine, she looked up. A tow truck idled on the road beyond the line of cars—and her bike.

She took a sharp breath, then grimaced. Her heart pinched. Her baby lay sandwiched between the Honda and a silver Mercedes: bars bent, headlight smashed, front fork seals blown. Brake fluid leaked like blood onto the wet road.

"Oh, no." A hollow ache that had nothing to do with her injuries filled her chest. She laid a protective hand over it.

"Back it up." The tow driver in a hooded windbreaker gestured to the driver of the Mercedes.

She limped to her bike. The frame didn't look bent, but the chrome was scratched, the gas tank dented. Deep gouges marred the leather side bags, but they were intact, and her sleeping bag and duffle still sat wrapped in plastic and bungee corded to the passenger seat.

"A Vulcan 750," the tow driver said with an in-church voice. "I haven't seen one of these in forever." He trailed reverent fingers over the one pristine side of her cherry-red gas tank. "What year?"

"'85." Sam glanced to the tow truck, grateful to see it had a flatbed.

A man in a rumpled business suit jogged up and stopped, too close. "I'm so glad you're all right. I came over the hill and you were right there. I tried to stop, but I just slid—"

She took a step back. "I didn't think I was going to stop in time, either."

He leaned in. "Here's my cell number and my insurance information." He handed her a business card with writing on the back. "Do you live around here? Let me drive you home. Or do you need a room for the night?"

Her eyes skittered away. "I'm just passing through. I'm fine. I don't need your help."

The man's face showed shock at the harshness of her voice. He looked her over, then shrugged and walked away. She turned to the tow driver's raised eyebrow and curious look. Heat pounded up her neck to flood her face.

Well, screw him, too.

The EMT stepped in front of her. "Look, I either have to take you to the hospital, or you have to sign another waiver."

"I think my ribs are just bruised." If she kept her breaths shallow, the pain only throbbed in cadence with the lugging truck engine. But the collarbone was another story. No longer distracted by the damage to her bike, the pain from her own damage cranked up.

"You really should let me take you in. Do you feel dizzy? Weak?"

"Not dizzy. I'm sure the weakness is from the adrenaline hangover. I've got to see to my bike, then find someplace to stay."

The tow driver said, "You go ahead to the hospital. I'll get her on the truck." When Sam opened her mouth to protest, he held up his hands. "I'll be careful, I promise."

He looked at the bike, then back at her. "We mostly work on foreign cars. But I'm a bike mechanic, and take a few in on the side. If you'd like, I can try to track down parts for you."

The sign on the tow truck's passenger door read Pinelli's Repair and Tow.

"Or I can haul her wherever you'd like. Just let me know."

She looked him over. Tall as she, with dark hair that was combed back on the sides and curling onto his forehead. He had a classic '50s bad-boy look. A cigarette pack would look right, rolled in the sleeve of the white uniform shirt peeking from beneath his windbreaker.

She remembered his light touch running over the gas tank as if it were a rare piece of art. "Are you in Widow's Grove?"

"Yep. Just off Main, near downtown." He tucked the clipboard under his arm, reached into a pocket, and handed her a business card. His open smile told her he knew he was being judged. He put out his hand. "Nick Pinelli."

With only a slight hesitation, she shook it with her left hand. "Samantha Crozier."

He noticed her wince. "You're lucky you were ejected."

She shuddered, imagining her legs taking the blow the bike had taken. "My body may not agree, but I'm with you."

Man, this is going to be a hassle. But the pain was already wearing her down, and she didn't want to imagine what the night would be like without painkillers. "Would you grab my stuff out of the saddlebags?" At his nod, she followed the paramedic to the back of the ambulance.

AT THE EMERGENCY ROOM, the paperwork took longer than the examination. X-rays showed a clean break in the collarbone, but luckily, the ribs were only bruised, albeit badly. By the time she walked out to the taxi they'd called for her, the drizzle had thinned to a fine mist.

As she eased in, the cab cocooned her in warmth and the smells of oily rags and old heater. She put her scratched helmet and bag of essentials on the seat, then snapped herself into the seat belt, ducking under the harness to avoid having it touch her shoulder.

The cabbie settled into the driver's seat, closed the door, and dropped the clipboard into a holder on the dash. He checked his mirror, waiting for a break in traffic. "Where do you want me to drop you?"

"Can you recommend a hotel in Widow's Grove?" She thumbed open the bottle of pills and, after reading the label, popped two and dry swallowed them.

He looked over his shoulder, then back to the mirror. "Are you looking for a room, or a bed-and-breakfast for a king's ransom?"

She smiled for the first time in what seemed like days. "Do I look like a B-and-B kind of girl to you?"

He shot her an assessing glance. "I've got just the place."

They rode two miles to the turnoff in silence, then slowed at the main street of town. The view made her forget the pain.

Wow. This is how to treat cottage architecture with respect.

Neat Victorian facades lined both sides of the street. She recognized Gothic Revival and Queen Anne styles, among others. Each house sported gingerbread scrollwork, and intricate spandrels above porches displayed traditional strong colors: green, maroon, yellow, or blue.

Sam looked around as they drove through downtown, wishing she had access to her camera. On the right, they passed a yellow, single-story adobe building with leggy wildflowers in the yard. The sign over the door said Santa Inez County Grange Building. From its look, she thought it probably housed the county library.

They idled at a four-way stop where a tall flagpole graced the center of the intersection. She couldn't read the weathered bronze plaque on the concrete base, but imagined it stood in memory of the founding of the town, or of its brave departed soldiers.

She glanced up the cross street lined with beautiful bed-and-breakfast hotels. Although the architecture had a Victorian flavor, they were spanking new. It reminded her of Main Street in Disneyland, everything so perfect and "in period" that it flirted with parody.

Nestled between them were antiques stores, art galleries and souvenir shops. The rain-drenched streets were deserted. They rolled through the intersection, past an empty coffee shop. White wrought iron tables dotted the patio, and a flock of small sparrows, looking as bedraggled as she felt, took shelter under the bright umbrellas. The entire town seemed like a carnival after hours—without the crowds it seemed pointless and lonely.

A half mile farther, the cab pulled in a graveled drive just past a sign for Raven's Rest, a cluster of tiny wooden cabins, their heyday probably dating to the '60s. Huge pines hovered over them, branches resting on moss-covered roofs. Each cabin had a small porch with a rusting metal chair that had once been white.

The driver glanced at her in the rearview mirror. "It doesn't look like much, but it's clean and safe."

"No, this is good." She unbuckled the belt, and bent carefully to retrieve her saddlebags.

She paid the driver from her dwindling wad of bills. "Can you tell me how far I am from Pinelli's Repair?

"It's less than a mile from here. Just turn left at Hollister. Nick's is a block down."

"Thanks."

The taxi backed out, then pulled onto the road. The rain began again, this time more of a cold, soaking mist. The office seemed a distant island in a vast sea of wet gravel. She almost sighed, but caught herself in time. She trudged, helmet and suitcase banging her leg, the pain in her ribs and shoulder pounding.

A buzzer sounded as she opened the creaking door and squeezed into a tiny office. Grumbling emanated from the recesses of the cabin, something to do with idiots out in bad weather. The curtain behind the desk whisked aside, and Sam faced…well, the first thing that came to mind was…a troll.

Old and stooped, the man had scraggly gray hair pulled into a messy ponytail. He wore a misshapen moth-eaten cardigan over a white shirt tinged yellow. A pair of Marine spit-shined wing tips peeked from under sagging pants at least a size too large. It took Sam several seconds to make out his words, as he was in need of an entire set of teeth.

"Lordy, whaddya have here?"

She could've asked the same question. "I'm looking for a room for the night."

"Well, you're in luck, missy. I have one left." Faded blue

eyes twinkled beneath grizzled eyebrows. "Forty-five dollars a night. No wild parties, no men and no room service."

Sam barked a surprised laugh, then winced. Reaching for her credit card, she said, "And here I had my heart set on champagne and cabana boys."

He turned the register for her to sign. "You look a bit like a drowned rat, but I guess you'll do."

"Do you know where I can get something to eat nearby?"

"The Farm House Café, just up the street. Not fancy, but good home cooking." He pushed the key across the desk. "You can have our executive suite."

"The Jacuzzi's fired up, right?" She opened the door, and his laughter followed her into the drizzle.

Luckily, he'd put her in a cabin close to the office. She put down her stuff and unlocked the door. A frayed chenille spread covered the swaybacked iron bed, and an old-fashioned radiator squatted under the window. Inside, she dropped the bags and crossed to the tiny bathroom. The pitted stainless steel hardware gleamed in the stark light of a bare lightbulb.

Sam turned the shower on full force and gingerly peeled off the sling and her damp clothes while waiting for the water to heat. She glanced into the mirror, flecked with black spots, and winced. A lump and an angry red impression of the bike's handlebar stretched from just below her sternum to her side. A purple goose egg rode her left collarbone. Damn. That was going to hurt for real tomorrow. She stepped into the hot shower, letting the stinging spray do its magic on her aching body.

Oh, heaven. Now if only the leprechaun at the front desk would just grant me room service...

Ten minutes later, when her body had stopped screaming demands and her bones felt soft and liquid, she stepped out of the shower. She wrapped the thin hotel towel around herself and walked the few steps to the bed.

She was hungry, but knew she was in no shape to walk anywhere tonight.

Lifting the covers, she gently burrowed in, shivering at the chilled touch of fresh sheets. She carefully rolled onto her uninjured side, creating a comfortable nest.

It looked like she'd be here awhile, and that suited her fine. The siren call of the open road had pulled her this far, but her travel account had reached warning levels. She'd need to find a job, but she was too tired to think about that now.

Her body relaxed and her exhausted brain drifted to the refrains of her road song and the sound of rain, dripping from the pines onto the roof.

Maybe this time she'd gone far enough, fast enough, to outrun her own guilty shadow. She sure hoped so, because she'd flat run out. Run out of time. Run out of money. And she'd run out of land to feed her restless front tire.

CHAPTER TWO

SAM JERKED AWAKE and in her panic, forgot. The ninja dagger plunged. She froze, panting in shallow rabbit breaths. Her heart slammed her ribs, which set them to throbbing.

Morning light slanted onto the bed through the white curtains. The nightmare seemed to drift on the dust motes. In the dream the cellar walls had transitioned to dirt. The rough cave opening had been only a darker shadow. Something had waited. Something that hammered her with soul-withering terror.

It's not real. It is not real. She knew the mantra would calm her, if she kept at it long enough.

Her nightmares weren't normal. She knew that. They washed her nights in an ugliness that lingered, the residue clinging to the inside of her skull. It leached out, leaving greasy stains on each new day.

When her lungs no longer begged for oxygen, she tried to roll onto her back and reach for the amber plastic pill bottle. *Stop it, stop it, stop it!* Her ribs' painful response was only the high soprano in the operatic chorus of her body's pain. Waiting until the wailing quieted to a whimper, she tried again. Slowly. That worked better. She swallowed the pills, grateful for the little white dots that promised relief.

Relaxing onto the pillow, she panted, waiting for the medicine to kick in. She glanced at the bedside alarm clock and did a double take. She hadn't slept until nine o'clock in years.

Her mind worried at the edges of the dream, like a tongue

on a broken tooth. But after a few minutes, her relentless antsiness kicked in; so long a part of her, it had melded to the myelin sheath covering her nerves. She moved, so gently, so slowly, that her medicine-lulled body only creaked. Easing herself to a sitting position, she slipped her forearm into the sling, and buckled it. She felt like the Tin Man, left out in the rain.

"Where is Dorothy, with that damn oilcan?"

She ran her fingers gently over the bruise on her chest. It felt swollen. She lifted her hand to the lump on her collarbone, and winced at her own touch. She had broken a collarbone before, thanks to a fall from a ladder; she knew a sling, Motrin, painkillers and time were the only cures.

Sam squinted through the worn, lacy curtains to the sunsplashed gravel parking lot. Evergreen boughs danced on the wind. Leaning over, she eased the window open a crack. A pine-scented breeze as clean as innocence and welcome as absolution swirled in, cooling her sweaty face.

"It's a physical impossibility to be in a bad mood on such a gorgeous morning." With hope that saying it would make it so, she stood and shuffled like an invalid to the bathroom.

After spending too much time dressing, she grabbed her helmet on the way out the door. It would be useless to her for a while; it belonged with the bike. She stepped out into the perfect day and pulled the door closed behind her. Yesterday's rain clouds had scrubbed the sky to Alice blue, leaving only a few puffy white ones behind. The sun flashed off quartz in the gravel, and in a pasture across the lot, the breeze led the live oats in a stadium wave.

She set off for the road. Between the distraction of the day and the sun on her shoulders, Sam's body eventually warmed up, walking fast enough to outpace a one-legged octogenarian. After a while, she came upon a bright red farmhouse on the left, a sign proclaiming it the Farm House Café that the old man had recommended.

Her belly sounded a rumbling timpani.

"Hang in there. Food's coming." Pushing the glass door to the café open, she was hit by the chatter of conversation, dishes clattering and the heavenly smell of bacon.

A blonde wielding a tray of dirty plates swished by. "Sit anywhere, honey. I'll be right with you." She had a tiny, pretty face, big hair piled in a riot of curls and perfect red fingernails. The white waitress uniform fit her busty stature as if she'd been dipped in it.

Sam eased herself onto a stool at the linoleum-covered bar that stretched the length of the room. Pretending to look at the menu, she studied the homey atmosphere. Customers filled the red vinyl booths, everyone talking at once. Small farm implements hung on the wall. Some of them, she could actually identify: a hand plow, butter churn, an oxen yoke. An old potbellied stove squatted in the back corner on a wood floor worn silver-gray with use.

The waitress appeared on the other side of the counter, coffee carafe in hand. "Sorry to make you wait, sweetie, this place goes nuts this time of day." Her head cocked. "You're not from around here, are you?"

"Nope, just passing through. This is a great place. Warm and cozy."

"Why, thank you, sweetheart. We're not fancy like some of those new places, but we try. I'm Jesse Jurgen, and that huge hunk of man behind me is my husband, Carl." Sam looked through the serving window. A blond giant filled it, looking like a modern-day Norse god, his white T-shirt riding high on heavily muscled biceps. He waved a spatula in greeting.

"What can I get you, sugar?"

"That bacon smells wonderful. Could I get some scrambled eggs and sourdough toast to go with it?"

"Sure you can. You want coffee?"

"You bet." Sam closed the menu. "What's with all the bed-and-breakfast places downtown? They look new."

"Oh, they're new, all right." The blonde pulled a coffee cup from under the counter and poured. "This has been ranch country for a hundred years, until some smart guy discovered the land hereabouts was perfect for growing grapes. Now we've got vineyards coming out our ears. Don't get me wrong, I've been known to sidle up to a nice glass of Zin now and again, but—"

The man a few seats down the bar broke in. "Oh, come on, Jesse. You can't complain about the business all those tourists have brought in."

"I'm not complaining, Hank, God knows. But this used to be such a sleepy town. You should see this place on a summer weekend now. The tourists swarm like termites."

"I can see why." Sam sipped her coffee.

"Can you believe there's a limousine service in town that will drive people to wine tastings? What will they think of next?" Jesse grabbed the coffeepot and swished around the bar. "I'm coming, Oscar. Hold your water."

"CaliFornication," said the older man on Sam's right.

"Sorry?"

"CaliFornication. You know, like the song. It's when you take a beautiful state and screw it up with too many people, too many houses, too many—"

"Don't listen to Don. He's just a bitter old man." A man on Sam's left leaned in. "This is God's country."

"At least so far." Jesse had returned and put a full plate in front of Sam. She stared at the sling, then the helmet. "Did you ride a motorcycle here?"

"Well, I tried to." Sam grimaced, then took a bite of fluffy egg.

Sam could see puzzle pieces fall into place and the woman's carmine lips opened. "You're the motorcycle chick. The one who got hit last night!"

Sam had heard of small-town jungle drums, but had never been the source of their pounding before. "Yep, that's me. Motorcycle chick."

"I mean that with respect. I'd love to ride myself, but I'm a hazard on the road as it is." She frowned down at Sam. "Are you sure you're all right? Shouldn't you be in the hospital?"

"Been there. Done with that." Sam stuck her knife in a mason jar of what looked like homemade strawberry preserves and slathered it on her toast. "I'll be fine."

The woman looked unconvinced, but asked, "Where are you coming from, honey?"

"Ohio, originally."

The blonde's brown penciled-on eyebrows scrunched. "You mean you rode a motorcycle out here from Ohio? All by yourself? Lord, weren't you scared? How long have you been traveling?"

Sam began to recognize that if you wanted to talk with Jesse, rather than listen, it would require using large amounts of duct tape. "I left Colorado two months ago, but it's been six years since I left where I grew up in Ohio. People have been great, for the most part, and I've seen more beautiful country than I knew existed."

"Well, I'm impressed. I'd never have the guts to do something like that."

Sam's mind skipped to the day ahead. Once she'd checked on the bike and picked up a rental car, she planned to cruise around and look for a job. "Can you tell me which direction is best to see some of the country?"

Eavesdropping diners tossed out suggestions.

"Zaca Station Road is real pretty."

"Yeah, but Foxen Canyon is better. The wineries are beautiful."

"They just repaved Calle Bonita."

As a heated discussion broke out, Jesse leaned over. "Oh, just head out of town and take any old road. It'll wind around and give you a pretty good lay of the land."

As Sam ate, the café got busier. Overall-clad farmers, who clearly owned their booths, spoke of yesterday's rain. A gaggle of teenagers bolted food while chatting loudly.

Sam ate her last bite of toast, grabbed her helmet and scouted the counter for her bill. Not seeing one, she walked to the cash register to pay for her meal.

Jesse stood behind the register. "That'll be eight twenty-three."

"I looked for the bill, but—"

"Oh, we don't mess with those things here." Jesse hit a button, and the drawer popped open.

"But how do you know how much to charge?" She handed over a ten.

"I just figure it in my head, silly."

"Tax and all?" Sam glanced at the dining area. "And you remember what everyone ordered, and what it costs?" There must have been twenty-five people here, and it had been more crowded when she came in. There was more to this blonde than big hair.

The waitress smiled. "That's easy. It's not like riding a motorcycle across country. Now, that's hard."

Shaking her head, Sam tottered out the door to track down her motorcycle.

"You need twenty-two foot-pounds at eighty degrees, then eighty degrees again." Nick leaned on the torque wrench, demonstrating. "Now, you—"

Next to him, his mechanic, Tom, made a low, quiet whistle through his teeth. Nick looked across the engine of the BMW M-Class to the windowed wall of his reception area.

The blonde biker stood checking out his photo collection, one hand in the back pocket of her jeans, the other in a sling. He couldn't blame Tom; she was a bombshell. Six feet tall, mostly legs. Lean, but the snug T-shirt didn't hide her long, capable biceps. Or the nice set of headlights.

He straightened, pulled a rag out of his back pocket and wiped his hands. Her features suggested innocence, but her full lower lip and the woman's awareness in her green eyes would set a man's pants on fire. Unforgettable. He sighed. Nick had no time for a come-n-go biker chick, even a stunning one.

It wasn't like he'd never asked a woman out before. Just not in recent memory. The business came first. *Yeah, but the business is secure, and growing. That excuse isn't going to work forever.*

When he'd been in L.A., getting his mechanic's license, he'd torn through the ranks of local single women. He'd had a high time. But Nick was still recovering from the fall off those dizzying heights. Since he'd come home to stay, things were more complicated.

In high school, good girls didn't date hand-me-down guys like him. Oh, sure, there was curiosity in their aloof glances, but between his grease-stained fingernails, out of fashion clothes and their daddies' admonishments, a glance was all he got.

To be fair, he couldn't blame them. After his life exploded, he'd done his damnedest to live down to those low expectations.

Besides, women tended to shy from men with murder in their family tree.

"Man, it's tough to be the boss." Tom jerked on the torque wrench.

"Watch what you're doing, or you're gonna strip that head." Nick stepped around the car and walked to the office.

"How are the ribs?"

Her look shifted as he approached, going from zero to red-line the closer he got. Realizing his gaze had wandered, Nick parked his eyes on her face. "You like my bikes?"

She turned back to his collection of glossy supersport photos. "Do you race?"

"No, those are bikes I wrenched on. It's kind of a hobby of mine." He crossed to the computer at the counter. "Riding never interested me. I just love trying to pull one more ounce of horsepower out of those sweet, compact engines." He jiggled the mouse to wake the screen. "I found you a new headlight and some fork seals online, but I wanted your okay to order them. After all, you were a captive customer last night. My rates are comparable with others in the area, but if you want to check around…"

Her studied gaze raked the reception area as she crossed the room and placed her beat-up helmet gently on the glass display counter. "You'd need to understand, I want only orig-inal parts used."

He nodded.

"I'd love for it to be done quickly, but I understand that the parts may be hard to find. I won't be here long, so I may need to leave it with you."

He nodded again.

"I'll be calling you, for weekly updates."

"Or I can call you."

Seconds ticked by as she studied his face. "I'll trust you."

Something about the tilt of her head told him she hadn't trusted him, before she walked into the shop.

"I'll take good care of your baby, you don't have to worry."

"I'm glad to know it. Now, do you know where I can rent a car?"

"Nope. But I can loan you one."

SAM FOLLOWED NICK around the outside of the shop to a ram-shackle one-car garage. Leafy vines climbed the warped, weathered walls as Mother Nature reclaimed her territory. "My insurance will cover a weekly rental," Sam said.

The old, spring coil door squealed as he lifted it. He turned to her and gestured to the car parked inside.

Sunlight filtering through the gaps in the boards shone off bright yellow paint. And green paint. And neon-orange glow paint. The...thing consumed the entire floor space.

"You couldn't pay me enough to rent this." There was a note of pride in his voice.

"No shit," she whispered.

He jogged around, opened the driver's door, started the engine and rolled the convertible monstrosity into the yard. She recognized the old Volkswagen Thing; a cross between a dune buggy, military vehicle and a Beetle—and none of those models should have been allowed to breed.

If that weren't enough, the eye-popping yellow paint was festooned with cartoon flowers, peace signs and rainbows in garish colors. It looked like the artist had dropped acid.

He shut down the engine and sat with a smug smile, clearly awaiting effusive acclaim.

She gulped, imagining all eyes following her as she drove around town. "I couldn't." Sam believed that your ride was an extension of your personality. Her Vulcan showed one side of her, her Jeep, another. She'd made snap judgments about people based solely on what they drove, and most of the time, they proved correct.

Her? Drive this—abomination? *No, really, I couldn't.*

He hopped out and gently closed the door. "The nearest car rental is Santa Maria, thirty miles that way." He pointed northeast. "So I offer my customers loaners, no charge." He patted the garish fender. "All of them are out right now, but hey, since you trust me with your baby, I'll trust you with mine."

She didn't owe him anything. She opened her mouth to decline, wondering if it would be too rude to ask him for the Yellow Pages to look up another shop.

But he worked on race bikes. She wasn't going to find a more experienced mechanic. She couldn't insult him. He sat there, beaming like a little boy offering her his prettiest marble.

The universe must be trying to keep me humble. Well, she'd just keep her head down and let her hair hide her face. It wasn't like anyone in town knew her, anyway. She swallowed. "Thanks."

CHAPTER THREE

A HALF HOUR LATER, top down, she scuttled through the weekend-busy town. She idled at the four-way stop at its center, feeling like she was sitting in a display window. Naked.

Hunching her shoulders, she peeked from behind her hair curtain. Reactions from the strolling tourists ranged from smiles of recognition to baffled expressions. The distinctive chug-whine of the old VW engine caught even more attention when she accelerated through the intersection. Maybe her bad-boy mechanic could get her bike back to her quick, or another loaner would get returned and she could swap.

Look on the good side. In the meantime, this beats walking.

She took the turnoff at Foxen Canyon, just because she liked the name. The sun warmed her shoulders and the wind tore through her hair. The radio played a perfect road song: Tracy Chapman's "Fast Car."

The road wound between hills in sweeping, perfectly canted curves. *This drive would be great on a motorcycle.* She tapped into the song's rhythm, accelerating on the straights and leaning just a bit into the corners, imagining her bike beneath her. Scenery blurred to slashes of blue, green and gold, rushing past the windscreen. The wind softened the engine's whine and carried the scent of freshly turned soil. Small champagne bubbles of joy rose in her chest to explode in her brain.

Topping a rise, a vineyard stretched ahead, rows precision straight. She passed a tasting room, a low adobe-style building with a broad, shaded porch. The winery was a sure tourist magnet. It looked like a large home, owned by people who would welcome visitors as family.

She let the road lead her deeper into the hills. Farmhouses appeared around a few bends, but for the most part, the hills stood as wild and empty as the first man who found them.

A few miles farther, she came out of the trees and saw it.

An old house, deserted and in sad disrepair, perched atop a hill overgrown with wild oats. Slowing, she pulled into the weed-choked gravel drive. The Victorian rose two stories, with a deep shaded porch dressed in broken gingerbread trim. A rounded gable graced the right front corner, the scalloped wood siding was worn and broken in places. Crossing the yard, Sam stumbled over a real estate agent's sign buried in the tall, straw-colored grass.

She circled the building and spied an old-fashioned garage, which had likely served as a carriage house in a former life. A property line of eucalyptus trees shaded the yard and the breeze blew their dusky scent to her along with the chatter of mockingbirds.

This house had good bones, from what she could see. It would be such a blast to restore the old lady to her glory. She itched to get her tools in her hands—to fix what was wrong here—to create a home out of a wreck.

She came around the corner of the house. The view past the sagging picket fence stopped her cold. Hills dotted with live oaks rolled away to the west like waves on a golden ocean.

Just that fast, she fell in love.

After fumbling with her cell phone, she dialed Homestake Realty, the company listed on the sign.

After setting up an immediate showing, she wandered back to the porch and lowered herself to the sun-warmed steps with a sigh. Leaning against the railing, she closed her eyes.

The heat eased the aches of the accident, and something inside loosened.

I've got to tell Dad. She actually lifted the phone, then, remembering, she let it drop to her lap.

His death hadn't been a shock. He'd battled the cirrhosis a long time. She'd spent countless evenings at the hospital after work, watching the baseball game and sharing the news of her day until he fell asleep. But one restless night, he'd wanted to talk.

"I thank God that you're a good girl, Sammy. I know I can't take credit for that. Hell, you took better care of me than I ever did you." He'd held his hand up to halt her protest. "One thing dying does is make you to take a hard look at things."

"Dad, I don't want to talk about this." She'd looked away.

"You don't have any choice, Sammy. I'm tired, and ready to join your mother. Now shut up a minute." His voice, soft as flannel, blanketed the sting of the words. The fluorescent light above the bed blanched his normally florid face, crumbling her wall of denial. He looked like a talking corpse.

"I can't give you any good advice, Sam. If I'd had any, I'd have made better decisions myself. But one thing I do know. Life is cold. You'll need to build a warm corner for yourself."

He fell silent a moment, fighting pain. She sank onto the mattress beside him to hold his hand.

"Working or not, I always paid two things—the mortgage insurance, and my life insurance, so you could have seed money to start your own business. It's time to make your own dreams, Sam, and let me go so I can stop mourning mine."

He'd put her hand aside and pushed himself up in bed. "Now, turn on the dang game, we're missing the first inning." He dashed his hand across his eyes, and they'd pretended to get absorbed in a game neither one cared about.

Three weeks later, he was dead.

Funny how she forgot that sometimes.

I miss you, Dad.

She'd drifted into a light doze when the sound of a car engine laboring up the hill roused her.

A petite blonde woman in an immaculate peach business suit and high heels alit from a new Cadillac sedan. From the looks, Homestake Realty did well. Sam glanced down at her T-shirt, jeans and motorcycle boots.

This should be interesting.

"You called about the property? I'm Honey Conklin, Homestake Realty." She watched her footing as she navigated the yard in a vain attempt to keep her heels from sinking in. When she'd tottered close enough, the woman extended a hand with bones as thin and delicate as a bird's.

Sam shook with her left hand. "Samantha Crozier. Thanks for coming on such short notice."

Honey stepped onto the porch, holding out her designer handbag as ballast, taking care that the heels of her pumps didn't stick in the cracks.

"This is a lovely old home. One of our founding families built it in 1902. It sits on four acres of land, and you can see, it has a beautiful view." She halted the pitch at the sagging screen door to search a full ring for the correct key.

When she opened the door, the house sighed the past into Sam's face with the unique smell of sunlight, plaster dust, and old wood that was inherent in old houses. Remembering her ribs, she only took small breaths of the rare perfume as she stepped over the threshold. A staircase on her right ascended a few steps, turned at a landing and continued upward. A tall, slim etched glass window let in as much sun as the dirt would allow.

Honey led her to the left, through glass-paned double doors into a small parlor with tall windows overlooking the front porch. She prattled on, reciting the home's selling points.

Blueprints unfolding in her head, Sam tuned her out, having assessed the retail market from the picturesque town.

They proceeded to the rear of the house. On the left, in a large formal dining room, a water-stained ceiling sagged in places. Windows, with a large fieldstone fireplace between them, opened onto the covered side porch.

A small door across the hall revealed a cubbyhole area under the stairs, saved from gloom by a round, beveled-glass window. The dog-trot hallway ended in a large, dark country kitchen. The green linoleum floor was worn through in places, the old-fashioned porcelain sink chipped and badly stained. A narrow opening beside the back door led to a laundry room, where the ceiling had collapsed entirely.

Sam interrupted the woman's chirping sales pitch. "Could I see the upstairs?"

Honey gave her a blank look, then recovered and pasted on her best sales smile. "Of course."

Sam could almost hear her thoughts. *I'm probably wasting my time.*

In the long hallway at the top of the stairs, several doors opened to small bedrooms. The reason for the ceiling damage below became evident when Honey opened the door on the left. Blinding sunlight streamed through the hole in the roof. The hardwood floor had rotted and buckled.

"Don't go in there. The floor's not stable." Honey pulled the door closed like a child with a messy bedroom—if you don't see it, it doesn't exist.

This house wouldn't work for everyone. But a young couple could love it.

This is what Sam did. As a building contractor, flipping houses was more than a career; it was her passion.

The last door at the end of the hall opened into a large bathroom. With a black-and-white checkerboard tile floor that was yellowed and cracked. An enormous claw-foot tub took up one corner.

This is even better than it looked from the outside.

They retraced their steps to the front porch.

"How long since anyone lived here?" Sam asked, while Honey vainly attempted to remove a smear from her designer skirt.

"Almost seven years."

"Has it been for sale all that time?"

"Yes." She sighed. "It was in better shape then, but the owners wanted too much for it." Her sparrow eyes brightened. "Now, of course, the area is in higher demand."

Sam cut in before Honey could launch into a discussion of the local market.

"Okay, I get it. So, keeping in mind that the roof is a complete loss, the left half of the house is severely damaged, all fixtures need replacing, not to mention any dry rot, termite damage, or structural unsoundness I might find—how much is it?" Sam calculated the balance in her business account.

Honey seemed dazed, but rallied and quoted a price.

Sam smiled; they must be desperate to sell, given the home's condition. Mentally decreasing the quote by twenty percent, she gave Honey her offer.

"Now, you don't know me, but please believe me when I tell you that this is my only offer. It is contingent, of course, upon a termite and structural inspection. How long until I can expect an answer?"

Honey looked at her as if she were from a different planet.

Sam took pity. "I'm sorry, I don't mean to sound rude. I just don't enjoy price negotiation."

"You want it? Just like that?" Her pouty voice made it clear Sam had taken away all the fun by cutting to the chase.

"I wouldn't put an offer on a property I didn't intend to

buy." Sarcasm was lost on the woman, who seemed confused that the deal wasn't proceeding according to her formula.

"I guess I could call the family when I get to the office." Honey jotted Sam's cell number, then wandered off through the tall grass to her car, dusty smears marring the butt of her peach skirt.

God save me from real estate agents named Honey. Sam went to investigate the carriage house.

She guessed the large structure could house six full-size cars. The large wooden door opened in a shriek of protest. Cool air washed over her. The smell of damp soil drifted from the dirt floor. She stood just inside the door, letting her eyes adjust.

A rough staircase against the wall appeared out of the gloom. She ascended it gingerly, testing the integrity of the staircase and her injured knee at the same time. The door at the top landing stood locked, so she peered through the glass panes into a large unfinished room.

Of all the homes she'd renovated, this one could be the most beautiful.

And bring in the most profit.

Roof replacement would top the long list of tasks. And the upstairs floors were so unstable it would be economically impractical to repair them. Her brain worried at the puzzle.

"Relax, Crozier, you don't even own the thing yet."

But I think I may have found the next dream, Dad.

CHAPTER FOUR

NICK STOOD IN Josh and Annette's backyard, alternately flipping burgers and throwing passes to their nine-year-old, JJ. The other twin, Courtney, was in the kitchen "helping," making cookies. He'd have to apologize for the mess when Annette got home.

He'd agreed to watch the kids for his friends' weekly "date." With two crazy-active children, they needed it.

"Go out long, JJ." Nick waited, then lofted a bomb, which JJ scooted under for a neat catch. "And the crowd goes wild!" The kid's face lit up. God, Nick loved spending time out here at the Bennetts'.

Thirty wasn't old, but lately he'd been thinking about wanting kids. But in his mind, kids didn't come without marriage. And marriage didn't come without dating. He fielded the wobbly pass from Josh, and fired back a hot one. If it were up to him, he'd skip the whole dating thing. Who needed the angst, the awkwardness—the judgment? Especially given his history.

Looking back now, from the long end of the telescope, it wasn't surprising when his home life had imploded that he'd gone a bit wild. He'd had so much anger built up and nowhere for it to go. Booze was the only antidote he'd found, and he made a career of partying for a couple of years, post high school. Thank God for friends; Jesse, Carl and several others staged an intervention, making him see where he was and where he was headed.

It actually worked for a while. He decided he wanted to be an auto mechanic, and enrolled in a school in Los Angeles. Once there, though, he'd gotten caught up in the bar scene, many days arriving for school in the same clothes he'd left in the day before.

That bender ended the day he'd woken up on someone's floor, and had been on his way to school when a kid darted out in front of his car. He swerved, took out a parked car and a fire hydrant, but thankfully, not the child. He still woke up some nights in a puddle of sweat, dreaming of what could have happened.

Luckily, since he'd finished his class work they allowed him to graduate, though he'd spent the day of the ceremony holding down a seat in a county drunk tank. When Nick sobered up, he looked around at the jail population and had a revelation—he fit right in with the drunks and losers. His mother would have been so disappointed. Hell, he was disappointed in himself.

Nick needed a plan. By the time he'd served his six-month sentence, he had one. He left L.A. with a twelve-step card in his pocket, an idea for a business and a bad case of homesickness.

Now he needed another plan. "JJ, go get washed up. Your parents will be here in a minute, and dinner's about ready."

Almost all the girls he'd known in high school were married now. When he first moved back, he'd tried dating, but between the hours he had to put in with the shop and the awkwardness of discussing his past, he gave it up. He hadn't met anyone who, an hour after spending time with them, he missed.

Time to check the cookie progress, and assess the damage to the kitchen. He turned off the grill and lowered the lid. The sound of the twins squabbling in the kitchen made him smile.

Maybe it was time to try again.

SAM CRUISED PACIFIC COAST Highway back to town, breaking into a goofy smile when she drove around a bend to see the ocean, stretching like molten metal, to the horizon. It had transformed overnight from a moody, white-capped, gun-metal gray to a California picture postcard. Foam rode the small blue rollers that combed the creamy beach sand. The ocean's chop fractured the sunlight into blinding silver slivers.

Turning inland, the road seemed guileless in the sunshine, but as she came upon the scene of yesterday's accident, a shudder rippled through her. Her shoulder protested with an electric arc of pain. She studied the scene, but still couldn't see anything she'd done wrong. Even if she had seen the Mercedes, she had nowhere to go. Now it appeared the accident had led her to another job.

Sam wondered how she'd look back at her time in Widow's Grove. Each of her project pauses on her way across country seemed like a separate lifetime—as if she'd tried on different lives, to see how they fit. When she shook her head, the thought blew away in the wind ripping through her hair. Nowhere fit. That was just the way of things. A dark wisp of the nightmare edged across her light mood. Best to keep moving.

She rolled back through Widow's Grove. The town had morphed overnight to a sparkling jewel. Tourists wandered, ducking in and out of shops. In the park, a group in bright spandex sprawled next to their bicycles. The coffee shop did a brisk business, the umbrella's flirty skirts flipping up in the breeze.

A picture-postcard town.

And that can only help the resale value of the house.

But time spent dreaming would be a waste if the owners didn't take her offer. She had learned the hard way not to want things—it was less painful.

Pulling up in front of her run-down cabin, she shut down the engine and unbuckled the seat belt. She ran her hand over the sun-warmed leather seat. Someone spent a lot of time and money restoring this; even the eye-scorching yellow interior was spanking clean and perfect. Nick, obviously, but why? Clearly he didn't take it out much. Why put good money into a garage-dweller? She stepped out of the car just as her cell phone belted out the first notes of an old Jethro Tull road song.

Her heart sped up when she recognized the soft voice on the line.

"Miss Crozier? It's Honey, from Homestake Realty. I was able to contact the Sutton family this afternoon. I've been trying to get you for an hour."

"I guess I couldn't hear the phone for the wind."

"Yes, well. I've been in touch with the family." She hesitated. "Look, I know you don't negotiate and I don't mean to offend you. But the sellers find it hard to reach a consensus, and…"

From the undertone of frazzled in Honey's voice, Sam could imagine what that conversation was like.

"The bottom line is that they won't take less than their original asking price."

Crap. This disappointment bit a layer deeper than most of her letdowns. She recalled the Victorian's stately bone structure, peeking out at her from under years of neglect. Uncovering those bones would have been such a challenging project. Fun, too. She sighed.

"Ms. Crozier?"

She realized it was the second time her name had been called. "What?"

"Why don't I call you in a couple of days? There's no reason to make a hasty decision."

Sam took a breath, fully intending to nix the deal. Instead, she heard herself say, "Let me think about it. I'll call you." She hung up, but continued staring at the phone.

This was business. Either a deal worked, financially, or it

didn't. This one didn't. So why did it matter so much? Sure, it was a neat project, but she'd learned there were great projects scattered all across the U.S.

So what was with the soft tug in her chest?

FOR THE NEXT WEEK, Sam didn't have much else to do but think. The rest was good for her battered body, but the forced inactivity wasn't good for her mind. The distraction of staying busy had always been her first line of defense against dark thoughts and bad dreams. That, and traveling. Grounded and idle, they were catching up with her.

She'd taken to walking, stalking the country roads around the cabins. Something about the green rolling hills and live oaks calmed her, but today she'd gone farther than usual, and her feet dragged the dusty roadside.

In spite of repeated admonishments, her mind kept returning to the puzzle of the house. Somewhere in the country miles, she'd solved the problem. If she demolished the top floor on the water-damaged side of the house, along with the rooms below them, the entire right side would become a master bedroom loft, looking down into a huge great room. That would leave the house with only one bedroom, but what a bedroom! She imagined the fieldstone fireplace, and the firelight reflecting off a burnished hardwood floor.

There was the carriage house—the second story was one huge open room. It could be converted to guest quarters. There was enough room for two bedrooms and a bath, easy.

Damn, that would be nice. She turned in at the cabins.

But she'd done the math more than once. She'd always turned a good profit, thanks to sticking to strict budget guidelines. This one didn't fit them.

But the location! Property values always skyrocketed near tourist towns. Maybe they hadn't peaked yet. If she took this deal, she'd be betting on the come.

But Sam wasn't a gambler. Gambling was for people who could afford to lose.

Screw it. I'll just move on. After all, there would be another project down the road. She opened the hideous car's door, gingerly lowered herself into the seat and fired it up.

Mind made up, she kicked the disappointment to a back corner of her mind. Maybe she'd head up the coast, see San Francisco. She liked the idea of working on a Victorian, and she heard they had a bunch of them up there.

I've got to pressure that mechanic to move faster on the bike. Without a project, she had no money coming in. She could have the Jeep sent from Telluride, but traveling was no fun on four wheels.

She turned at the Farm House Café parking lot. Listening to local gossip would be a good distraction from her thoughts. She'd just grab a cup of coffee. Her phone rang with the distinctive drum riff to "Radar Love." Only having full use of one hand was getting old, fast. She zipped into a parking place, put the car in Park and picked up the phone.

"Ms. Crozier? It's Honey, Homestake Realty."

"I was going to call you, later today. I've done the numbers, and they just don't add up. I'll need to—"

"Would you still be interested if I told you the family would be willing to split the difference with you? It was a fight, but I got them to agree to accept ten percent lower than the asking price."

Sam stepped out of the car, recalculating the spreadsheet in her head. That would work. Just.

"When can we sign papers?" She kept her voice deadpan, a hard task while grinning ear-to-ear.

"Would you like to meet me in the office in the morning, say nine o'clock?"

Sam hung up, and did a gingerly happy dance, complete with fist punch. "Unh." Stabbing pain made her pay for forgetting her ribs. She grimaced, taking shallow breaths. But it couldn't wipe her smile.

Sam hobbled inside, holding her ribs.

"Well, that looked like good news. I think." Jesse stood watching, hands on hips, behind the counter. Her hair was in a different style than the last time Sam had been in, but it was just as big, and the short dress just as tight.

A book lay face down on the counter. Sam read the title. *Mensa Sudoku.*

"The best news. It looks like I'm going to be your neighbor for a while. I just bought the Sutton place."

"You what? What would you want with that wreck?"

Sam's stomach woke, growling to the delicious aroma of grilling meat and frying potatoes. "I'm a building contractor. That house has potential."

"From what I've seen, the biggest potential that house has is to fall down."

"Well, it will be a challenge, I'll admit. My biggest to date. But I've renovated four other houses on my way across the country. I can handle it."

Jesse glanced at Sam's sling, but said nothing.

Sam claimed a stool at the afternoon-empty counter and dropped the DayGlo flower keychain on the counter.

Jesse's penciled eyebrows shot up and she raised her head to look past Sam to the parking lot. "I heard about that."

"Heard about what?"

"Nick must have thought a lot of you to let you borrow the Love Machine."

"And here I thought I had the booby prize."

Jesse's solemn look stopped Sam midlaugh. In a quiet voice, Jesse said, "That's his mother's car."

Before Sam could ask for that story, Jesse turned a sharp eye on her. "You are a surprise, sweetie. How did you ever get involved in that career?"

"I'll tell you, if you promise to explain the math-whiz thing to me, sometime."

When Jesse nodded, Sam picked up the menu in front of her. "My dad wanted a boy—bad. My mom was the love of his life and she died when I was born, so I was as close as he was going to get. He taught me what he loved. Growing up, partially built houses were my playground." Sam perused the menu. "By the time I was old enough to realize that all kids didn't spend their summers crawling around construction sites, I was hooked."

"Well, then I'm glad you're buying it. Fighting over the estate, the family priced it out of the market. By the time they got real, it was in such bad shape, it wasn't worth much. I'll bet they just jumped at the chance to unload it."

Jesse started to fill Sam's coffee cup, but paused, midpour, looking off with an unfocused stare. "It used to be such a beautiful thing. I went to a Christmas party there once when I was a kid. You should have seen it. White lights strung along the eaves, huge Christmas tree in the front windows. It sure was pretty." Jesse finished pouring, then raised her voice. "Hey, everybody—this is Samantha, and she's just bought the old Sutton place. I expect y'all to make her welcome."

Embarrassed to be singled out, and unsure of her reception, Sam glanced around to see smiles and some curiosity, but none of the suspicion or animosity she expected. Being a woman, traveling cross-country on a motorcycle, she was used to people not knowing how to react to her. A few customers raised their coffee cups in salute.

Jesse smiled down on Sam. "Well, honey, anything we can do to help, you just let us know. That hunky guy in the kitchen is pretty handy. And I can help you plan the housewarming!"

"Whoa up a minute, Jesse. It'll take me close to a year to complete the renovation, since I do most of the work myself. I think it's a little early to be planning a party." She smiled.

"But I appreciate the support. It can be hard to fit in to a new town."

It is, usually. But a tiny dust bunny of contentment had nestled in her chest, the past few days. It felt odd there, but she thought she liked it.

SAM CONTACTED THE storage company in Telluride where she'd finished the last project and arranged for them to send her meager furnishings, the Jeep and her father's precious tools to Widow's Grove. She planned to bivouac in one of the rooms while she worked on the rest of the house.

One morning a few days later, she glanced out her cabin's window to see the old manager shuffling by, huge wrench in hand. His attire hadn't improved, except he now wore mirror-shined brogans.

Sam stepped onto the porch. "Excuse me, Mr. Raven?"

He stopped and squinted at her. Sam was relieved to see he'd put in his teeth.

"Could you tell me where I'd find a lumberyard or a hardware store around here?"

"Well, there used to be Lincoln Hardware, downtown." He frowned, and his lip curled, just a bit. "But they cancelled Dave's lease last year. Guess the landlord thought he'd make more money off another antique store. Now there's just Coast Lumber, on the way to Solvang."

Sam stepped off the porch into the morning sunshine. "Mom-and-pop yards can't compete with the big chains anymore. But it's the local builders that suffer, since the smaller places catered to their localized needs. The box stores couldn't care less."

He extended a gnarled, arthritic hand. "You've been here a week and a half—the name's Tim."

Those fingers looked painful. She shook his hand gently. "And you can call me Sam."

"Sam it is, then. Give Coast a try, they're better'n most. I traded with them when I had my plumbing business." His blue eyes twinkled as he hefted the iron wrench. "That's a'fore I retired, you see."

Sam smiled. "Thanks, Tim." She turned and walked to the borrowed car where it sat looking like a tavern slut in a church pew.

The drive to Solvang only took twenty minutes.

Sam had the same emotional connection with hardware stores that many women had with lingerie boutiques. She stood in the tool aisle, inhaling the clean scent of cut pine, debating the quality of power saw brands with a clerk.

She noticed a man eavesdropping. He examined a band saw, but glanced at her often. As her conversation ended, he approached.

"Excuse me. I don't mean to be rude, but I overheard you say you're a contractor, starting a large project. Do you mind if I ask what it is?"

Sam eyed him. He was short and round, a fringe of dark hair around the edge of a bald head. His demeanor didn't seem threatening, but there was no reason to announce that she'd be living alone, way out of town.

"Let me explain why I'm interested. Then you can tell me to get lost if you'd like." His smile was harmless, anyway. "I'm Dan Porter, the shop teacher at Widow's Grove High. I teach occupational programs to give the kids usable skills. I'm always looking for sites for my kids to get some real-world experience." He extended a broad, hairy paw.

After a brief hesitation, Sam shook it. "So you stalk the aisles of lumber stores, springing yourself on contractors?" She smiled, imagining this little Friar Tuck in his Hawaiian shirt, stalking like a big-game hunter.

"Yeah, something like that. I've approached several about my idea, but haven't had any takers yet."

"Fear of lawsuits, right?"

"No, I've worked that out with insurance through the school. They just don't want to be bothered. Not that I blame them. They're in business to make money. But I know they'd see a benefit to their business as well as the kids if they'd give it a shot."

That's all she needed—a bunch of left-footed teenagers, falling off her roof. "How much experience do these kids have?"

"Some of them are really good. They've gotten all the classroom experience I can give them and they're familiar with all the tools from my class."

She thought of the deep-grunt demolition work ahead. And her damned collarbone. Much as she hated to admit it, she needed help. "I'd need a lot more information. By the way, I'm Sam—Samantha Crozier. I bought the old Sutton place outside of Widow's Grove."

He let out a low whistle. "Now, that *is* an ambitious project. Are you planning on subbing out the work?"

"I'll do most of it myself."

"Not for a while, you won't." He eyed the sling. "Why don't you stop by the school sometime, to see our setup? You'll get an idea of the kids' skill levels, and I could introduce you to some of them."

"Let me think about it."

"I only teach shop classes, so you could stop by anytime during school hours." He pulled a wallet from his back pocket and handed her a business card. "You have no idea what this would mean to these kids. And remember, you'd be getting young muscle, cheap!"

Sam didn't notice the products on the shelves as she wandered the aisles. The hardware store ambiance was a soothing backdrop to the battle waged in her head. She liked working alone. The projects took longer to complete, but at the end, she could admire the quality result and know she'd left a mark on the landscape as she passed through. She'd know she was more than an anonymous biker in leathers. She liked working in peace, no one talking, interrupting or getting in the way.

Oh, sure, she usually subbed out plumbing, and an occasional electrical job. But teenagers? They were a seething batch of hormones with big feet. Unsafe, unfinished, unknown.

When she lifted her shoulders to shrug off the idea, her collarbone shot a bolt of pain down her arm.

Dammit. She didn't have six weeks to wait to heal. Every day, money was trickling out of her account. She could hire professionals, but they came dear, and had opinions about how to do things. With kids, she could be sure it was done her way.

But was she prepared to take on a babysitting gig?

Since work couldn't begin on the house until the deal closed, Sam found herself once more, with too much time on her hands.

Late afternoons, she usually walked to the Farm House Café. During slow hours, she and Jesse would sit drinking coffee and "shooting the poop," as Jesse called it. Sam got acquainted with the town through Jesse's stories. Sam considered it research, learning more about the market without having to meet the people.

She'd also found Jesse a fascinating study in opposites; she looked like Flo, from the old sitcom, *Alice*. But she also appeared to be a savant with numbers, and Sam had seen enough to know that she was the force behind the diner's popularity.

Today, she'd sat at the counter talking to Jesse long enough to get the coffee jitters.

You don't have to like asking for help with the house; you just have to do it. "Jesse, do you know Dan Porter, the shop teacher at the high school?"

Jess refilled Sam's cup. "Of course I do. Why?"

"I'm looking into the possibility of using a couple of his students for a couple of weeks." She lifted her damaged arm, then winced, and put it down. "Only till I heal."

"Oh, Dan's one of the good guys. He got Teacher of the Year, back in '09. Kids who aren't going off to college need skills, to get a job. He's helped out a bunch of them."

The clanging of the cowbell against the glass café door brought Jesse's head up.

"Hey, Nick."

Sam's mechanic sauntered to the counter. "Hey, Jesse."

Sam leaned away. It wasn't that he stood close. His presence itself seemed to crowd her, taking more space than his body. His scent enveloped her, an odd blend of smoky aftershave with an undertone of engine oil that shouldn't smell pleasant, but did. He smelled like a blue-collar man. He smelled electric. He smelled like danger.

He looked down at her. Not with the "hunting coyote" look. More of a "who are you, under the Biker Chick?" look. The open curiosity seemed kind and well-meaning. She wouldn't have trusted just a look—faces were just masks men wore. But something in his loose posture, his sincere mouth, his quiet waiting telegraphed his question; she knew it as true as the skill in her hands.

He slid onto the bar stool beside the one she'd begun to think of as hers. Her skin prickled with awareness. The hair on her arm rose, waving like a charmed snake.

God, she hated this. She lived well by herself, but every once in a great while, her traitorous body craved touch. Not a jump-in-the-sack touch. Just a simple longing for human contact that was almost stronger than her ability to quell it. It hit at random—in line at a store, she'd be suddenly and completely aware of a stranger ahead of her. Time would slow. Details would come into sharp focus: working hands with heavy-boned fingers, dark hair on a tanned forearm, set off against a stark white cotton shirt. A core-deep ache would bloom in her chest and she'd have to fist her hands to keep from reaching to touch the pale, vulnerable skin at the inside of a stranger's elbow.

She shuddered, shivering the feeling off like a dog shakes off water.

"You know, Jesse," Nick tipped his chin to the pie safe next to the cash register "That pie looks familiar. In fact, I think it's the twin of the one I found on my front porch this morning."

Jesse raised her pert nose and sniffed. "I have no idea what you're talking about, Pinelli." She turned to the kitchen window to pick up an order.

"I do appreciate it, Jess, but I'm not in high school anymore. I *can* cook, you know."

Eyes straight ahead, Jesse swished by, a food-laden tray gracefully balanced on her shoulder.

"Hey, Samantha." He turned his attention back to her. "What did the doctor say?"

She fingered her empty coffee cup. "Who needs a doctor? What I really need is a time machine to speed up the healing."

Nick gave her the hairy eyeball. He opened his mouth, but apparently thought better of it. "I've been checking online parts boards every day, but nothing new has come up for the Vulcan. From the look of things, this may take a while."

"That's okay. As it turns out, I'm going to be here awhile." She told him about her plan to buy, renovate and sell the house. "My Jeep will be here in a week or so, and I can return your car then."

"No rush." Nick pulled a menu from the stainless clip at the edge of the counter. "Did you feel like the bomb, riding around town in the Love Machine?"

Jesse walked by frowning, and gave her a barely perceptible headshake.

Sam said, "Yeah, the bomb." *Nuclear bomb.*

A stout middle-aged man stopped on his way to the register, dollar bills in hand. "Hey, Nick, I thought you were coming by this morning. Are you picking up bread tomorrow instead?"

"I don't have a car at the moment, Bert. Can I make it Wednesday?"

"Sure, that'll work. I'll leave the back door open at seven."

Jesse strolled up. "Nick picks up day-old bread at the bakery and takes it down to the homeless shelter once a week." She glanced at Sam.

Through the years, Sam had enough people try to set her up to recognize the matchmaker gleam. Sam ignored Jesse's grin as an awful thought surfaced. "Did I take *your* car?"

Nick looked up. "Nah. That's my mom's car. I don't own one."

Remembering Jesse's cue, she wasn't going near that one. She closed her open mouth. "You run a garage that fixes cars, but you don't *own* one?"

"Nope. Don't need one, most of the time. When I do, I just use one of the shop's loaners."

Ah, an opportunity! "Why don't I swap your mom's car for another loaner? I'd hate to have something happen to—"

"Nah, you keep it as long as you need. It needs to be driven now and again."

He snapped the menu closed and ordered a burger with fries from Jesse, then turned his attention back to Sam. "So where are you from? Originally?"

"Ohio." Sam felt speared, by his interest and his gaze, as the moment spun out. Caffeine zinged along her nerves.

He cocked his head. "That's odd."

"What?" Her tone teetered on bitchy. "A woman shouldn't ride a motorcycle? Shouldn't be on the road, alone? Shouldn't have a man's job? What?"

His open smile disarmed her. "I'm just surprised anyone would want to travel so far from home."

She examined the dregs of coffee in the bottom of her cup. "Well, not everybody grew up in Mayberry, Opie."

He chuckled, but it didn't sound happy. "And not everywhere that looks like Mayberry, is."

Hmm. Maybe, like Jesse, there was more to Nick than bedroom eyes and a great smile. "So, tell me how a guy who doesn't own a car came to own a tow and repair shop?"

"I've been a mechanic for a long time. I came into some money about eight years ago." His eyes sidled away. "I bought the shop from Bud Proctor, who was retiring. I added towing—" he looked up, and winked at her "—and wrenching on injured classic babies, which I do for pure love."

Damn, he's good-looking. But it was his focused interest that made her hop from the stool and make a hasty exit.

CHAPTER FIVE

TWO WEEKS LATER, Sam packed her belongings. After extracting a promise from Mr. Raven to visit her, with new house keys tucked in her pocket, she drove to the house. Pulling into the driveway, she stared at it. Her house. For a while, anyway. She pictured it complete—a stately grande dame, holding dignified court over the tan hills that bowed at her feet.

She was itching to get back inside, to see if her idea of a loft would really work.

Her fingers ached for her tools as she looked forward to mindless hours spent restoring a windowsill, to listening to the old house whispering its secrets.

Why this house should stand out from her other projects, she couldn't say. Perhaps the secret would be revealed in the renovation.

Sam gathered as much stuff as she could with one hand, navigated the weed-choked sidewalk and climbed the steps to the front porch. She looked out over the sleepy hills. Puffs of eucalyptus-scented breeze touched her face and fat honeybees droned in the overgrown shrubbery at her feet. No traffic noise, no human voices—only the sounds of spring, and the countryside drowsing in the heat. Sam closed her eyes, feeling the edges of the hole in her chest where the restlessness usually lived. Peace stole in. Her mind quieted.

"Come on, Crozier, start hauling ash." Realizing that her father's words were literal in this case, she smiled, dropped her stuff, unlocked the door, and went in search of a broom.

She was attempting to clean out the pieces of ceiling in the dining room with one hand and a sling, when the sound of a large truck laboring up the hill disturbed the quiet.

She walked to the front parlor and looked out the tall front windows to see a moving van towing her Jeep, turn in the drive. She directed the men to put her single bed in the front parlor, along with her boxes of clothes and sundries. Most of her furniture would go into storage for the duration of the renovation.

Last off the truck were her red toolboxes. After rolling them into the kitchen, the movers left. For a half hour, Sam indulged herself, pulling and closing the long flat drawers, hefting mallets, rearranging hardware, stroking her father's antique hand plane. The world tilted to a more familiar axis and the ground settled under her feet. Traveling was fun, but nowhere was home until her tools arrived.

I so miss you, Dad. With a last lingering caress, she closed the drawer and got to work.

She spent the rest of the weekend settling in. After driving the Love Machine to town for much-needed supplies, Sam did a good cleaning of the bathroom, the kitchen and front parlor, her chosen bedroom for the duration of the remodel.

Surveying the roof, she judged the framing solid, but everything else would go—from the sheathing out. She took measurements and visited the lumber company to order supplies. Her body hurt just imagining the labor involved. She pictured herself, on the roof, trying to tear off sheathing with one hand.

Dammit! She *liked* working alone. Liked knowing at the end of a job that the satisfying result was hers alone. Others may not realize after Sam had moved on, that the mark left behind was hers, but *she'd* know. And that had always been enough.

But wanting didn't make it so. Given her injuries, she'd

have to get help. She'd curse the accident, but if not for that, she wouldn't have found this great house. Reluctantly, she decided to stop by the high school on Monday.

You can always bite the bullet and pay through the nose for professionals if students turn out to be a hairball idea.

Nursing a cup of coffee on her porch after dinner, Sam imagined pioneer wagons carrying tired families coming over the hills. How would they have felt, after facing unbelievable hardships on their way west, seeing this beautiful land for the first time? The view from her porch probably hadn't changed much since then, and she liked that.

The self-satisfied purr of an expensive engine disturbed her reverie. A sleek black Mercedes convertible slowed, and then pulled into her drive. Her muscles snapped to attention like guard dogs on a leash.

Probably a lost tourist. She set her cup down.

The driver glanced in the rearview mirror and smoothed his hair before climbing from the car's cream leather interior, a bottle of wine in his hand tied with a blowsy scarlet bow. Squinting into the low sun, Sam recognized the man who'd hit her motorcycle that day in the rain. She stood.

He found the edge of the sidewalk in the weeds and, head down, followed the trail in the tall grass. As he neared, he looked up with a broad smile. "I'm here to officially welcome you to Widow's Grove."

She felt the house's empty rooms at her back. "How did you know where I live?"

"Well, now, that tells me that you didn't grow up in a small town. When I heard a biker chick bought the old Sutton place, I knew it had to be you." Smiling, he bowed over the bottle of wine like a maître d', awaiting a diner's approval.

Sam tucked her good hand in her back pocket. "Thank you. But I don't drink." She did, but she wasn't telling him that.

His smile went a bit stale. "That's okay. You can save it

for your housewarming." He extended his hand. "We never had the chance to be properly introduced. The name's Brad Sexton."

Not knowing what else to do, she took his hand and gave it a quick shake. "Samantha Crozier." She let go. He didn't.

"I just wanted you to know how very sorry I am for the accident." He gave her hand a gentle squeeze, then let go. His bored-with-my-life, family-man eyes took a tour of her body. "You look like you got the worst of it."

She wrapped her good hand around the arm in the sling, covering her chest. "I'm fine."

He glanced up at the house. "I used to play in this place as a kid. Sure looks different than I remember."

Sam studied his faded-handsome face. He looked like a former high school quarterback, gone to seed. Middle-age thickness had crept up from his waist to his heavy jowls. Age and easy living had begun to assault the skin at his neck.

But his eyes, when he glanced back to her, seemed innocuous. "Mind giving me a tour?"

Her shoulder muscles tightened as the sound of "no" moved from her brain to her lips. She'd always been a lousy judge of character—trusting those she shouldn't, and spurning offers of friendship from well-meaning people. It was as if some internal compass constantly pointed her in the wrong direction.

But Brad didn't see her hesitation, because he'd turned and walked through the open front door.

"Hey!" Shrugging off the ice-water trickle of déjà vu at the back of her neck, she hurried inside.

She stepped to the doors of the front parlor and pulled them closed, hiding the tortured pillows and rumpled sheets of her narrow bed. When she turned back to Brad, there was a flash of something at the back of his eyes. Something oily. Her stomach twisted, remembering that her closest neighbor was a quarter mile away.

Maybe it was just her uneasy brain, superimposing the past on the present.

He walked to the stairs. "Donny Sutton and I used to slide down these banisters." He patted the newel post. "I remember when his mother ordered that window." He tipped his chin to the ornate fleur-de-lis etched in the tall glass window at the stair landing. "His dad bitched up a storm about it. Must've cost a pretty penny, even back then."

When he bent to place the wine on the top step of the landing, a late afternoon sunray caught his diamond-studded wedding ring and threw dancing sparks up the shadowed wall of the staircase.

"I want to thank you for this. It's not often you get to walk into your past." His face formed a mask of sincerity.

Maybe it wasn't a mask. Maybe she was wrong, this time.

"Could I see the upstairs? Donny and I spent a lot of time in his room, conspiring on world domination."

"Um. I guess."

He stepped back, gesturing for her to lead. She pictured him watching her butt as she climbed, and waved him on ahead.

"Old man Sutton died about ten years ago, and his wife, two years later." His voice echoed in the narrow space as he turned at the landing and started up. "Donny and his sisters have fought over this place ever since."

Sam stayed well back, not wanting to watch his pudgy rear end struggle up the stairs, but not able to stop herself. On her way by, she grabbed a screwdriver from the window ledge and slipped it in her back pocket. The weight of it there somehow felt right.

He was huffing by the time he reached the top landing. "I don't know why I'm telling you all this...." He wandered down the hall, opening doors as he went.

"Don't go in that one!"

He stood at the doorway of the ruined room. "Wow. Donny sure would be pissed to see his room now."

He wandered down the hall. Sam closed the door to the room.

"Oh, my God." His voice echoed from the large bathroom at the hall's end.

Sam hurried, wondering if he'd hurt himself on something. She had liability insurance, but sure didn't want to have to use it.

He stood in the center of the bathroom, pointing. "The black-and-white checkerboard tile, the old claw-foot tub, the light fixtures. It's all the same!"

She touched the scarred molding of the doorway. "I'm going to keep it as original as I can."

He took a step closer.

Even without looking, she felt the brush of his glance, against her skin.

"Can you imagine the hours Donny spent in here as a teenager, whacking off?"

At the low, creepy tone, her head jerked up, though she knew what she would see. The concentrated, unfocused stare. Ruddied cheeks. His lips glistening, as if he'd just licked them.

She stood in flash-frozen shock, her heart fluttering in scared-rabbit beats. *Not again.*

His eyes roamed, lingering, as if he already possessed her. He addressed her breasts. "You know, I've got money. You could have a sweet deal, here."

Shaking her head, she took a step back.

His pudgy fingers, reaching to touch, shattered her taut stillness. She ran.

Her feet pounded a hollow beat on the old wood of the hall. Halfway down the stairs, a knife of pain in her ribs forced her to stop. Her chest and shoulder screamed, but her lungs trumped everything. She leaned over, taking small breaths, trying not to throw up.

She hadn't heard him coming, but he was there, hands all over her. Her body jerked away in an involuntary spasm and she stumbled to the landing, her brain spinning in freewheeling panic. Random thoughts pinged inside her skull. Snips of memories. Nothing useful.

Off balance, she threw out her good arm to keep from plunging headfirst into the wall. She spun to face what would come next.

A small voice whispered, *You knew you'd end up here again.* The forgotten-familiar weakness of lassitude pulled at her. *Give up. You know it'll go easier if you do.*

The smell of nightmare-sweaty sheets drifted from the open collar of her shirt. The stench of fear.

He must have sensed victory because, face flushed and breathing heavy, he took the last step to the landing.

Sam stepped back. *He's stronger. No one is going to believe*—her back hit the wall. Something clinked and bumped her butt.

Triumph-laced adrenaline zipped through her, cutting off the little girl's whisper midsentence. Jerking the forgotten screwdriver from her back pocket, she held it in front of her like a madman in a slasher film. "Get. Out."

His flat shark eyes gauged her resolve. "Now, you don't want to be that way." He reached out a hand, but jerked it back when she thrust the screwdriver at the exposed veins of his wrist.

"You've totally misunderstood my intentions. I don't mean to hurt you." His lips peeled back from his teeth, but it wasn't a smile. "Unless you want me to."

Her stomach heaved in a hot, greasy wave. "This may not kill you, but it could take out an eye." The blades of rage in her throat made the words come out ragged, torn.

He hesitated, absently touching the skin of his forearm. His fingers stroked the hair, smoothing it in gentle circles.

He was imagining stroking her—Sam knew it as clearly as if she'd read his mind.

And maybe she had.

Their heavy breathing echoed loud in the hushed stairwell. Time spun out to a thrumming wire of tension. The tension sprung from different sources, with different motivations, but it paired them in a dark dance—one they both knew.

Sam stood, waiting for his next move.

Brad sighed, his lips twisting into an entitled pout. Straightening, he sucked in his gut and hiked the waist of his expensive dress slacks. "The guys at the club told me a biker chick had to be a lesbian."

"Get the *hell* out of my house." She pointed the screwdriver down the stairs. "Now."

"Guess I lost that bet." Hands raised, he eased past her, not turning his back until he was out of range. He took the last three steps to the entryway.

Sam followed him, screwdriver at ready. "The only thing I sleep with is a snub-nosed Colt." He stepped through the open door. "You ever come back here, you'll find out its sex."

"Shit, I knew better." He walked through the door, then turned and looked down his patrician nose. "Stray dogs may be fun to play with, but they've got no manners." He shot his cuffs, squared his shoulders and walked down the porch steps.

Gravel shot from the tires as he backed out. When he hit the asphalt, the car surged and fishtailed, tires squealing for purchase.

Still shaking, Sam watched from the top step of the porch. What was it about her that made men think they could get away with that shit? There must be some kind of mark on her forehead that only perverts could see—something that told them it was safe to approach. Many times, she'd studied her face in the mirror, trying to make it out. But she only saw what everyone else did—cursed, unwanted beauty.

The car disappeared over the hill. She waited until the sound faded, then her knees gave out and the screwdriver fell from her hand. Clinging to the support post, she sank onto the wooden step. Shivers ran from her neck through her body in pulsing, shivery spasms. She hunched over her knees, staring at the ground, her thoughts years away.

Some untold time later, she stood, rubbed her sore buns, straightened her shoulders and went back to work. Mulling over the past was a waste. If you never put it down, you wouldn't stand a chance at moving beyond it. Just because that philosophy hadn't worked to date, didn't mean it never would.

She couldn't afford to contemplate the alternative.

CHAPTER SIX

Nick LOOKED UP from the computer screen. The late afternoon splashed window-shaped sunshine over his polished waiting room floor. No new Vulcan parts for sale. Hell, there had to be junked Kawasakis all over the country—just his luck they'd be owned by the technologically challenged.

Not that it would break his heart to see the biker chick as a fixture around here.

Gold hair, full lower lip, her long and elegantly boned face. He liked her small shoulders and long legs, in denim. But even a killer body could easily be dismissed, once you had an eyeful. Instead, Nick's attention snagged on the air of mystery that surrounded her like a gossamer shawl. It was more than her odd career and her mode of transport. He sensed she had walls. He got a vague sense of them from her conversation, but their true magnitude lay in what she didn't say.

Intriguing. He thought about calling her. But with what? Non-progress on her bike?

Wake up, dude, you're dreaming. She'd made it clear she was gone as soon as the remodel of the Sutton place was complete. And he was in Widow's Grove to stay.

But regardless of the facts, Samantha Crozier remained a puzzle his brain wouldn't put down. He wasn't even sure why he'd offered her his mother's car, that first day. He hadn't had that car out except to keep the battery charged since—well, since forever.

Sure, she was gorgeous, but it was more than that. Other

beautiful women had needed loaners and it never occurred to him to offer them his mother's car. He sensed that Sam didn't need help often, and wouldn't have asked for it if she did. That made him want to help.

He looked up at the sound of the door opening. He sat up straight and watched his puzzle walk in, a neon daisy keychain dangling from her fingers.

"I've brought the Love Machine home."

"Hey, Sam." Nick ripped off his horn-rimmed glasses, stuffed them in the lap drawer and slammed it closed. "Good timing. I'm starving. Want to go to lunch?"

She walked to the desk and dropped the key in his hand. "Sorry, I can't. I've got to get back to work at the house."

He snatched his blue jacket from the back of the chair. "Come on, Sam, let me take you to lunch."

"Thanks, but I'm just walking down to Jesse's. She'll run me home."

There were those walls again. "Oh, come on. Carl is a great cook, but aren't you tired of eggs and burgers by now?"

"No. Thanks, but no." She turned for the door.

There had to be a way around her walls without pulling a muscle climbing. "You don't want to pull Jesse away from work to drive you home, do you?"

She winced. "I'll just call a cab."

He strode across the room, pulled the glass door open and held it. "Don't be silly. I know a place that serves killer crab." He yelled, "Tom, I'm going to lunch. Hold the fort."

She stood there, waffling.

"Sam." He stood, watching her. "It's just lunch. Promise." What had made this woman so wary? Well, he intended to find out. She was like no other beautiful woman he'd ever met.

"Thanks. I guess that would be fun." Her smile transformed her from worried waif to magazine model.

He walked ahead to open the passenger door of the Love

Machine for her, then trotted around the car, opened the door and settled into the driver's seat. "Glad you left the top down. It's a perfect day for a ride."

It was, too. Nick cranked a rock 'n roll station, and they cruised through town. He drove, one hand on the wheel, the other hung over the door, waving every few feet to a pedestrian who hailed him, feeling as if he were chauffeuring the homecoming queen in a parade.

Springsteen's "Pink Cadillac" blared as they turned onto Pacific Coast Highway. Sam kept the beat with her hand on the car door, singing in what he supposed she meant as harmony, but wasn't, quite. *Well, thank God, she isn't perfect.*

The smell of hot sand and salt whipped by on the wind, and Sam pulled her hair back to keep it out of her eyes. She laughed, looking like a carefree teen playing hooky.

Ten minutes later, they passed a sign welcoming them to Pismo Beach. The town looked like a throwback to the '60s, when surfers were gods and before the term *yuppie* had been coined. The small, gaudy painted stucco buildings held an odd charm, and the Love Machine fit right in.

He pulled off PCH and parked in front of Dougie's Place, a long, flamingo-pink building sprawled at the edge of the surf, like a fat, bikini-clad woman.

He held the thick metal front door for her. "Don't judge it by the exterior. They have the best seafood for fifty miles."

"If you say it, I believe it. I think." She ducked under his arm.

A jukebox belted out the Beach Boys in the corner, and the bar stretched along the wall to the left. Behind the bar, where a mirror would normally reflect liquor bottles, stood a saltwater fish tank, stretching the entire length of the back wall. It was brightly lit from above, but the back had been blacked out, so the exotic fish stood out in bold relief. Schools of small bright yellow, red and blue fish darted around the huge tank like pennants fluttering in the wind.

He led the way past the bar to a dining area, where empty tables sat, dressed in red-and-white checked tablecloths. She followed him down a step to the patio. A glass wall blocked the wind coming in from the ocean side. Red and white umbrellas touting Mexican beer shaded glass-topped tables. The patio extended to the high tide point of the surf, the waves nearly lapping its base.

"Oh, I take back everything I was thinking. This is even better than the California I heard about, back in Ohio. How did you find this place?"

"It's a closely guarded secret. The outside is to discourage tourists, I think."

He led Sam to an unoccupied sun-filled corner. At a square table he pulled out a chair facing the ocean, and settled her into it before taking the one alongside. The waitress arrived, wanting their drink order.

She ordered a glass of the house Chablis without ever pulling her eyes from the long low waves combing the beach.

He took the proffered menus and ordered a Coke, thinking how pretty her hair looked, glinting platinum in the sun. With a bit more tan, she could pass for a vacationing movie star.

"Can you give me your mother's address, Nick? I'd like to send her a little thank-you, for the use of her car."

To avoid her look, he opened a menu and scanned it. "My mother died, fifteen years ago."

"Oh," She sounded like she'd stepped in a hole. "Nick, I'm so sorry." Her fingers touched the back of his hand. Long, elegant fingers. Soft skin. Touching him. He kept his eyes on the menu.

Don't drag out the dirty laundry basket. Not on a first date. When he fisted his hand, her fingers hovered for a moment, then withdrew. For the best. He didn't want her sympathy. Besides, sympathy evaporated fast given the blowtorch of his past. "It happened a long time ago. Do you want to try the crab?"

"Sure. But you'll have to show me how. I've never had the guts to tackle those leg-cracker things."

He glanced up to see if she was joking. "You're not going to tell me you've never eaten crab?"

"Give me a break. Ohio isn't exactly Mollusk Mecca, you know."

"I guess not." He gathered the menus, trying to hide a smile. "Crab is a crustacean."

She waved a hand. "Whatever."

Time to test those walls. "What's Ohio like?" It was a bonus that he got to watch that gorgeous mouth move.

"Just about as different from this as you can get." She looked out at the sea, squinting a bit in the glare. "California is like a teenager, all brash and full of energy. Ohio is a middle-class, middle-aged grown-up. Flat, staid and earnest."

"Your family still there?"

She stopped, just long enough for him to realize he'd never seen her still. "My mom died when I was born. My dad died six years ago."

"No brothers or sisters?"

"I was first, and only." She pulled a strand of wind-blown hair away from her lips. "But my mom was it for him—he never remarried. So he had to make do with me." She smiled. "It was lucky for me, though. In the summer he had to take me to work with him, and I learned my love of building from him. If there had been a brother, Dad probably wouldn't have thought to teach me."

He ignored the heat in his chest, warmed by the smile that wasn't meant for him. "Sounds like a fun childhood."

Her smile faded. "It sounds that way, doesn't it?"

When the waitress interrupted, he ordered for them. She asked if Sam wanted another glass of wine. Sam looked down as if surprised to find the glass empty. She shook her head, and the waitress left.

Sam folded her arms on the table. "What about you? Where did you come from?"

"Right here, in Widow's Grove. I thought you knew."

She looked him full in the face, eyes round in shock. "Jesse said something about it, but I thought she was kidding. You've never lived anywhere else? Ever?"

"Well, my trade school and internship was in L.A., but I scooted back here as soon as I could."

Her lips quirked. "Homesick?"

He thought about the jail cell that had been his home for six months. "More than you can imagine. Like every other teenager from a small town, I couldn't wait to blow this place. But L.A. didn't suit me. Too many dazzling lights. Too many people. Too many bars." He took a sip of Coke to make himself shut up, and kicked the laundry basket full of past to a dark corner. "Why did you leave home?"

She looked out to sea so long he thought she wouldn't answer. Maybe he wasn't the only one with an overflowing basket.

"About a month after Dad died, I was sitting at the kitchen table drinking a cup of coffee. You know how when you're thinking, you don't see what you're looking at?"

She couldn't have seen his nod.

"When I came to, I was staring at the kitchen cabinets. I really saw them. The white paint was dingy, and worn around the handles. The section over the counter actually sagged in the middle. I looked around the room. The linoleum was worn almost through, in places. The porcelain sink was rust-stained and the white tile on the counters was chipped."

He knew she wasn't seeing the waves she focused on.

"So I wandered to the living room. It was so weird. This was the house that Dad and I had worn for years, like a pair of well-loved slippers. On the other hand, I saw the house as a professional. What a disaster! How could we not have noticed that?

"Anyway, I figured I owed it to the old girl to spruce her up. I quit my job to work on the house. I needed a goal. I was kinda lost after Dad…." She shook her head, a sad ghost of a smile lifted a corner of her mouth. "By the end of the year, that house was a jewel. Walk-in closets, bay windows, curved archways. Man, that was a sweet place."

He watched emotion flick across her face, sensing this woman didn't divulge her past often. Or easily. "Why did you leave?"

She shrugged. "When I finished the renovation, I realized the house wasn't mine anymore. I could just see a young mom, cooking dinner in the kitchen…."

"And so?"

"So, I contacted a real estate agent about selling. The offer that came in floored me. It started me thinking. Maybe I could make a living renovating houses and reselling them. I looked for another run-down house, but then I realized—it wasn't only my house that didn't fit me. Ohio didn't, either." She straightened the silverware in front of her. "Maybe it never had."

When the server brought their meal, he wanted to shoo her away, afraid Sam would abandon her story. The girl must have sensed it, because she laid out the plates and left with only a smile.

Sam sat straight and put her napkin in her lap. "So I hit the road. I saw a lot of the country, and took on projects in places I liked: Florida, Texas and the last in Colorado." She looked from him to the plate. "So here I am, on the California coast, with a plateful of crab and no skills for eating it."

He flexed his knuckles. "Ah, but you are lucky enough to be dining with a master crab cracker."

Through the meal, they discussed getting-to-know-you topics: music, food, movies, books. They lingered, talking long after the dishes had been cleared. He'd had female friends, but he'd never felt this relaxed on a first date. Hell, on any date.

Sam's nostrils flared, taking in the salt air. "It never occurred to me that I'd live within driving distance of the ocean. Do you ever get tired of the view?" She leaned back in the chair and crossed her legs, her hair lifting on a stray breeze.

He couldn't pull his eyes from those long legs. "No, and I don't think I ever will."

At his reverent tone, her brow furrowed. Turning her head, seeing his smile, her eyes narrowed.

Wrong move, Slick.

Her face settled into tight, polite lines. "Well. Just look at the sun—what time is it?"

"I don't know, Sam. Does it matter?" *Note for the future— don't gawk.*

If there was a future.

She tossed her napkin on the table, scooted her chair back and reached for her small slouch purse. "I need to get back. I'm right in the middle of a big project." She opened her purse and pulled out some bills.

He rolled on one hip and pulled his wallet. "I've got it."

"I'll pay for my own, thanks." Her formal tone matched the cool in her eye.

He knew better than to argue with that tone. Damn. He'd known she had strong boundaries; he should have known better. But she'd been so relaxed, and he'd been enjoying himself so much that he let himself forget.

Now he may have blown his chance with the most interesting woman he'd met in eons. *Idiot. No wonder you're alone on Friday nights.*

SAM KEPT QUIET on the way back to the house. *This was a bad idea. You knew it.*

Just loosen up a bit, the little girl whispered in a singsong voice.

If you loosen up, stuff is going to fall out.

Sam gathered her hair into a ponytail with her fist, pulling tight the tender hairs at the nape of her neck. Maybe the pain would wake her up. She'd been in denial. The nightmares were the rumble of thunder, signaling an approaching storm. Now was the time to hunker down—find some shelter.

Because it's surer than hell gonna rain bad stuff.

She snuck a glance at Nick's profile. He looked like a bad boy thanks to an unlucky arrangement of features. But she learned today he was really just a small-town homebody. Sweet, but…

Too sweet to get sucked into the funnel cloud heading her way.

A shudder rattled down her spine. She didn't know what was going to happen when that storm hit, but it wasn't going to be pretty.

Nick slowed, and turned at her driveway.

She reached to the floorboard to pick up her bag, before the car stopped. "Thanks for lunch, and for the ride."

He turned, the questions in his eyes grazing the skin of her face, as if looking for a way in. "I had a good time, Sam. It felt like I've known you a lot longer than I have. I'd like to find out why. Can I call you?"

So he'd felt it, too. Usually she didn't relax so easily. Lunch with Nick had filled more than her stomach. She'd enjoyed him way too much. When had that ever happened to her? Exactly never.

But within her, a harbinger wind whipped the small hope away. She scrambled out of the car. "I don't think that's a good idea. Besides, I'm going to be really busy."

"What are you afraid of, Sam? Me?"

"Not you." She felt her lips twist, but the result probably wasn't a smile. "We've both got things to do, Nick, and my things aren't in Widow's Grove. Better to just let it go."

"Better how? Look, Sam. I know you're going back to the road as soon as the house is done, and I have no intention of leaving Widow's Grove, ever again." He lifted his hand from the passenger seat, turning it palm up. "Doesn't that make me safe?"

"Safe?" She dropped her hands and stepped away from the car. "I don't know that word." She turned to trudge up the drive, hearing the throb of the car's engine, and feeling the familiar throb of separateness in her chest.

CHAPTER SEVEN

SAM SPENT A RESTLESS night awash in dreams that were complex and dark. She'd struggle almost to the surface of consciousness, only to be pulled under by another black wave. At dawn, sleep's undertow pushed her onto the beach of Wednesday morning. Her muscles ached, as though she'd spent the night swimming against the current.

After brewing a pot of coffee, she sat on the front steps to strategize. Once the basic task of keeping the rain out was complete, maybe she'd install a porch swing. How great would it be to sit out here in the morning, watching the cloud shadows shifting over the landscape?

Besides, a swing would add a homey touch. Make it show better.

Later that morning, she drove into the packed parking lot of Widow's Grove High. Much as she hated it, she had to face facts. She needed help.

The school was a cluster of single-story stucco buildings connected by covered walkways, outlined in flowerbed borders. Her alma mater in Ohio had been a stone block prison in comparison. Heading for the large double doors, she wondered if things would have been better if she'd attended a school like this.

Yeah, right. Like pretty scenery would have changed anything. Now, if you'd never met Mr. Collins, that would have made a difference.

She opened the heavy glass door and stepped into the past.

Amazing how all state-run learning institutions smelled the same: a mixture of old library books, decades of cafeteria food, dust and teenage hormones. She checked in at the office and received directions to the shop classroom.

Sam forced her shoulders back and her chin up, reminding herself that she was no longer a gangly, scuttling misfit. Strange how walking the halls brought back the sharp-edged emotions that memories themselves did not. A tall, awkward, tomboy from the wrong side of town might have skated under the radar of the cool girl clique—if she hadn't had the audacity to be *friends* with their boyfriend pool.

Clllannnggg! At the bell, the cavernous hall became a flash-flood river of students. They wore cutting-edge fashions, piercings and blatant attitude. The girls chattered behind their hands about the boys, who postured in studious disregard. Exotic fragrances competed with sweet, immature ones, combining in a miasma of perfume and teenage sweat. Raucous laughter echoed off the cinder block walls and every voice ratcheted decibels, competing. Sam breathed in the youthful energy, the air fairly crackling with a potent mix of potential and angst.

It was one of those rare times when she stood at the edge of a double-sided mirror: on one side was the awkward teen outcast, on the other, a grown woman. A professional. A contractor.

An emotional mess.

She found the correct room number and dropped out of the flow of students.

Maybe so. But at least in one aspect of her life, she'd achieved her dream. A rare bubble of pride rose in her chest.

Dan Porter stood at the front of the classroom in dress slacks and a blue collared shirt with the sleeves rolled up.

"Samantha. You came!" His tone told her he hadn't been

at all sure she would. He hurried over on stubby legs to pump her hand.

The front of the large room was a typical classroom, with chairs in rows facing a blackboard. The back transitioned to a wood shop, with high ceilings and windows marching down one side.

"Class is about to start. Do you have the time to sit in? It would give you an idea of the kids' knowledge levels. At the end, would you mind talking a bit about what you do for a living? I try to remind them that there will be life after high school. Or am I asking too much?"

Sam chuckled. "What would I expect from a man who prowls home improvement stores, springing on unsuspecting contractors? I'd be happy to talk, but I'm not ready to commit to hiring them."

"That's fair enough."

She slid into a chair at the back as the bell rang. Several students slipped in as Dan closed the door. Sam was gratified to see both sexes represented; she'd been the only girl in her shop classes. The boys had accepted her, once they realized that she took it seriously. The girls weren't as forgiving.

Dan began the class by asking them to recite the rules.

Smart way to get the kids to buy in to safety.

"I want to introduce Samantha Crozier, a local contractor."

Heads turned, chairs squealed and the heavy regard of a tough audience settled on Sam. She sat still, squirming relegated only to her stomach.

"Ms. Crozier is going to speak with us at the end of class. You're free to work on your individual projects, now. Anyone has questions, come see me."

Sam followed the noisy crowd to the business side of the shop.

Wandering past the floor saws, she stopped to talk to several students. Their projects ranged from simple bookshelves to birdhouses.

One boy was using power tools to carve a long chunk of cedar. Tall and lanky, stringy black hair obscured most of his pale face. Clad totally in black, he had a safety pin through his eyebrow and homemade tattoos etched the backs of both hands. He ignored her, concentrating on his intricate work with a scroll saw.

When he paused, Sam asked, "What is it?"

"A sign for a band I know."

Gothic letters spelling "Long Goodbye" stood in bold relief, an elongated dragon winding through them.

"It's beautiful."

"Huh."

"Do you want to work in wood as a career?"

"Dunno."

"You should think about it. You have talent."

"Yeah. Thanks."

The buzz of the electric router made further conversation impossible—though *conversation* seemed too ambitious a word. She moved to the next station.

At the end of class, Sam spoke for ten minutes about the building trade and the future of the industry.

When she was done, Dan spoke up. "We've got a few minutes for questions. This is your chance, people. Do you have anything you've wondered about the career that Sam could answer?"

The blonde girl in the front row raised her hand. "Have you run into prejudice, being a woman contractor?"

"Great question, but I can't really speak to it. I apprenticed under my dad, then started my own business. I've never worked for anyone else. I can tell you that I've had some odd looks from other contractors, and a few clients, but no prejudice. Don't let fear hold you back."

A gangly boy with acne raised his hand next. "How do you decide what kind of contractor you want to be? Electrical, plumbing, woodworking…there's a lot to choose from."

"And isn't that a great problem to have? Actually, you'll choose based on what you're drawn to. The cool thing about this field is that it's more than a career. It's a skill, and an art, too. What makes an artist choose sculpting over painting? It's a combination of what they're good at, and what calls to them. Don't be afraid to try everything. You'll know when the time comes to choose."

Dan thanked her as the bell rang. She walked over to him as the students made a mad dash for the door.

"I've seen the students and your shop. It's only fair that you see their potential work site," Sam said. "Why don't you stop by after school sometime? It's a hundred-year-old Victorian, and the first order of business is the roof. You may see that pitch and decide you don't want the kids anywhere near it. I'm not saying I'm for this, but I'm willing to keep an open mind."

"That sounds good. After that, we should both have enough information to make a decision."

That afternoon Sam climbed onto the roof slow and easy. Luckily, she'd thought to have the movers put the ladder up for her; she couldn't have wrestled it up with one arm. But she needed to assess the damage and survey the area so she could order supplies.

The jackhammer in her collarbone drove home the fact that she had to get help.

But only until I'm healed.

Straddling a roof beam, she looked around her. The view was even better from here; the hills seemed to march into the marine layer cloud bank advancing from the coast. Her eyes followed her eucalyptus fencerow, down the hill to her nearest neighbor, a small cottage. An old woman in a flowered housedress and straw hat knelt in the backyard, gardening. As if feeling Sam's gaze, the woman looked up. Sam waved, but the woman turned back to her work.

"I hope she's not the Welcoming Committee." Sam turned back to her computations, reminding herself to stop and introduce herself soon. After all, two women living miles from town needed to check in on each other.

When Dan stopped by that evening, he whistled when he saw the roof. "That is a tough one. You're going to need help."

"At least until the bone heals. Your kids seem to have good safety habits in the shop, but this is dangerous. I'll teach them what I can, but I don't have time to babysit."

"Hey, you're the employer. You choose whom to trust. If they break the rules or give you a hard time, fire them. One of the most important things they need to learn is what employers expect, and how to behave. Most haven't held jobs before, but I can vouch for them, they're good kids."

"I guess I'll give it a shot, then—for now."

"The kids are going to be excited." His round face beamed and he rubbed his hands together. "I'll announce it in class, and have those interested apply in person after school."

"Who was the kid with the wood-carving project? He's good with his hands."

"Oh, that's Beau. Beauregard Tripp the third, no less. His parents have more money than God, though you'd never know it to look at him. He's been suspended a couple of times for excessive absences; mine is the only class he attends regularly. He's been on the edge of trouble for years, with school and the local cops."

If she hadn't had her father to take care of, would she have rebelled in high school? Something about the boy's defiance made her wonder about his home life. *Takes one to know one, I guess.* "He sure didn't look like a poor little rich kid."

"I'm not sure what his problem is, but things don't seem

to be getting better for him—mostly due to his own choices." Dan shrugged. "He's talented enough to work for you, but I'm not sure you want to take on the attitude." They walked through the grass to his car. "I'd better get moving. I've got to get up early to go surfing."

"You surf?" She couldn't hide a smile, imagining Friar Tuck in Hawaiian-print swim trunks and flip-flops. "But hey, I'm a biker chick. Who am I to throw rocks?"

The backyard was crowded with shadows by the time Sam pushed the screen door open with her butt, a glass of iced tea in one hand, a sandwich in the other. She sat on the stoop. The full moon had just peeked over the hills, softening the reality of the backyard, cloaking the choking weeds and flaking paint. By squinting, and allowing for exaggeration, she could see the place—trimmed and in order, with the rows of a vegetable garden to her left, and a grape arbor to the right, tucked up next to the carriage house.

She inhaled the freshly-pressed smells of evening. A cricket orchestra tuned up in the knee-high grass of the yard. Content, she took a big bite of her bologna and lettuce sandwich.

"Grrrrine."

Her butt muscles tightened. That was not a cricket.

"Grrrrine?"

The growl came from the brush-filled eucalyptus fencerow at the back of the property. Surely this wasn't wolf habitat. *Yeah, but I bet there are coyotes in these hills.*

"Grrrrine?" Louder this time.

Maybe rabid ones. Clenching her sandwich too hard, she squinted in the ghostly moonlight. She caught a glint. Off teeth? Bottom teeth. When the animal moved, its eyes flashed a flat, haunted green.

She shot up and was through the screen door in two heartbeats. Slamming the heavy inside door, she locked it. Between the wild animals and rabid men, maybe she *would* be wise to buy a gun.

THE RADIO PLAYED a Paganini violin concerto as Sam worked the next day. Rock anthems ruled the road, but she liked to work to classical. The old music lent her perspective, whispering in a soothing voice that there were no problems that couldn't be solved by time.

She stood on a ladder in her dining room, surveying her demolition. Frustrated with the restriction of the sling, she'd taken it off, never intending to use it again regardless of the pain.

The floors upstairs were dangerous, so instead, she worked on the ceiling of the first floor. Decades of mummified spiders and hundred-year-old debris rained on her head. It was only noon, and the left side of the house looked like a blitzkrieg-bombed building.

The sound of a knock at the front door snapped Sam to attention, her nerves surging to DEFCON 5. Sledgehammer in fist, she backed down the ladder and stalked through the hall. She stood, hand on the locked door. "Who is it?"

"Jesse and Carl. We come bearing food and muscle."

Sam's held breath whooshed out. "Hold on." She unlocked the door.

Jesse and her husband stood on the porch, holding what looked like box lunches from the café. Sam's heart slowed from a panicked gallop to a fast trot.

Jesse looked Sam over. "Lord, honey, do you know you're coated in plaster dust? You look like the ghost of Pig-Pen!"

Sam unlocked the screen door and pushed it open. "You're going to run screaming when you see the mess."

Jesse stopped halfway down the hall, gaping. "Oh, my God, did the ceiling collapse?"

"Not without a lot of swearing." Sam swiped her hand down her jeans and took the bags of food from Carl. Inhaling the decadent smell of warm French fries, her stomach growled. "You didn't have to do this. I don't want you to feel like you have to help."

Carl stepped around Jesse and took the hammer from her hand. "I've been looking forward to this," he said in a quiet voice, walking into what remained of the dining room. "I'll eat later." Sam and Jesse retired to the kitchen and dug in, serenaded by strains of Mozart and Carl's sledgehammer.

"So?" Jesse draped her arm on the chair back in slouched nonchalance. "Heard from Nick?"

Sam took a sip from her soft drink. "He calls a couple times a week, updating me on the parts hunt for the Vulcan."

"That's all?"

"Don't even start getting ideas in that blond head of yours. He's my mechanic."

"I know, you've told me before in our afternoon chats that you're not looking for a relationship. But don't you think he's a nice guy?"

"Yes, Yenta, he's a nice guy." Someone save her from well-meaning—but misguided—matchmakers. "Thanks to you, I know that he's—" looking to the ceiling, she ticked the points off in her catechism voice "—a local volunteer for the homeless shelter, runs some kind of meetings at the Knights of Pythias a couple times a week, is mechanic for the police force and fixes town kids' bicycles for free." She looked back to Jesse. "Did I forget anything? Has he rescued any drowning kittens since I spoke with you last?"

"No, but—"

"Don't you get that look in your eye. I don't know why you're trying to turn this into something it's not, and never will be."

"I know I shouldn't butt in." Jesse shrugged. "But I never let that stop me before."

Sam rolled her eyes, but Jesse barreled on.

"I just don't understand. You've got a body to die for, a face that could be on a magazine cover yet you live like a hermit. I *know* you're not gay. So what is it?"

"Not everyone wants a husband, a house and two point five kids, Jesse."

"I know that. But everyone has *someone*. From what you've told me, you don't: no friends back home, no relatives, no one to call when something bad happens. Or something good, for that matter." Jesse leaned in, too close. "And that's not normal—unless you're schizophrenic. And come to think of it, they at least have other people in their heads."

"Look, it's not like I don't date. I haven't since I've been here, but I can. I mean, I have. I go out with perfectly decent men. Perfectly normal men."

"Sounds like you're choosing a computer."

Sam sat, skewered on the pin of Jesse's logic.

"Look, I care about you. I can't help wanting you to be as happy as Carl and me. If you'd ever felt something like that, you'd know what I'm talking about. It's like finding a part of you that you didn't know existed, and after, you wonder how you ever lived without it."

Sam dropped the remainder of her hamburger in the bag. "You're giving me a sugar rush, Jesse."

"Do you know that I was scheduled to go off to college when Carl asked me to marry him?"

Sam stopped crinkling paper.

Jesse looked out the window to the backyard that Sam was sure she didn't see. "Carl and I went together all through high school, and afterward, he was going to Cal Poly, just up the road. I had a full ride scholarship to Princeton." She patted her hair. "What can I say? Math's my anomaly.

"Anyway, the summer after graduation, Carl's dad was

killed in a car wreck on Coast Highway. His mom was a mess. Carl had to take over the café.

"When I told him I was staying to help, he told me I was going to Princeton, if he had to carry me over his shoulder and take me there himself. So I went." Her mouth tightened. "I *hated* it. The people were stuffy, the weather was dismal and I missed Carl and Widow's Grove like a piece of me had been torn away. By November, I had enough. I packed my stuff and drove back here—hardly stopping until I parked in the lot of the café. I walked in, and at the top of my lungs told Carl that if he didn't marry me, I was driving to Pismo and throwing myself off the pier."

Sam smiled, imagining what that would have done to Jesse's hair. "So? Did you get wet?"

Jesse shrugged. "Okay, so I got a little dramatic. But once he got over being mortified, he asked me to marry me. Right there, in front of a roomful of people."

At her sweet smile, something pinched in Sam's chest. But when she tried to imagine staying in one place for years and years, claustrophobia expanded like an octopus's ink cloud. What was it about this town that made people hate to leave it? First Nick, now Jesse and Carl. Sam made a mental note to drink nothing but bottled water from then on.

"Jess, I'm glad for your 'happily ever after' story. I really am. But don't you ever, on a bad day, look around you and think about the road you didn't take? I mean, jeez, woman, you could have—"

"Could have what? Been some egghead math whiz at the Pentagon? Been a professor at a university? Yeah, maybe I could have." She put her forearms on the table. "So, what? What good is a gift, if it doesn't make you happy?

"I'm not unaware, Sam. I know I look like a cliché—the ditzy blonde waitress in the diner." She raised her hand to her neck, checking for any stray hair that dared to fall out of her sprayed helmet. "But you know what? I don't care. I am exactly where I want to be, doing what makes me happy, with the man who makes me happier." She sat back with a moony smile. "Isn't that what everyone wants? Happiness?"

Maybe happily ever afters could happen, outside of kids' books. But they sure didn't happen to biker chicks hauling her kind of baggage. "I'm truly happy for you, Jess. But what is right for you doesn't work for me." Sam stood and gathered the garbage that littered the table. "Besides, you're wrong. I'm not alone. I've got you."

"You do." Jesse stood. "But I refuse to give up. I'll keep nudging in my oh-so-charming way, and you can tell me to shut up anytime."

"Jess, a bulldozer 'nudges.' You're more like a force of nature."

"Why, thank you, darlin'. I think that's the nicest thing that's ever been said of me. Listen, I want to help with the remodel, but I don't want to break a nail if I can help it…." She pulled a nail file and polish from her purse. "Are you sure you don't want to do your toes with me?"

Sam snorted. "How did I end up friends with a poodle like you? Never mind, that was a rhetorical question." She left Jesse to her toes, and went to find Carl.

The afternoon passed quickly. They demolished ceilings in the remaining two rooms and hauled the debris to the two oversize Dumpsters that had been delivered. Carl seemed a sweet man, though a quiet one. But considering his spouse, his silence was probably self-preservation.

Watching the couple walk arm-in-arm to their car hours later, Sam felt a stab of loneliness. She'd learned today that happy endings *could* happen. But for some reason, knowing it didn't make her feel better.

THAT EVENING, SAM sank onto her back stoop and settled her napkin-wrapped sandwich on her lap. "You were right, Dad, I am a porch potato." She missed being in the outdoors all day, traveling on the bike. Being in nature grounded her, helping her keep perspective; her problems were small put up on the backdrop of the timeless earth. After a day working indoors, she'd always gravitated to the porch.

But not all her porch memories were good. Following her dad's funeral, she couldn't make herself care what came next, so she'd taken bereavement leave from work. During the day, she'd float around her empty rooms, a becalmed ship. In the evening, she'd sit on the porch, where she and her father had spent so many sundowns. But when night closed in like a cold, comfortless blanket, there was only howling emptiness. Many mornings, the sun found her stiff and cold on the back step.

"Grrrrine?"

The sound snapped her from the past.

The shrub at the edge of her property rustled.

The half-eaten sandwich fell from her lap. She pulled herself up by the support post to crouch on the step, ready for flight. Or fight.

"Grrrrine?"

A pink-white muzzle poked from the shadows.

Wolves aren't white. Neither are coyotes. Just the same, she reached for the hammer, her constant companion since Brad's visit.

A white head emerged. Wrinkled skin hung from drooping jowls. Small crumpled ears. Pugnacious nose. She'd been so prepared for a snarling predator that it took her a minute to place the features. A bulldog?

The dog emerged from under the bush, scooting on its belly. It pulled itself upright and teetered on short legs. *"Grrrrine?"* It took a wavering step, then another.

Sam tightened her grip on the hammer. It didn't have to be wild to be mean. Or rabid.

One slow waddling step at a time, the dog crossed the yard, never looking at her directly.

White and pink? What kind of dog was pink? And red. An open gash bisected the length of its short back, angry and inflamed. She winced.

As the dog neared, she understood its piebald coloring. Pink skin showed through the fur in gaping, scaly patches.

"Mange?" A thread of pity mingled with revulsion.

The dog stopped and cocked its head. *"Grrrrine?"* It dropped onto its belly and pulled itself the few feet to the steps, stumpy tail going like a manic metronome.

Dogs didn't wag their tails, then bite—did they? Never having owned one, she wasn't sure. Eyes downcast, the dog shot her tentative glances from under expressive eyebrows.

Maybe if she gave it something it would go away. Still clenching the hammer, Sam inched her other hand to where her sandwich lay scattered on the dirty porch boards. Pulling out a piece of bologna, she tossed it at the dog.

Jaws snapped so fast Sam jerked back.

The dog ducked and cringed.

Someone had abused this hideous animal. Pity beat out revulsion. "Damn."

Taking her statement as forgiveness, the dog's tail started up again. It looked directly at her for the first time, a look of love in its eyes.

At least, that's what she thought it was. She tossed the rest of the sandwich the few feet between them. The dog wolfed it in one bite.

"That's all I have. Now go away." To be clear, she made shooing movements with her hands.

"Grrrrine."

The whimper sounded like, "Mine."

The dog rolled over, showing her a dirty, mangy belly. And that it was male.

"Oh, no. Uh-uh." She stood, brushing her hands on the seat of her jeans. "I'm a short-timer, dog. Go find a local to sweet-talk."

It lay, dirt sticking to lolling lips, eyes closed, panting.

Sam turned, took the last step, then crossed the porch to the door. She snuck a look over her shoulder.

The dog hadn't moved.

Jerking the door open, she walked in the kitchen, letting the screen door slap behind her. Stepping to the sink, she grabbed a clean glass from the drain board, filled it and drank. Then looked out the window.

The dog hadn't moved.

It was sick. Probably feverish from infection in that gash.

She crossed to the refrigerator, opened it. Leaning on the door, she peered in, looking for an alternate dinner choice. She had to remember to get more bologna at the store. And bread. And…

The way the mangy mutt was lying, that cut would be in the dirt.

"Oh, hell." Straightening, she slammed the door. She crossed to the window and looked out.

The dog hadn't moved.

If it died there, she'd have to bury it.

"I don't have time for this." She snatched her cereal bowl from the drain board and filled it with water from the tap. Careful not to spill any, she carried the bowl outside and down the porch steps to set it down next to the oversize head.

Smelling the water, the dog struggled to stand. Balancing on shaking legs, it lowered its head to slurp the water, splashing more out than it drank.

When the bowl was empty, it looked up at her, panting,

water and drool dripping from distended, liver-spotty lips. It lifted a broad paw, reached out and tapped her tennis shoe.

She stepped back.

"Grrrrine?"

It took a rigged sling and a lot of grunting and moaning, but a half hour later, the dog lay tucked in a blanket on the passenger-side floorboard of the Jeep as she drove into town. "I can't stand to see anything suffer. I'll take you to the vet, but then you're on your own."

A call to Jesse had yielded the name of a vet. He'd been closing when she called, but agreed to stay until she could get there. Just outside of town, she pulled into the parking lot of a small building. It looked like a doctor's office from the '60s. Large aluminum-framed windows gave a view of a lit, deserted reception area.

She shut down the engine and got out. Gravel crunched underfoot as she walked to the passenger side and opened the door. "Come on, mutt, let's go."

The dog lifted its head, but made no move to stand. Skin rippled as a shiver traveled the length of its body; then again. It laid its head on thick, gnarly-knuckled paws.

"How the heck I get myself into things like this…" She bent, wrapped the sling around the shaking, muscular body and lifted.

If felt like someone had hit her collarbone with a hammer. "Damn, you're heavy." She backed up and slammed the car door with her butt. "Mange just better not be catching, that's all I'm saying."

A tall, thin man with red hair opened the clinic door, and seeing her grimace, took the dog from her.

The lobby was just as she'd expected—cinder-block walls, green linoleum, orange plastic chairs lined up against the window and a Formica reception desk. Pine-scented disinfectant couldn't mask the odor of years of four-legged patients.

She followed the veterinarian to an exam room. He looked the dog over thoroughly and determined that, in addition to mange, the dog had a raging infection and a bad case of dehydration. But even lying on the cold stainless exam table, the dog's stump tail ticked at redline RPMs. An IV line snaked from a bag of saline to his front leg.

"Why didn't you bring him in earlier?" The vet fiddled with the IV line.

Sam glanced up. "Not my dog. He crawled out of my bushes an hour ago." She took a step to the door. "I really need to go—"

"Well, I'll drive him to the pound when the infection clears, but…" As he straightened, the surgeon's lamp glinted off hair the color of copper wire.

"But what?" She tucked her hands in the front pockets of her jeans.

"Well, if I take him down there with mange, purebred or no, he's not likely to be adopted."

The dog lifted his head and stared right at her. Drool stretched from distended lips to the exam table. His brow shifted with every eye movement, giving the liquid eyes an almost human expression of loving devotion. He laid his head back on the steel with a sigh.

She retreated a step toward the door. "Look, I'm committed here for ten months, max, then I'm in the wind. I've never owned an animal. Never wanted one. I—"

"Well, then, that shouldn't be a problem. I can give you medicine for the mange. His coat will grow back in a few months, once the scabies are gone. You can take him to the pound when he's all pretty again." He dusted his hands, as if it were already decided. "You know what happens to unwanted animals at the pound, right?"

The dog lay still. Except for the tail.

She knew manipulation when she heard it. She didn't have

time for this. But the damn animal looked so pathetic. And she knew what it felt like, being a stray. "Oh, hell." She took a step toward the table.

"You're a good sport." The vet ruffled the dog's ears. "Thank you."

"I'm a sucker." She pulled her wallet from her back pocket. "What do I owe you?"

"Nothing. I volunteer time at the shelter, so I'd have seen him there for free, anyway."

She leaned down to look the dog in the eye. "This is temporary, mutt. I just want you to know that up front, so there are no hard feelings later. Got it?"

The dog's tongue shot out, aiming for her chin. She jerked back just in time. *Maybe Jesse wants a pet.* She straightened. "I don't know the first thing about what to do with a dog."

"Well, the first thing he needs is a name." He ran his hand gently over the patchy coat. "You can't call him 'Not My Dog.'"

Sam considered. "How about Bugly? Because he is one butt-ugly animal."

The dog raised its head, glanced at her, then away.

"Aww, I think you've hurt his feelings." He scratched under the dog's scaly pink chin.

Sam winced. *Yuck.* "Well, I'd hate to damage his delicate self-esteem. How about just Bugs, then?"

The dog panted in what looked like a smile.

"I think he approves." The vet patted the dog's side. "I've given him antibiotics in the IV, but you'll need to give him pills for ten days. I have dust for the mites and ointment for when they're gone. Then—"

"Hang on, I don't even know what to feed it!" She grabbed a pad and pen from the counter. "You better start at the beginning."

Once they arrived home, it took two days for Sam and

the dog to negotiate the logistics of his sleeping arrangements. She began by closing him in the carriage house with vet-supplied dog food, water and a nest of packing blankets. When his panicked barking told her that was not acceptable, she tied a long rope to his vet-supplied collar, and left him tied to the back porch. With the same results. Grumbling, she brought him inside and made a bed for him in the closet under the stairs. He seemed to settle better there.

Until an hour later, when she bolted awake to a cold nose and dog breath in her face. Stumbling, stupid with sleep, she retrieved his blankets and made a pallet for him on the floor next to her bed.

He plopped there with what she hoped was a contented sigh, and was finally quiet.

Until the snoring began.

CHAPTER EIGHT

SAM AND THE DOG worked their way into a routine over the next few days. Sam erected a sturdy clothesline in the backyard, sinking the metal end-posts in concrete. She bought a braided wire running line at the pet store and clipped one end to the clothesline, the other to Bugs's collar, well within the radius of the huge shade tree and a bowl of water. He slept most of the day away, presumably healing.

Monday dawned too pretty to spend amid the debris indoors. A perfect day to introduce herself to her neighbor in the Victorian cottage at the bottom of the hill.

Sam left Bugs napping and walked the gravel drive to the road, stopping to do a few stretches and practice deep breathing. Her collarbone didn't hurt, as long as she didn't pound nails with that hand, or pick up a dog. Her ribs had improved, as well.

She'd found that traveling quieted the tension that braided in the nerves of her spine. When her finances forced a sabbatical from the road, the wire vibrated, traveling through her body in a low-frequency thrumming that left her shoulders hunched near her ears and put a fine tremor in her hands. A white-noise background to her days, the tension owned the night. She'd toss and tear at the sheets, trying to relax. But her mind and body craved movement. The blessed exhaustion of walking was the only thing she'd found to lull the wire.

She thought about the afternoon with her mechanic, Nick. She'd had a great time, right up to when he started hitting on her. Why did guys feel like they had to do that? They sooner or later started with the compliments and the hungry eyes. Why wasn't enjoying each other's company enough for an afternoon?

He was good-looking, though, with his olive complexion and expressive eyes. With a last name like Pinelli, he must be Italian and looked every bit of that from his thick dark hair to his lithe body. They'd enjoyed the afternoon to that point. She admitted to herself that she'd like to see him again.

You don't even know this guy.

But Jesse's known him since he was a kid, and she's a fan.

He's dangerous in other ways. You know it.

Sparrows cheeped in the wild oats growing on either side of the road, and a fresh breeze ran fingers through her hair. As she walked another road song dropped onto the turntable in her brain: Lynyrd Skynyrd's "Free Bird." Her tennis shoes scuffed the pavement and her mind gentled.

Feeling more relaxed, she threw her head back and squinted into the sun.

After cresting the hill and walking down the other side, Sam approached her neighbor's house. The small cottage was a real gem, with scalloped fish-scale siding, and fanciful Mary Hart fretwork in the eaves, all painted a blinding white. Intricately turned columns supported the roof of the deep porch. Rosebushes used them to climb to the sun.

She opened the gate of the thigh-high white picket fence and stepped into a riot of color. Small delicate blooms hid under splashy, flower-covered bushes, in stark contrast to the golden desert outside the fence. That this much fragile beauty could exist in such a harsh landscape was a testament to hard work and a huge water bill.

Sam walked up the steps and across the porch to knock on the wooden screen door. The sound echoed from the shadowy interior. After a moment, she retraced her steps, following a terra-cotta stepping-stone path at the side of the house. An old woman knelt, using a trowel to loosen the dirt around a plant. She wore a flowered housedress that must be an old favorite; the flowers on it were blurred, the cotton worn to soft shapelessness. Green gardening gloves covered her hands and a broad-brimmed floppy straw hat obscured her face.

"Excuse me," Sam said.

The woman started, clutching her chest. Steel-gray laced through the black hair peeking from under the hat. Her wrinkled cheeks flushed pink.

"I'm sorry. I didn't mean to frighten you." Before Sam could reach to help, the woman scrambled to her feet.

"What do you want?" She glared, gripping the trowel as a weapon.

"I'm Samantha Crozier. Your new neighbor?" She pointed up the hill to her house. "I thought I'd stop to introduce myself."

The woman stood mute, staring.

Sam inspected her faded denim overalls, a T-shirt that ended at her midriff, and her scarred tennis shoes. Nothing out of the ordinary. "I'm sorry to have frightened you. I thought you heard me walk up. Are you all right?"

"Yes."

More silence.

This is going well. "And your name is…?"

"I am Anajuschka Strauss," the woman said in a slight Germanic accent.

"My friends call me Sam." Flashing a peace-offering smile, she reached out a hand. The woman recoiled as if it were a snake. She reminded Sam of an animal in a trap, baring its teeth at someone trying to help. "I'd love to learn more about your beautiful flowers. I could use some advice."

"I am busy." She barely moved the grim line of her lips.

The woman appeared angry, but the naked fear that Sam

glimpsed underneath felt familiar. It felt like her own. Sam spoke in a calming voice. "Some other time, then. I'll stop by and we can get to know each other a bit."

"There is no need. There is nothing for you here." She turned back to her plants.

"Okay, but if you ever need anything please let me know. We're two women, all alone out here." Sam let herself out of the gate and turned toward home. Cresting the hill, her heart stuttered at the sight of a sleek new BMW sedan parked in the drive.

Brad. Her stomach did a loop, then plunged, like an amusement park ride. *Not the Mercedes.* She forced her feet to keep moving. *No law against owning two cars.* Without taking her eyes off the car, she slapped her pockets for her screwdriver. They were empty. Well, she'd have to improvise. Squaring her shoulders, she marched to the house.

She walked to the backyard, only to see Bugs, drooling in the lap of a teenager. When he looked up, Sam recognized the woodcarver from the high school.

"Cool dog. What's his name?"

"*His* name is Bugs. What's yours?" The fear made the words come out hard.

The kid must have realized he was being rude, because he pushed to his feet, tucked in his shirt, brushed off his drool-damp black jeans. "I'm Beau. I met you at school. Mr. Porter's shop class? He told us you might have a job...." He trailed off, seeming to have expended his meager supply of words.

This was a really bad idea. *I can get by without help.* She rolled her shoulders. Her collarbone disagreed.

She sighed. "Mr. Porter said he'd talk to his class. He didn't say when. Have a seat." She walked to the tree and sat with her back against the trunk, out of Bugs's drooling range. "So, why do you want to work for me?"

The boy gave her a flat stare, as if this were the last question he expected.

She glanced at the expensive car, then back at him. "Look, this isn't the local grocery store, or an office environment. This job is dirty and physical. It can be dangerous. I need to know your attitude and motivation. I'll probably ask some questions that may seem weird to you, even personal."

She took his silence as assent. *I sure hope this kid isn't the cream of the applicant pool.* "Why do you want a job?"

His shoulders slumped. Strands of hair fell in his eyes when he looked down. "My parents are pushing me to get a job." He pulled at the grass with nervous fingers.

"Why?"

"They think if I stay busy, I'll stay out of trouble." He blew out a breath. "I wouldn't make it two days working in a grocery store or an office, so when Mr. Porter told us about this job, I thought…"

This was going nowhere. "How about looking at me?"

His head whipped up, eyes narrowed.

"I am *trying* to help you. Your James Dean attitude won't get you a job."

"Who's James Dean?" The anger in his voice shifted to confusion.

"Don't you ever watch classic movies? He was Hollywood's original bad boy."

Why am I wasting my time? "Look, I'm willing to talk to you without judging. Think you can do the same?"

He brushed the hair back, and his eyes met hers. "I guess that's fair."

She relaxed against the tree. "Okay, let's start over. Tell me about yourself."

"I'm not sure what you want to know. I live in Widow's Grove, and you know I go to the high school."

"Do you like it?"

"School?" He snorted. "Hate it. Not shop class, but every other subject is a waste of time. I can't see how math and history are going to help me once I get out of school."

She remembered feeling exactly that, in high school. "You might be surprised how much of that comes in handy. You can't build anything without math—surely you know that by now. I've been traveling the past couple of years, and what I knew about the civil war helped me in the South. History isn't so bad when you see where stuff happened, and how it shaped people. Anyway, if school isn't it for you, what do you like to do?"

He looked as if no one had ever asked him that question. He thought a moment. "I don't know. Mess around with friends, play video games, watch TV—the usual stuff."

"What kind of trouble have you been in?"

His hand jerked, pulling up a fistful of grass. His eyes cut away.

"I need to know."

He shrugged. "Nothing bad. Mostly skipping school, or hanging out too late with friends." Straightening his shoulders, he looked at her. This time, his eyes didn't waver. "You wouldn't be sorry, hiring me. When I like something, I'm dependable. Even my mother says that."

"Now that," she said pointing at him, "is the kind of attitude an employer wants to see." She pushed to her feet. "I'll tell you about the job. By the time I get done you may not be interested."

Did she really want to take on a potential train wreck? Hell, no. She didn't want *any* help. But she needed it. She looked him over, piercings, tattoos and all.

If she'd had the normal life of a teenager, would she have ended up like this kid? Maybe. In a way, she'd been lucky to have her dad to care for. When you had to ride your bike to a bar at thirteen to drive your drunk dad home after dark, you grew up fast.

He stood, watched her and waited.

"Come with me." She led him inside and upstairs. She opened the door to the ruined bedroom. "This would be way too expensive to repair. So I'm going to demolish the rooms on this side of the second story, shore up the remaining floor with posts below and create a loft that looks down into the great room I'm going to create down there."

"Oh, wow." The indifference was gone, his eyebrows pulled together in a frown of concentration, and a ghost of a smile lingered on his lips. "That would look *awesome*."

She led the way downstairs. "I'm leaving the parlor, but demolishing all the rooms down here, back to the kitchen." She walked the few steps to the closet under the stairs and pulled the door open. "This will become a powder room. A true 'water closet.'"

The kid stood in the doorway, stroking the curved wood molding of the doorframe.

She led the way to the kitchen.

"Oh, man, this is fugly."

Sam smiled. "Won't be when I'm done with it."

By the time they returned to the front yard, his stoic facade had slipped, revealing the excited kid beneath.

"I never thought much about houses." He waved his hands to illustrate. "You know, how they're put together. It can end up looking however *you* want, not just the way some architect thought it should." He winced. "Our house is stupid looking. Like somebody took a Southern plantation house, slapped a bunch of wedding cake frosting on it and plopped it in Widow's Grove."

She chuckled. "The creativity is one of the best things about this career. I'm given the basics, but I can create anything I want from there." She couldn't help but react to the look of wonder on the kid's face. That, more than anything, sold her. "So are you interested?"

"If you'll hire me." The wariness was back in his narrowed eyes and tight muscle of his jaw, as if he were waiting for rejection. Steeling himself for it.

He may be petulant and immature, but she couldn't resist anyone who got excited about building. "I need a copy of the waiver your parents signed for the school." She tried to focus on the business instead of the kid's big, goofy grin. "You'll also need written proof from Mr. Porter that you're covered by insurance. You bring these to me, and you can start."

"Wow." He looked up at the house as if she had just given it to him as a gift.

"I need you right after school until full dark. Since I'm kind of out in the boonies here, I'll feed you dinner as a part of your wages. If you work out, when school's out for the summer, we can renegotiate your work schedule." She led him down the weed-encroached sidewalk to his daddy's car, then turned.

"One more thing." She paused until sure she had his full attention. "If I ever see you screwing around, not following my instructions, being unsafe in any way, you'll be fired. Immediately. Understood?"

"Sure." He smiled at her and tucked his hair behind his ear. "This working gig may not be so bad."

"Wait until you try to get out of bed after the first day to tell me that."

As she watched him drive away, it occurred to her that she was starting to collect people. And animals. She'd been carefully separate from the outside world since Dad died, preferring to remain an anonymous shadow in the towns she'd waylaid in. What had changed?

Well, the dog was suffering. She hadn't had much choice there. She glanced down the hill to the cottage. So was that old woman. And Tim Raven had no one in the world. Stopping and talking to him, being sure he was okay was no big deal. There was Jesse, but she was different—you couldn't very well chase off a force of nature.

But that's it. No more strays for me. She didn't need strings that would break when she roared out of town on the Vulcan. Strings could be painful, and she'd had enough of pain.

OVER THE NEXT few days, several students showed up looking for work, and she selected two from the group. Pete Carter, a bulky starting lineman on the JV football team, wanted a physical job to help him stay in shape over the summer. She chose him for the heavy work. Her last hire was a lanky girl with an unlikely name, Sunny Skyes.

"My parents are the last of the hippies," the girl explained with a grimace.

"I like strong names. They give you something to live up to."

Sunny rolled her eyes. "You can't imagine the crap I get about it."

"See, it did give you something to live up to." Sunny laughed. Sam liked her immediately, not able to escape the comparison to herself at that age.

Definitely not boring.

NICK TURNED THE KEY in the door of the shop, then looked to where his younger employee stood outlined by the streetlight. "Good night, Tom. Happy hunting."

"You should come with me, boss. The beach has some great nightlife."

Yeah, been there, done that. Got the orange, county issued T-shirt. "I've got somewhere to be, Tom."

"Yeah, so you've said. But you should see some of those coeds from UCSB."

His low whistle made Nick smile. "All the more for you, buddy. See you in the morning."

He walked to the stairs at the side of the shop, a wave of loneliness scouring his chest hollow. His past relationships mostly revolved around a bottle. Turns out, when you hang out in a bar, you meet women who drink. Not a recipe for a love match.

These past years he'd been busy with the Big Three: building his business, building trust in himself and building back the damage done to his family name. He'd dated, but his love life fell way down on his list of priorities. Besides, imagining a gaggle of giggling coeds made his head pound. The drama factor of that age group held no appeal for him.

He remembered the bar-night hopefulness on Tom's face. He'd almost forgotten that. Maybe it was time to move his love life up a few notches on the priority list.

Nick pulled his cell from his pocket, and touched the screen till her name came up. Climbing the stairs, he listened to her phone ring.

"Hi, you've reached Samantha, of Crozier Contracting. I'm looking forward to helping you with your remodel needs, so please leave me a message and I'll get back to you as soon as I can."

Beep.

He'd been so busy listening to the husky alto voice with an undertone of sexy that he hadn't thought what he'd say. "Sam! It's Nick, and I was wondering if…"

There was a click on the line. "Hey, Nick." She sounded out of breath. "How's the Vulcan coming?"

She's leaving. Don't forget that.

"The gas tank is the tough nut at the moment. I found a couple online, but they're in worse shape than yours."

"Isn't it possible to pop the dents out of mine?"

"Yeah, but the bike is a classic, and everything else will

be pristine. It would be a crime to slap Bondo on it. It'd be like…supergluing a crack in the *Pieta*."

She chuckled. "I love my bike more than anyone, but I've never compared it to a Michaelango masterpiece."

"Well, I just meant—"

"You're some mechanic, Nick."

Her praise warmed him like summer sunshine. "Hey, I've got lots of hidden talents. Wait 'til I show you my first-grade artwork."

"Are you inviting me up to see your etchings?"

It was his turn to chuckle. "Maybe that's a little forward. I was thinking along the lines of showing you around the area. What do you think? Are you busy on Sunday?"

She hesitated so long he was beginning to think they'd been disconnected.

Then he heard her sigh. "You found my soft spot, Pinelli. How could I turn down a guy who worships my motorcycle?"

"Great. I'll pick you up around two on Sunday. You choose what you'd like to see."

"Deal. Thanks, Nick."

He hung up, excited about the prospect of a date for the first time sober. He unlocked the windowed door at the top of the landing and stepped into his kitchen. Flipping on the light over the chef's island, he opened the fridge and pulled out the calzone he'd made over the weekend, set it in a baking pan and turned on the oven.

After a quick shower, he padded barefoot to the kitchen and put his dinner in the oven. Canned spotlights created a warm circle, reflecting off the copper-bottomed pots on the hanging rack, to hit the gray Venatino marble countertop. His fingers itched to work some dough into capellini.

Instead, he wiped the wet hair drips from his neck, poured a glass of iced tea and carried it to the living room. He paused, fingers on the lamp switch, glancing out the picture window that looked down onto the high-rent district of Hollister Street.

When he returned from L.A., his luck changed. He couldn't believe that a developer offered him an ungodly amount of money for his family's dump of a house. Nick was more than happy to unload it—and all the secrets within its walls.

The sale gave him seed money to buy his business, a busy garage right at the edge of downtown. But the rabbit-warren apartment above it was another story. He'd gutted it to the studs and started over, creating space as he'd need it—a huge kitchen, bedroom and living room. A small dining nook and bathroom. The result fit him like a custom pair of steel-toe work boots.

When he switched on the light, the picture window became a mirror. He turned away. Plopping on the couch, he hit the remote for the sound system. The haunting strains of Verdi's *Rigoletto* poured over him. He relaxed, his mother's music melting the day's tension.

Sipping tea, he picked up the framed photo on the glass end table—an old studio portrait of his mother. She'd been a beauty, with the classic features of Sophia Loren; long black hair and high sculpted cheekbones. A seven-year-old version of himself stood close, hand on her shoulder. He remembered the sitting. He felt like a man. As if his hand had grown big enough to shelter her.

Another wave of loneliness broke over him. He'd finally managed to build a life his mom would be proud of. God, she would have loved grandkids—and to see him settled. He could almost hear her lecture, echoing in the back of his mind.

His eye caught on a thin crescent of a white shirt at the very edge of the photo; the reason the portrait sat off center in the frame. He'd cut away his father's swarthy image, but kept the rest.

Just as he'd done in life.

After dinner, Nick strolled the three blocks downtown to the Knights of Pythias building. He greeted a few people clustered around the coffeepot on his way to the podium.

"Let's get started, people. You want to take your seats?"

The clusters broke up. He waited for the scrape of chairs to settle, and murmur of voices to trail off.

"Hi." He bent, putting his mouth closer to the mic. "I'm Nick. And I'm an alcoholic."

DEMOLISHING THE CEILING hurt too much. Sam decided to save that for the students. Instead, she worked late on something she could do: sanding the window trim in what was becoming the great room with a small hand sander. The solid white oak she unearthed from years of water damage, paint and abuse made her throbbing collarbone worth it.

She stood in the middle of the room and rolled her shoulders. Her collarbone protested, but at least her ribs seemed to be healed; her morning walk hadn't elicited even a twinge.

"Maybe Arnie at Coast Lumber can tell me where I can get some used oak to replace a couple of pieces."

Bugs, comfortably ensconced on his pink sherpa throw blanket, lifted his huge head and yawned.

"Well, that's easy for you to say, bub. You want to take a turn at sanding?"

When she'd seen the almost hairless dog shivering outside on his clothesline run, she'd brought him in. Only until the weather warmed up. During the day, he followed her as she worked. After noticing his naked and painfully red elbows, Sam bought the softest blanket she could find in town, which he now dragged with him, from room to room.

She walked over, slid down the wall beside him and rubbed her shoulder. "I sure wish you had opposable thumbs. I could use a back rub."

Nick's strong capable hands popped into her mind.

Bugs looked at her out of the corner of his eye.

"I know. I should have turned him down." Her voice echoed in the empty room. "Better to scare him off now. I don't have time for a guy. Don't want one. Besides, I've put a moratorium on picking up any more strays."

Bugs dropped his head onto his paws and farted.

"Well, how do you *really* feel?" The delicate scent of eucalyptus from the open window dissolved in a miasma of bulldog flatulence. "Jesus, Bugs!" She slapped a hand over her nose and scooted away. "We have *got* to work on your diet!"

Expressive eyebrows shifted guiltily, but his head stayed on his paws.

"You've overstated your point, but I get it." She tested the air before uncovering her nose and scooted back beside the dog.

At the thought of Nick, tiny bubbles of excitement had risen in her core. Tightening her stomach muscles, she squashed the little buggers. That lunch a week ago had been too easy. She, too, felt a connection—as though they clicked on some fundamental level. That, coupled with the low-voltage jolt when their eyes connected…

You don't have to be an electrician to know voltage is dangerous.

For her, closeness with a man just wasn't possible. She'd tried committed relationships in the past. She was a dismal failure at the physical part, but worse, her secrets always kept her separate. Even if the guy didn't notice that she wasn't really present for sex, eventually he couldn't help but notice her emotional distance, and the holes in her past. The price of feeling normal for a while, dating, was a piercing, depressing reminder of her failure. So when she dated, she made sure to keep it light, strings-free and short-term.

But for some reason, Nick's smile seemed to flow through

unchinked cracks in her walls she hadn't even known were there, trying to snuggle next to her heart.

The little girl whispered in her ear. *It's no good, wanting what you can't have.*

Living on the periphery was safe. It was enough.

Bugs let out a loud snore.

Oh, well, thanks to the student work crew, the house would be complete by Christmas. That was only eight months away. Then she'd hop on her bike and ride south. Or, if her bike wasn't ready, she'd take the Jeep on the Northern route, up to Washington, then east. It didn't really matter where—there were houses in need of remodeling all across the country. After Nick finished the motorcycle, he could ship it to her.

With a sigh, she lifted her hand from the long patch of intact fur on the dog's haunch and got back to work.

CHAPTER NINE

SOMETHING CLAWED AT *the back of her brain. She shut off the belt sander and pushed the safety glasses to the top of her head, listening, sensing the fat hollowness of an empty house.*

There's something wrong.

The afternoon light slanted through uncovered windows, dust motes swirling. She stood, her knees popping like pistol shots in the hush. Brushing the sawdust from her jeans, she walked from the large country kitchen to the entrance hall of the log home. She tested the front door. Locked, just the way she'd left it.

There is no one here. Is there?

The silent house gave no clue, but danger crackled like static in the air. She stepped to the sidelight window of the front door, her fingers twitching at the lacy curtain, as she peered across the covered porch. The dense tangle of evergreens seemed to loom closer than earlier, a result of the advancing dusk.

Nothing.

Nothing physical, anyway.

Now where had that thought come from? She'd like to think she was merely spooked at being alone in the old house. But it was more than that. Much more.

Unseen eyes crawled over the back of her neck, like something forgotten at the edge of her memory.

Something she'd remember soon. Something...

Not good.

"Now you're really out there, Crozier." Her own voice, high-pitched and shaky, scared her even more.

Awareness crashed in her brain.

It's in the basement.

Her terrified thoughts scurried like cockroaches, looking for a way out. She froze midstep. "There's something in the basement that...could drive me mad if I see it."

She didn't know how she knew it. But she did. Her soul had whispered to her before. And it was never wrong.

Her gaze fell on the cellar door. Two needs plucked at her—an undeniable need to put her hand on the knob, and incredulity that she'd consider something so foolish. But beneath that, a thrill-seeking pull of attraction stood stronger than the terror. She wanted to open that door.

SAM WOKE WITH a start, then lay staring at the ceiling until her body accepted that it was just another dream, and unlocked her muscles. When a shower didn't wash off the dream's hangover, she decided to take Bugs for a walk. The dog spotted the leash in her hand and ran, nails clattering in the hall, to jump against her legs.

She shrugged into a fleece-lined denim jacket. "Patience, mutt." She clipped the leash on his collar and they stepped out onto the porch. Damp brushed her cheeks and eyelids. Beyond her front porch, a fog-shrouded yard waited. They walked into the clinging, silent world, revealed only a few grudging feet at a time. Not wanting to get lost in the gray sameness, she stuck to the road. Bugs dragged her from one side to the other, probably scenting rabbits.

Her unoccupied mind circled back to her dream. How could she possibly want to open that door? She wanted to deny the crazy urge, but it drove her as hard as the incredible feeling of terror at what lay behind it. Where the heck did that dream come from? Well, she probably knew the answer to that. But would she be haunted by it for the rest of her life? If so, it would be a short life—even if her mind could handle it without breaking, one day her heart would give out. Could a person actually die of fear?

Sam came to herself, standing in the middle of the empty road. While she'd wandered her nightmare, the sun had burned through the fog and the fields flanking the road appeared out of the mist. *Where's the leash? Screw that—where's the dog?*

"Man, I am losing it." She scanned the fields for the mutt, or any landmark that would help her get her bearings. The pavement rose ahead. She trotted to the summit. Her neighbor's cottage lay ahead, her own house behind. One problem solved. She ran down the hill, scanning the brush for movement. She heard a noise ahead, like someone throwing dirt against a barn door.

She sprinted to the cottage.

Bugs joyfully dug in the rich soil of the cottage garden. Nose snuffling, he flung dirt through his short legs. The sound she'd heard was the mud, splattering the pristine white picket fence.

"Stop!" The dog happily ignored her, as engrossed in his excavation as Sam had been in her thoughts.

She vaulted the gate, too late seeing the plastic sheeting covering the dirt. When she landed, her feet flew from under her. She just had time to think, *Oh, this is going to hurt,* before slamming onto her back, staring through tree branches at the sky. She sat up, collarbone hollering, holding her ribs, dazed.

A new batch of mud flew out from the rear of the frantically digging dog. It smacked her face and open mouth.

The screen door of the cottage banged open. Sam turned, almost afraid to look. Her neighbor stepped onto the porch, brandishing a broom like a baseball bat.

Sam spit mud. "Oh, crap. We're in for it now." Bugs ducked his head and scrambled behind her.

"Coward." She peered through muddy hair at the advancing woman. Mrs. Strauss's look shifted from thunderous to something else. Halfway down the sidewalk, she dropped the broom, covered her mouth and giggled.

Sam couldn't have been more surprised if her neighbor had flown off the porch on the broom. The woman laughed until tears rolled down her face, then retreated to the porch steps to catch her breath. Sam scrambled to her feet, brushed dirt from the seat of her jeans and grabbed the delinquent's collar. She dragged him behind her to the porch.

"I am so sorry, Mrs. Strauss. He slipped the leash, and when I found him…"

The woman waved her hand, clearly trying to get herself under control. "Oh, my, I have never seen anything the like! Your feet went completely over your head—like something from a *Three Stooges* show." She paused to take a breath. "Then the mud. You looked so shocked. Oh, my." She fanned her face with the edge of the apron tied around her ample waist.

Sam glared at Bugs, who looked everywhere but at her. "I am so sorry. I'll pay for any damages he made to your beautiful garden."

"Keep your money. It is what dogs do." She put her hand to her chest. "It was worth the mess to laugh like that." Ana squinted down at Bugs. "I do believe that is the ugliest dog I have ever seen."

She lifted herself from the porch step. "You smeared mud all over your face. I will get you a rag." The stern look had returned, but Sam thought she heard a snort of laughter. The screen door slapped shut.

"Well, dog, we've made a great impression. First, I scare her half to death, then you practically give her a stroke, laughing. Let's try to be on our best behavior from now on, shall we?" She frowned at the pink, white and mud-colored bull-dog. "It's a bath for you today, bud. That's the price you pay for giving in to baser instincts."

Mrs. Strauss returned, handing Sam a warm wet rag.

"Thank you," she said, scrubbing her face. "Again, I am sorry for the trouble. We'll be getting out of your hair now." She handed the rag back.

Mrs. Strauss stared at them for a long moment, her mouth pulled to a stern line. "Do you want coffee?" The old woman's eyes shifted to the road, the yard, the garden. "If you don't, be on your way and do not bother me."

Sam stuttered, "Oh, no, please, I would love a cup."

In minutes, Sam found herself sitting on the porch steps, a cup of coffee in hand, Bugs tied securely to the porch rail, the silence lying thick on the porch.

"Your house is beautiful. How long have you lived here?"

"Many years."

Sam waited to see if Ana would explain. She didn't. "Where did you learn to garden?"

"I've always known."

The birds chirped.

"I'm focused on the house right now, but before I put it up for sale, I'm going to have to do something with the yard."

The roses nodded in the faint breeze.

"Um. Well. Do you think you'd be willing to give me some tips when I get to that point? I'd love to plant a grape arbor, next to my carriage house."

"It is not hard. You can get a book."

"Yes, but I'll bet you have secrets. I've never seen roses with dozens of blooms on every bush." It seemed as if the old woman was out of practice with conversation. Didn't she get any human contact? But Sam kept trying.

After a bumpy ten minutes of Sam's questions, the old

woman seemed a bit more at ease, explaining the finer points of rose care. Sam admired the splashy flowers. "Have you ever entered your roses in the county fair? They'd win for sure."

"I would never do that."

"But why not?"

"Why do you push your nose where it is not wanted?" She snapped like a drill sergeant. "The arrogance of young people." She glared, stood and stalked into the house, the slam of the wooden door a clear rebuke.

Sam was getting used to the woman's lightning mood shifts. She set down her empty mug and glared at the ugly dog lying asleep on her feet. "Well, time to get home, mutt. You have a date with a washtub." Bugs woke when she grabbed the leash. His toenails clicked down the path to the gate. Opening it, Sam turned to look toward the cottage. The curtains on the front window twitched.

The woman's wariness poked Sam's heart. She understood fear.

AFTER WASHING AND medicating the dog, Sam made a huge pot of chili, and put it on the back burner to simmer. Her recipe wouldn't win a chili cook-off, but at least there was a lot of it. She knew teenagers could put away food.

The students showed up shortly after two o'clock. She got them sodas and sat them in the backyard. They sprawled on the grass petting Bugs.

"I told you this in your interviews, I will tolerate no horseplay. If I see any, or if you're not following my instructions, you'll be fired immediately. Is that understood?" Sober nods all around.

"Then let's get started." She pointed to the stocky football player. "Pete, I want you to mow the front and back yards. Don't you roll your eyes, you said you wanted a physical job.

You'll thank me for helping you build up those shoulders." She turned to the other two. "Sunny and Beau, come with me. I need help hauling stuff."

That afternoon, three extra sets of hands and youthful backs filled a construction-size Dumpster. The house looked gutted, but it no longer resembled ground zero.

At five, she called for a break and led them to the kitchen. They each grabbed a plate with a sourdough bread bowl and filled it from the pot of chili on the stove, then carried it to the front porch to eat—it was either that or sit on the floor in the kitchen, since she only had a card table in there, covered in blueprints.

"Hey, good chili, Ms. Crozier," Pete mumbled, mouth full.

Sunny stared at Pete's progress through a second helping with a cross between fascination and disgust. "How would you know? You eat like my dog. Wolfing it so fast, there's no way you could taste it."

"Call me Sam, and I'm glad you like it." She kind of enjoyed the sight of the kids sprawled on her porch.

"Hey, Sam." Beau cleaned the sauce on his plate with his last piece of bread. "When are we going to get to do some real construction, not just the grunt work?"

"Yeah, I want to learn some new stuff," Sunny said.

"We'll get to that, but you've got to realize that a lot of construction *is* grunt work. No job is just the fun stuff. That's why I pay you to do it."

Beau put down his dish and leaned against the porch railing. "My old man does nothing but bitch about his job, and I can't see why. He just works from home on the computer. What's to hate?"

"What does your dad do?" Sam asked.

"Something with stocks and stuff. He made a ton of money in the dot-com thing."

Pete spoke between shoveling bites. "I don't see what's so

tough about that. My mom works at the Walmart. She's beat when she gets home."

"What about your dad?" Sunny asked him. The kids knew each other from shop class, but apparently ran in different circles.

"Don't have a dad. He bailed before I was born. It's just me and my mom." His look dared them to judge.

"Hell, it would be okay with me if my old man disappeared. Especially if he took my mom with him. You don't know how lucky you are." Beau didn't sound like he was joking.

Sam broke in. "Okay, I'm going to play Simon Legree. Back to work."

"Who's that?" Pete set aside the empty bowl.

"Another reason to stay in school. You haven't had to read *Uncle Tom's Cabin* yet? Now *they* had a tough job."

The kids looked at her with blank faces.

How can I sound old at twenty-eight? Supervising high school kids was going to be a humbling experience.

The crew took out their angst by demolishing the remaining walls on the left side of the house. They had just gotten that mess hauled out by the time darkness fell. Sam called it a day. The kids dragged themselves to their cars, barely mumbling goodbye.

Sam called out, "More of the same tomorrow."

The chorus of groans made her chuckle all the way to the shower.

Yeah, definite advantages to a work crew.

She had to admit, it was nice having conversation and laughter in the house. The students distracted her from her worries, and the dream that ran over and over like a skipping record in her head. That was something that, up till now, only a motorcycle ride had been able to do.

Tomorrow, they should be able to finish the demolition.

If future days went like today, this student work crew could turn out to be a good thing.

She thought of her dad, teaching her on a job site, when she was in high school. How strange was it that she'd now be the one doing the teaching? *Wow, Dad, who would have ever thought?*

HAIR IN A TOWEL, Sam stood in her underwear before the closet beside the upstairs bathroom. Every item of clothing she owned fit in the standard coat closet, with room to spare. She shifted hangers. Mostly work clothes, with a few dressy shirts, a pair of dress slacks and a structured jacket for business meetings. And her leathers. Remembering the damage to her riding suit, she pulled it out. The hole wasn't huge— maybe she could repair it. She hung them back in the closet. Reaching to the top shelf, pulling down a fresh pair of skinny-leg Levi's from the pile next to a towering stack of T-shirts.

"Any color, as long as it's blue." She sighed. Had her closet always been so…bland?

She'd indulged in a half hour of worry after listening to Nick's voice mail last night, then called him, suggesting a wine tasting today. She wanted to have a few bottles on hand when Jesse stopped by, and besides, she liked the clean orderliness of the wineries. The regimented vines marching over the hills soothed her.

She checked through her choices one more time. No business blouse on a date—even she knew that. Plaid flannel sure didn't make the cut. Ditto the denim. Damn. Hangers slid faster. Sweatshirts, baggy sweaters and equally dismal choices flew by.

Wait. She stopped at a fitted white eyelet blouse with cap sleeves. "It's April. You'll freeze your nipples off." Maybe, but nothing else in her closet was remotely appropriate. She squirmed, imagining Nick walking up, staring at her boobs. The eyelet would show her bra.

Well, she'd just wear a jean jacket over it. She snatched the blouse from the hanger and went on a hunt for a bra without a safety pin holding it together. She blow-dried her hair, dressed and ran a wand of mascara over lashes. She checked the bathroom mirror. Blah. She needed some color. Inspiration hit. She tore back to the closet, dropped to her hands and knees, digging for her box of gift wrappings.

"Aha!" She pulled a silky pastel strip of cloth ribbon from the tangle.

The doorbell rang. Bugs barked.

She stood, stepped into loafers and shrugged into her fitted jean jacket. Jogging to the bathroom, she tied the ribbon as a headband and checked it in the mirror. Better. Marginally.

Her loafers clattered on the wood of the hall, echoing as she ran. Out of breath, she opened the door, stooping to grab the dog's collar when he tried to muscle himself past her.

Nick stood at the far edge of the covered porch, leaning against the railing. His hands in his front pockets, he telegraphed nonthreatening.

God, he was gorgeous. Cowboy boots, jeans and a white button-down shirt, the high rolled sleeves displaying tanned biceps. He didn't move, but his eyes crinkled and the corner of his mouth lifted in that smoking bad-boy grin.

She stood, snared by the clean heat in his look. Most men's eyes looked at her with a scary, out-of-control conflagration—all smoke and molten sweat. Nick's was more like a pilot light on a furnace, a soft blue flame that beckoned her to cup her hands around it and warm herself. The heat jumped the space between them to spread to her body; she was conscious of the blood, pounding warm at the backs of her knees, her throat, her temples.

Bugs barked and lunged, breaking her trance.

"Hi." He pushed away from the railing. "Jesse told me about your new dog."

"*Not* my dog. I'm just giving it medicine until it's presentable enough for the pound."

"Of course. So what's his name?"

"Well, Butt Ugly seemed to hurt his feelings, so I shortened it to Bugs."

He just grinned at her.

Blood pummeled her collarbone on the way to her cheeks. "Well, the darned thing was going to die on my back step. What was I supposed to do?"

He chuckled. "Can I pet him?"

"Prepare to be slimed." She allowed Bugs's squirming hindquarters to pull her across the porch.

Bugs, as always unaware of his repulsiveness, plopped on his side and gleefully offered his belly for a scratch. Nick squatted. "Wow. What happened to you, big guy?"

"I wish I knew. He just appeared out of my bushes one day." Sam tucked her hands in her pockets, not trusting her fingers. They wanted to brush back the coffee-colored hair, to slide their backs against his tanned neck. "It doesn't make sense that someone would dump a pedigreed dog. Jesse's asked around in town, but no one's claimed him."

With a last pat, Nick stood. "Well, at least he's found a good home now."

"He's found a hotel." Sam grabbed Bugs's collar and dragged him to the open door. "But I'll make sure he finds a permanent home, once he's completely healed." Bugs staged a sit-in protest. She had to put her hands on his butt and scoot him through the door, then pulled it closed before he could sneak back through.

Nick led the way to where the Love Machine sat parked in the driveway, top down. When she reached the car door,

Nick was there to open it. She paused, taking in a lungful of fresh air. "Don't you just love the smell of eucalyptus?"

"You know the town was named after those trees, right?"

"Widow's Grove?"

He nodded. "They're tall and leafy, so farmers planted them at the edge of their fields as a windbreak." He glanced to her fencerow. "But the root systems are small, and grow shallow. In a high wind, they can come down without warning."

Nick touched her elbow, helping her into the car. "They used to call them 'widow makers.'"

She shivered.

"Are you going to be too cold with the top down?"

And here she'd liked the trees' grace, and scent. *Why would they name a town after something like that?* "I'm fine. A goose just walked over my grave."

SAM SET THE empty tasting cup of Buttonwood Syrah Rose on the bar. "We've been to four wineries, Nick, and you haven't tasted a thing."

"That's not true." He lounged against the oak bar, watching her. She'd been catching him at it, all afternoon. "I tasted the chocolate at the Sunstone Winery, and the licorice, here." He took a bite of the red twirl of licorice whip in his hand. "A rich cherry flavor, mellow and—"

"You don't drink."

His body shifted from relaxed lines to hard angles. His jaw tightened. "I'm an alcoholic. Eight years sober, this past Christmas." There was pride in his words.

"I kind of figured. Good for you." That explained the connection she felt with him. Her subconscious, recognizing the familiar cloud of her childhood.

Eight years sober is seven years, eleven months and twenty-seven days more than Dad ever managed.

She mentally shook herself. *Doesn't matter, because you're not getting involved.*

His breath huffed out, as if he'd been holding it. "You hungry?"

"Sure."

They strolled outdoors to the manicured lawn, where a half-barrel barbecue threw off smoke and the delicious smell of grilling pork. The day had turned warm enough that Sam had abandoned her jacket in the car, but she shivered when Nick touched the inside of her naked elbow.

"I'll get us lunch. Why don't you get us something to drink and find us a spot to eat?" He stepped into the food line.

A woman at a table beckoned to Sam with a bottle of Chardonnay, but she shook her head and grabbed two cans of soda from stainless steel buckets beside the table instead.

Her lips twisted at the metallic taste of irony—only she would invite an alcoholic on a wine-tasting date. She carried the cans to an unoccupied picnic table and sat.

Suddenly a yearning tugged her insides; to be on the bike, leaning into turns, a road song filling her head. The nervous chatter in her mind quieted as, closing her eyes, she imagined the scenery blurring, and the roar of the wind in her helmet as the guitar riff of AC/DC's "Thunderstruck" rumbled through her mind.

NICK CARRIED THE two loaded plates to the table where Sam sat, eyes closed, a look of peace on her beautiful face. *Wonder what she's thinking?* Had he blown it, telling her about his addiction? *Well, if I did, this wasn't going to work, anyway. Better knowing now than—*

He heard her humming. *"Thunderstruck"?* He wasn't sure what that signified, but maybe it wasn't bad. At least it wasn't "One Bourbon, One Scotch, One Beer."

"AC/DC?" He stepped over the picnic table seat, putting

down the two loaded plates before sitting himself. She glanced up—her shuttered expression told him more than he wanted to know. His confession stretched on the table between them like a pregnant porcupine, bloated, awkward and prickly. "I'm sorry I've ruined your after–"

"My dad was an alcoholic." She pushed coleslaw around her plate.

He winced as that fact bit. Looking at the pork sandwich on his plate, his stomach churned. He could no more eat it than two-week-old roadkill.

"He was a great dad."

He raised his head at the strength of truth in her tone.

She stared out at the grapevines, eyes narrowed. "Life just threw more at him than he was equipped to deal with." When she turned her head, the naked pain in her eyes hit him like a slap. "You know?"

Better than you can imagine. He nodded.

"I took care of him from the time I was a little kid. And in his way, he took care of me." Her glance slid away. "The best he was able to, anyhow, given what he knew." She sat straight and flicked her hair over her shoulder. "I'm not going to judge you based on your past, Nick." Her shoulders dropped, just a bit. "I can only hope you'll be able to do the same for me."

"You loved your dad a lot, didn't you?"

She just nodded. The heavy conversation seemed to weight the afternoon, smothering the life out of it.

As they pretended to eat, the air developed a nip, so he helped her into her jacket, then into the car. They did manage some normal conversation on the way home, if you could call yelling over the wind normal.

He pulled in the drive and turned off the ignition. They sat a moment, listening to the tick of the cooling engine. He unsnapped his seat belt and twisted in the seat so he faced her, his leg within inches of hers. "I'd like to see you again, Sam, if my history hasn't scared you off."

SAM KNEW NICK was giving her an out—a chance for a graceful retreat. It was her wisest choice, given her hyperawareness of the proximity of his knee to her thigh. And his hand, hanging from the back of the seat, long-fingered and heavy-veined, only a few short inches from her shoulder.

But if she were wise, she would have said no when he invited her out to begin with. "I'm game if you are."

"Great." He got out of the car, and walked around to her side.

His smile was disarming—literally. This guy made her want to drop her guard.

Nick Pinelli made her feel safe, normal and so desired. Worse yet, Nick Pinelli made her *feel*.

She reached behind the seat for her two bottles of wine. When he opened her door, he reached to take the bottles from her. She snatched them to her chest.

"Sam. I'm not going to go off on a binge because I carried two unopened bottles of wine to your front door. I promise."

Cheeks flaming, she let go of the bottles as if they burned her palms. She led the way to her front porch, turned soft and golden by the setting sun. She put the key in the lock. The dog barked, once, then she heard him snuffling on the other side of the door.

"It looks like you've got yourself a guard dog." Nick handed her the bottles.

"Yeah, maybe he's good for something, after all." She turned to say goodbye.

Nick put his arm over his head and leaned on the doorframe, bringing his face inches from hers.

She froze.

He took his time, as if memorizing her features before

tipping his head. His lips brushed hers. A soft, chaste kiss, with only the barest flick of the flame she'd seen in his eyes. It made her want to get closer. Much closer.

The bottles bumped his chest. His lips lifted in that bad-boy smile. He pushed away from the doorframe, and leaned in again. But this time he only opened the door. Bugs's mashed-in snout appeared in the crack.

"Thank you, Samantha." He brushed the back of his fingers across her cheek. "For everything."

Oh, you are so in trouble here.

He turned, walked across the porch and practically bounced down the stairs, striding the broken sidewalk to his car, hands in pockets, whistling "Thunderstruck."

CHAPTER TEN

As PROMISED, SAM kept in touch with Tim Raven, stopping to visit him at the hotel on her frequent forays to the hardware store. Today, though, she had a problem with plumbing, and hoped he knew of a local who could help. She pulled the Jeep into the parking lot of the Rest.

Tim stepped out of one of the cabins, blinking in the bright sun. As usual, he looked like a garage sale fugitive, rumpled clothes hanging off his bent frame.

"Hey, Tim, what's with the formal attire?" She stepped out of the Jeep.

"I've got a date at the opera as soon as I finish this job." Tim walked over, ignored her outstretched hand and hugged her.

Frozen for a moment in awkward surprise, she patted his back once and took a step back.

"You've got a guard dog, I see." He tipped his chin toward the Jeep.

"Not my dog." Bugs stood, front feet against the dash, drool stretching from his panting lips, watching them through the windscreen. "As soon as he's presentable, he's off to the pound. I'm starting to think he's trying *not* to grow hair as a delaying tactic."

She turned her back on the smiling mutt. "Tim, you know everyone around here. Can you recommend a good plumber? My pipes are in sorry shape, and I always farm that job out."

His blue eyes twinkled from under gray caterpillar eyebrows. "You're looking at him, missy." He threw his shoulders back, then snatched at his sagging pants just in time to save them both embarrassment. "I wasn't always living in the lap of luxury, you know."

Doubt must have shown on her face. He thrust out his whiskered chin. "I was a plumber for thirty-five years. Did quality work, too."

She cringed, imagining the fragile old guy carrying heavy tools, much less cast iron fittings. "Well, Tim, it's just that this is a pretty heavy job."

"I'll make you a deal. You've got a couple of kids working for you, right? I'll charge you half my usual rate if you let me use one of them to do the grunt work. That way, I'd make some extra money and I won't be killing myself doing it." He scratched under his moth-eaten Tyrolean felt hat. "What do they call that nowadays? Consulting." He chortled. "That's me, a consultant!"

She smiled, remembering the polished yuppie consultant she'd done a remodel for. "Far be it from me to keep you from a new career. But if this turns out to be too much—"

"No problem. From what I hear, consultants never break a sweat."

Together, they worked out the details of their agreement right there in the parking lot and shook on it. Tim led her back to the Jeep. Bugs stretched his head out of the driver's side window, and Tim gave him a good scratch. "Have you had a chance to meet your neighbor at the bottom of the hill?"

Sam told him of the disaster in Mrs. Strauss's garden.

"Anajuska is one of the finest women I've met. She's been through a lot."

"I wouldn't know. Getting to know her isn't easy." Sam opened the Jeep's door, shooing the dog to the passenger side, then snatched a rag from behind the seat to wipe drool from the steering wheel. "She seems reclusive. Do you know why?"

Tim frowned. "If she wants you to know, she'll tell you. I ain't no gossip."

Sam recognized a wall when she ran into one. But Tim's answer only made her more curious. Maybe she'd stop by Ana's soon.

WHEN THE STUDENTS showed up that afternoon, Sam had them set up scaffolding in what was becoming the great room. Since her collarbone wouldn't allow overhead work, Sam got the kids started, then put the finishing touches on the spaghetti. She'd been afraid the teenagers would be picky eaters, but quantity seemed more important than quality. Sam drained the pasta and called them to fix their plates. Pete showed up first, Sunny and Beau right behind.

He grabbed a plate. "Spaghetti. Great, my favorite!"

"You say that every day," Sunny called from the back of the line. "Leave some for the rest of us." They served themselves, then walked to the front porch to eat.

"Monday, we'll have another instructor on-site. A plumber."

"Plumbing. Gross." Sunny's mouth turned down. "Do I have to learn that? I'd rather just work on the construction part."

Sam settled on a plastic chair, balancing her plate on her knee. "As a contractor, you have to at least understand every aspect of the trade, even if you sub out some parts. Otherwise, how do you know if you're being overcharged, or if the work is substandard?" She pushed the dog's nose away. "Besides, I don't think you're giving plumbing a fair shake."

"You're kidding, right? Toilets?" Sunny shook her head. "I'd hardly put the invention of plumbing up there with the creation of the internet."

"I don't know about that." Sam swirled spaghetti onto her fork. "I think indoor plumbing is *the* most important invention, especially for women. Plumbing isn't just toilets. It's running water." She pointed to her plate. "This dinner would take three or four trips to a well, if you include washing the dishes."

It was refreshing to hear how teens saw the world. She hadn't spent time around them since she'd been one herself, and found their incomplete perspectives fascinating, and was surprised by the subjects they discussed.

She snapped her fingers. "Back off, dog."

Bugs walked across the porch to sit at Pete's feet and practice his starving-dog routine.

"How many baths a week would you take if you had to pump and heat every bucket? Plumbing is civilization."

"Yeah. Whatever." Sunny took a sip of iced tea.

"I think it's kinda cool," Pete said. "Like a puzzle. How do you get the water where you want it to go without losing any? Like you're controlling nature or something."

Sam said, "I'm glad you feel that way, because plumbers have to be strong. I was going to suggest that you help Mr. Raven."

"*Tim* Raven?" Beau broke in. "You mean the old guy with those dumpy cabins at the edge of town?" He set his empty plate on the porch rail, ignoring Bugs's pleading whine. "You've got to be kidding me. He's one step above a homeless person." He lounged, uniform intact: scuffed boots, a faded black T-shirt and artfully holey jeans. He was in full body armor as well, with studs in his eyebrow and plugs in his earlobes. Lank hair hung in his eyes.

The spaghetti she'd eaten churned in Sam's gut. Having been on the wrong side of people's prejudices most of her life, she wasn't listening to more. Especially about her friends. "You've got room to talk." She stabbed a fork in Beau's direction. "Look at you. You're a hot mess. But that's okay, because you're cool, right? You're the first one to jump on adults who judge *you*."

Ignoring them all, she stood, sniffed and walked to the door. "Sometimes you all irritate the crap out of me." Bugs scooted in when she opened the door. She let the screen door slap closed behind her.

She walked a few steps, but stopped when she heard Beau's voice behind her. "Don't look at me—what did I do?"

"Aside from being a dick, you mean?" Sunny said.

"You got no manners," Pete added.

Walking to the kitchen, Sam realized that mentoring may involve more than just teaching kids a trade. How did they feel comfortable being so frankly judgmental? Surely she hadn't been like that at their age? Sure she had. But somehow that didn't make it easier to deal with now.

THE WEEKS PASSED, and Sam's injuries healed. Nick began calling at night, as Sam lay in bed dreading sleep. Something in his deep voice soothed the jitters from her hands and the long muscles alongside her spine. Listening in the dark, she'd relax into the sheets, mind focused only on that disembodied voice.

"How the heck did you learn to drive at thirteen? Did your dad teach you?"

"In a way, yes. If it got to be close to my bedtime and he wasn't home, I'd walk, or hitch a ride to the bar. He'd be sprawled on his usual bar stool, passed out, or close to it. No way to get him home except in the car, and I sure wasn't letting *him* drive."

"Did you ever get caught?"

"Thank God, no." The last thing they had needed was another social worker visit. "How did you learn to drive?"

There was a hesitation before he answered. "My mom taught me. In the Love Machine. God, I was so embarrassed to be seen in that car. We'd get in, and I'd head out of town, hoping I wouldn't run into anyone I knew."

"So the car grew on you over the years, huh?"

"How could it not? A piece of artwork like that?"

Trying to stifle a snort, she swallowed wrong and choked. He chuckled, and she laughed long and hard.

They got to know each other in those small hours. Sam found it easier to answer questions when she didn't have to face the asker. She didn't tell him the bad stuff. But hearing the focused attention on the line made her want to.

She learned more about Nick in the small hours of night: his internship in L.A., his drinking, his time in jail, his sobriety. But there were gaps—missing years—in his childhood stories, making her wonder if he, too, held back some of the bad times.

Working late gave her a good excuse to decline when he asked her out, but it didn't stop her from looking forward to his phone calls.

Sam found an odd coal of pride burning small in her chest, watching the kids morph into a working team. She taught them how to replace the roof, but she handled the gable solo, judging the pitch too dangerous for beginners.

They then moved on to installing a lapped-wood ceiling inside. The varnished oak would lend a warm, casual look, at odds with the formal Victorian facade.

While Tim and Pete replaced every pipe in the house, Sam assigned special projects to the other two. Beau would design a custom parquet inlay in front of the fireplace, and Sunny, a wooden scrollwork railing for the loft. When that was complete, she'd put them to work on the carriage house build out.

Despite their initial reluctance to work with Tim Raven, the crew eventually accepted the old man. Even Beau. Tim seemed to puff up with the attention, and Pete followed him around the house like a puppy.

IT WAS FULL DARK when Sam stepped out of the car at Pinelli's garage on Friday night. The blank windows eerily reflected the streetlights on Hollister, but warm yellow lamplight spilled from the second-story picture window.

You're having dinner with a friend, and watching a baseball game. That is not a date.

Crossing the pavement to the stairs, she tightened her stomach muscles, squelching circling butterflies.

Yeah, but he's cooking. At his house. That makes it intimate.

It walked like a duck.

And, she'd put on makeup.

It talked like a duck.

Only blush, mascara and lipstick.

Yeah, but you didn't own lipstick. You had to go out to buy it.

Did that make it a duck?

Nick's voice she knew, from their conversations in the dark. But put a man's body with the voice? That complicated things. She settled the bottle of sparkling cider on her hip and climbed the stairs at the side of the garage, listening to the muted strains of classical music through the wall.

He must have heard her, because when she reached the landing, he threw open the door.

Seeing him, she realized—this man was almost a stranger.

He wore a white chef's apron over jeans and a short-sleeved denim work shirt. But it was the look on his face: welcoming, anticipating, delighted—that jostled her heartbeat to a dirt-road cart ride. She stood, falling into eyes of dark chocolate, so deep brown they were almost black. They made her want to step close, right up close, to find the man behind them. Time spun out.

I am so not ready for this.

His smile turned serious. *"Benvenuto alla mia case, amico."*

As the warm voice of Sam's nights poured over her, her stomach unclenched and her skewed viewpoint righted. She smiled at her friend. "Ciao." She handed him the bottle. "You have now exhausted my entire repertoire of Italian."

Stepping into the kitchen was like entering an Italian cocoon—warm, close, with a delicious redolence of garlic.

He put his hands at her neck and she started, but he only wanted her jacket. While he hung it in the closet, she stood, amazed. Sheets of what appeared to be homemade pasta, hung drying from a wood rack on the counter. A pan of white sauce steamed on the stove, a huge boiling pot next to it. She peeked through the small window into the oven. She'd bet her leathers those doughy baguettes were from scratch, too.

Nick returned to the chef's island.

She shook her head. "After seeing this, the only meal you're ever getting at my house is takeout."

He just grinned. She colored, realizing she'd just intimated he'd be invited.

"I'll bet you're a good cook." He pulled a huge knife from a block on the counter.

She remembered her spaghetti—sauce from a jar, pasta from a box. "You'd be so wrong."

"You have choices, here, Sam. You can sit and talk to me—" he waved his knife at the small table with two chairs against the wall "—or you can help, and talk to me."

She frowned. "I'll help, but only if you have something a third grader could do."

"How about washing the romaine and cutting it for the salad?"

She stepped to the opposite side of the island, where fresh lettuce rested next to a large stainless steel bowl. "I think I can manage that."

It felt awkward at first, working together. But the music, the mindless repetition of her task and his funny story of the mayor's wife and the masseuse loosened her clumsy hands. Apparently the woman had walked into a parlor off a back street in Big Sur, and gotten a different massage than she'd bargained for. Soon they were laughing, bumping hips as they vied for room at the sink.

Her job done, Sam leaned her hands on the counter and watched him work at the stove. "Where did you learn to cook?"

He carried fresh-cut pasta to the stove. "I'm full-blooded Italian." His back to her, he added, "My mom taught me. Those are my best memories—she cooked to Verdi and while the pasta boiled, we'd dance in the kitchen." The soft pain in his voice sounded like a bruise—an old, deep bruise.

He turned and held out a hand. "Will you dance?"

She stood like a scared rabbit. *You don't want to give him mixed messages.*

The violin wove through the music, a crying thread of sadness.

He doesn't want you, he wants a memory. You could give him that.

"Sam."

She looked up.

His hand hung outstretched. "It's only a dance."

His soft smile convinced her. She stepped forward and took his hand.

It was large and warm, the calluses a reminder that this dance partner was also her mechanic. He swept her away, gliding across the kitchen, his steps sure and graceful. He held her classically, giving her space. But his pheromone-loaded working-man smell bridged the gap. She took a long breath of him and held it, feeling no guilt—she was doing *him* a favor, after all. His strong arms supported her but didn't push, suggesting movement rather than demanding. Relaxed in his surety, her awkward body shifted—to something petite, fragile, almost graceful. She felt like Cinderella, at the ball. When he spun her, a bubble of joy rose in her chest until it burst from her mouth in a laugh.

If this man loves like he dances, any woman would be toast.

Not that she'd ever know. She stiffened, her fairy-tale moment popping like a soap bubble.

He danced her back to the stove and pulled her into a brief, fierce hug. Lips beside her ear, he whispered, *"Grazie, bella signora."* He released her and stepped back.

She curtsied low. She had no idea why; surely it was the first curtsy of her life. But something in the formal passion of the old world music and his courtly manners made her feel…womanly.

He turned to the oven, missing her blush. *You're a little old to play princess, Crozier. And a tiara doesn't fit under a motorcycle helmet.*

NICK LED HER to the table, seating her farthest from the door.

"Now for the best part." He prepared the plates and delivered them to the table with a flourish. He poured the sparkling cider in wineglasses, lit the two ivory tapers in the center of the table, then sat.

Her skin glowed in the candlelight, and it caught highlights in her blond hair.

She looks like an angel.

But that couldn't be right, because an angel wouldn't have this effect on his body. He shifted in an attempt to gain some room in his jeans.

She closed her eyes, inhaling the steam rising from her plate. "What is this amazing dish?" She opened her eyes and pulled her napkin into her lap.

"Shrimp linguini alfredo. The Casa Pellini is the Mollusk Mecca tonight." When he lifted his glass, the candlelight flickered in her eyes. *"Per cent'anni."* He touched his glass to hers. "For a hundred years."

"That's beautiful." She sipped the cider, then set the glass down.

They dug in. The pasta was rich and textured, the shrimp delicate.

Not bad.

Sam closed her eyes and moaned.

He watched her long throat as she swallowed. Heat shot to his crotch so fast he was almost dizzy from a lack of blood flow to his brain. He felt a rush of his limbs loosening, as if his glass held real wine. He could get drunk on this woman.

"I'll take that as a favorable review." When his voice came out low and rough, he cleared it.

She must have noticed his stare, because pink tinged her cheeks. She raised her glass, touching his. "You chose the wrong business, Nick. Tourists would pay dearly for this."

He took a sip, set down his glass and picked up his fork. "I cook for myself, and for my friends. To turn it into work would ruin it."

"I never thought about it that way. I guess I'm lucky to be able to make a living at what I'd be doing for fun, anyway."

I could make a living, looking at you. He'd love to cook for her, every day. To have their nightly conversations take place with her wrapped secure in his arms. To watch the morning light come in, to touch her sleeping face.

He sensed her interest in him, too. But he also knew when she hit one of those walls. The light in her eyes clicked off, and she backed away, wary. He understood enough to know that at those times, her focus was inward; it had nothing to do with him, but still, it stung.

The Cleveland Indians were playing the L.A. Dodgers tonight, so in stark contrast to the romantic beginning, they trash-talked at the end, finishing dinner as the game was about to start. They piled dishes in the sink and adjourned to the living room.

SAM SANK INTO the leather couch, her stomach humming with happiness. Nick was a great cook, and a great dancer. She glanced at his full lips, wondering…

Distraction. She needed distraction. "One-season wonders. The Dodgers won't make the playoffs. Never gonna happen, grasshopper."

Nick dropped onto the cushion next to her. "Are you kidding? We're gonna beat you like a jungle drum."

From the first pitch they ranted, yelled and cajoled their teams through nine innings. Baseball hadn't been so much fun since she watched with her dad. When the Tribe's closer threw his last strike, she jumped up, pumping her fists and doing a war dance in front of the TV. Looking over her shoulder, she cocked a hip and patted her butt. "Next time, try not to brag until the fight is over, bubba."

Nick snatched her hand and jerked. Laughing, she tumbled back onto the couch. Into his arms. She stopped laughing.

His gaze seized hers as his fingertips brushed up her neck, along her jaw, to tip her head back. Out of breath from the victory dance, her panting was the only sound in the room. Well, maybe not the only sound—her heartbeat slammed out a frantic SOS.

His eyes, full of questions, never left hers. "This okay?"

Hearing the deep, soothing voice from her nights, Sam closed her eyes.

She'd been able to ignore the times his knee touched hers during the game. She'd hardly noticed when their hands brushed, reaching for their sodas at the same time. But ignore his lips, inches from hers? That would take a stronger woman. "Might as well find ou—"

His lips met hers. Strong, but soft. Asking, not demanding. Sweet.

So sweet. She tilted her face to get closer, the smell of him swirling in her head, making her dizzy. When his tongue met hers, she ached to open. And not only her mouth. Her treasonous body relaxed, flowing to his. Her nerves shot bolts of awareness to her brain; his lips, her nipples, his breath, on her cheek. A warm ball of heat formed in her chest.

Desire.

Awareness slammed into her brain and she jerked, breaking the kiss.

He backed away. His eyes still held questions, but his gentle smile promised not to ask them. "Well, I guess that answers the question about chemistry."

Scooting to her own cushion, she tucked her hair behind her ear. "Yeah, well."

She turned to the TV to collect the thoughts that had blown away like leaves in a gale.

Desire? Me? She couldn't deny the visceral craving pooling in her chest.

Oh, sure, she'd dated. Perfectly adequate men. Middle-of-the-road men: middle-management, middle-aged, middle-class men, carefully chosen. She snuck a glance to the end of the couch. No part of Nick Pinelli was remotely near the middle.

Or safe.

What were you thinking? When had she dropped her carefully executed social plan? She dated for company, and for human contact. Nothing more.

Nick was more. More than a pleasant diversion to stave off isolation. And after that kiss, more than a friend. She touched her temples; her head ached. Her nerves echoed the ache, as if the cumulative tension of the past months were an acid, frying the ends.

"You okay?"

She turned to Nick's frown. "I'm fine, thanks. Just a little headache." Recognizing her thoughts were better left scattered, she focused on the television screen.

Nick stood. "Would you like some tea? I'm sure I have some from Jesse's last care package."

"Sure." Anything to give her a bit of space.

The game had segued into an investigative news program. The host sat in a darkened room, interviewing a shadowy figure, his inhuman voice a product of electronic distortion. He explained how he paid "scouts" from all over the United States to bring him young girls. Runaways, mostly.

A trickle of ice rattled down her spine.

The camera cut away to a city at night. Cars rushed by. The clandestine camera bounced, then focused on a couple, standing across the street beneath a garish neon sign. Pedestrians hurried by, oblivious. The man was dark and sketchy, in a leather jacket and jeans, his hand a manacle around the thin arm of a young girl. She was slight and blonde, wearing a cheap faux-fur vest, a tiny, too-tight miniskirt and knee-high stiletto boots. The camera zoomed in on her face.

Sam dug her fingers in the edge of the leather cushion, frozen in horror. The girl wasn't more than thirteen; her cheeks still held a preadolescent plumpness and pimples showed plain, in spite of a heavy layer of makeup.

Older than you were.

When the man leaned in, his shadow falling over half her face, the girl flinched. Her eyes darted, searching for help. For a microsecond, she stared straight into the camera.

The tortured panic on the girl's face shot a matching bolt through Sam. Her hands twitched as adrenaline mainlined into her blood. Sweat popped on her forehead. But that wasn't the worst.

It was the too-old look of anguished resignation in the girl's eyes—as if she knew there'd be no reprieve.

And she was steeling herself to survive what came next.

"What is it, Sam?" Nick stood over her, a cup of tea in his hand. The alarm in his voice made her aware the fear must show.

She shot to her feet. *Get out.* "I have to go. Now. My head is killing me." She sounded like an automaton. A defective one. "And I forgot something. At home."

She tried. Focusing on her feet, she tried to walk slowly. But by the time she hit the door, she was running. She scrabbled at the handle, twisting and pulling at the same time, getting nowhere. She sniffled, focusing only long enough to jerk it open. Then she was flying down the stairs into the cold, welcome night.

CHAPTER ELEVEN

HER FEET POUNDED pavement to the beat of the words in her head. *Get. Away— Get. Away.* It was late; the streets were blessedly empty. The streetlights were cold circles of revelation. She sped up, her feet flying until they barely touched the ground.

He saw. He knows. You told.

Shame slicked the inside of her mouth. When a shadow-filled street opened on her left, she plunged into the cold arms of the dark.

Her lungs were bellows, fired by adrenaline. Her collarbone screamed.

After six years of running, her past had caught her. Shadows, deep in her mind had exploded into the light.

Now she understood why she'd fled Ohio.

She must have known on some deep level that if she stopped, her secret, the one the little girl whispered of, would catch up.

Dark, shrouded houses gave way to black, empty spaces. She ran, her stomach roiling. Tonight it had awakened.

The horrible monster she hid in the closet all these years was loose. *And someone saw!*

She had always remembered. The bruising of unwanted hands. His rancid breath in her face.

Her years from nine to eleven had been the iceberg in the cold waters of her childhood.

What she realized tonight was that she'd held only the

physical memory. The emotional memory—what it *felt* like—was the terror lurking beneath the waterline. And everyone knew the bigger part of an iceberg lived underwater.

She stumbled to the side of the road and, leaning over, vomited into the weeds. Her lungs screamed but her stomach clenched like an iron fist, heaving. *Can't. Breathe.* Dizzying white spots whirled behind her eyelids. A wave of vertigo dropped her to her knees.

Something grabbed her. She flinched, and her breath hitched. She choked in a coughing spasm. A fist pounded her back. Her throat unlocked, and she sucked icy air in huge lungfuls. She rocked, helping her body pull in more.

"Just relax."

Nick's calm voice flowed over her, soft and quiet. She didn't try to know the words, but they wound around her like a spell. Her stomach, still a burning fist, loosened, and her gorge settled.

She sat back against her heels, wiping a sleeve across her face. It came away damp with tears and spit.

His hand at her elbow guided her to her feet. "Here, get into this. It's freezing out." He shrugged out of his fleece-lined leather jacket and helped her into it.

Nick's denim shirt was a lighter shadow against the blackness of the March night.

"Let's go." Hand on the small of her back, he steered her to the asphalt. Their footsteps carried in the stark air. She shivered. No, that was like calling a tornado a breeze. Her skin prickled, deep muscles contracting until her bones shook. Her teeth chattered in cyclical spasms. Her soul was a desiccated husk, ready to flake away in the cold wind that howled through her emptiness.

She stepped away from Nick's touch.

"If you want to, tell me." The calm voice of her nights came from the dark. "Or not."

They walked on.

Her mouth opened. Words came out. *The* words. A sliver of her awareness stood apart, shocked. After all, this was the first time the story had been told out loud.

"Have you ever been so wrapped up in something that time seems to stop? You know, 'the zone.' Working with my dad that day at a job site was first time I ever felt that. Like time was suspended." Her shivering made the words shaky. Or maybe it was the words themselves.

He made an I'm-listening sound.

"I was carving a newel post. The wood worked like hard butter—like I didn't need the detail knife—I could shape it in my bare hands." She remembered the heft of the wood, the smell of pine sawdust. "I felt eyes on me. I looked up. Mr. Collins was staring at me like he was starving. And I was turkey dinner."

His face appeared in front of her: greasy nose, snaked with tiny spider veins, weasel eyes and pudgy, questing fingers. The smell of ancient cigarette smoke that hung on him like the stench of the grave.

"I was nine that first summer my dad gave me small jobs to do. I was so happy." Another shudder ripped through her. "My dad supervised me, but that day, Mr. Collins sent him to the lumberyard. They were building a house in a new subdivision, on the edge of town." She crossed her arms, shoving her icy hands under the jacket. "Mr. Collins said he needed my help—something only I could do. He led me to the back of the house. It was too quiet.

"When I asked where everyone was, he told me the crew had left for lunch, in town. He led me down the hall to the master bath, where he'd dropped a coupling under the sink, into the wall. His hands were too big to reach it."

Stop. Right now, stop. But her confession spewed like the vomit had: bitter and unstoppable.

"So I knelt and stuck my head under the sink. I put my arm down the hole. I'd just touched the fitting, when he touched me." Her throat clicked when she swallowed. "I jumped, and smacked my head on the counter—knocked myself silly. He pulled me from under the sink and acted all concerned—said he'd make it feel better." She turned her head to spit out the vile taste the words.

She turned to where Nick's face would be. It was suddenly, critically important he understand. Maybe if she convinced him, she'd buy it herself. "I wanted to get the hell out of there—but Mr. Collins was my dad's *boss*. He reminded me that my dad was a drunk. Like I needed reminding. He said if I 'played nice,' he'd keep my dad on. Otherwise, he'd kick us out, and I could figure out how we'd survive.

"My dad had been 'laid off' from so many jobs that even a kid like me knew this was his last chance."

Nick touched her arm.

She hugged herself tighter and stepped away. "I really did try to weigh my options. But I didn't see any. The social worker had already been to our house once. I saw the doubt on her face. If she had to come back again, they'd take me. What would happen to my dad? What would happen to *me?*" She dragged in as much breath as her taut muscles would allow. *Almost done.*

"Mr. Collins must have seen the answer on my face. He sat next to me. Told me I was his 'good girl.'"

Her teeth chattered over the words. Her mind jittered over the pictures.

"Then he put my hand on his crotch."

Nick growled, low in his chest.

"It went on like that, about once a week. I started doing badly in school, and I lost weight. But Dad was so wrapped up with his demon, he didn't see mine."

Nick reached across the gap between them, his hand hovering a moment over her arm. Then it dropped to his side.

"You know, it's funny—you kind of dig a hole in your mind and bury the bad stuff. The memories become something that *just happened.* Some kids' parents divorced, or siblings died. We recognized darkness in each other, passing in the hall. We knew things the other kids didn't. We knew there were things that grown-ups couldn't fix."

The words ran out. She cast about in her mind, to see how she felt. Only hollow silence echoed back.

When they approached the lights of Hollister, she glanced at Nick. Did he buy her excuses? His profile looked like the faces on Mount Rushmore looked, at night. Cold, white, shadowed.

"How long?" The anger threading through Nick's voice held the words tight—like rebar in concrete.

She ducked her head. "About two years."

"How did it end?"

"It turns out, you can't live scared forever. One day I just got *mad.*" The echoed memory of that anger heated her guts, banishing the shivers. "I woke up one day, and knew it was *over.*"

They'd reached Hollister and turned right, toward the garage. "I told Mr. Collins if he touched me again, I'd tell. I'd tell the police. I'd tell my teacher. I'd tell anyone who would listen."

"He said my dad was as good as fired." Sam stepped into the street to avoid the exposing circle of streetlight. Nick walked close, but not too close.

"Then the answer popped into my brain, fully formed. If he fired my dad, I'd tell then, too. In fact, my dad would keep his job forever. I'd paid that debt in full, the past two years.

"Of course, I was bluffing. I didn't know what would happen if I *did* tell. Would anyone believe me? Could I live with everyone knowing? Talking behind their hands, 'there's that poor girl…' But it didn't matter. Nothing could be worse than having his hands on me. Ever again."

"Did you turn him in?"

They'd reached her car. The past fell back into the past. She shrugged. "Why would I? He kept his part of the bargain. I kept mine."

Air whistled through his teeth.

Her keys jingled as she pulled them from her pocket. "My dad worked for Collins Construction until the cirrhosis got bad. Mr. Collins continued Dad's medical coverage, even though it was obvious he'd never work again."

Nick's mouth opened, then closed. A deep line formed between his eyebrows. "Are you saying that no one *ever* knew?"

She stood, hand on the door latch. "Not until tonight."

NICK DROVE HIS loaner Toyota slow, keeping the taillights of Sam's Jeep in view. He knew she didn't need his help; she'd made it across country, on a motorcycle, alone. Tonight, he'd learned that wasn't the bravest thing she'd done.

Jesus. He shivered in spite of the heater blast of hot air. How could a person survive something that twisted, that *evil*, that young, all by herself?

Josh's little girl, Courtney, just turned nine last month. He imagined Sam at that age: tall and thin with bony foal legs, blond hair still in pigtails. His knuckles blanched white on the steering wheel in the moonlight. All he wanted was a half hour with that guy, a live battery and some jumper cables.

At the turnoff onto Foxen Canyon he idled, waiting for her to get ahead a bit. Another car on that back road was rare during the day. She'd worry if she saw headlights behind her at night. It wasn't like she was in danger, anyway, out here in the country. He followed more for himself. It was as if he wanted to save her, retroactively. He knew sleep wouldn't come if he didn't see her safely in her door.

He also knew that what she shared tonight hadn't been given freely. He was only a witness to the meltdown, not a confidant. He shoved the heater gauge to max. Sam had no way of knowing that he understood the shame she felt. If this relationship was going much farther—and he wanted it to— he was going to have to tell her about his own family. His own shame. Maybe it would help her, knowing that he, too, understood the darkness.

Was that why she never stayed in one place? Did she think if she kept moving that the past wouldn't catch up? Well, to-night it had. Not that he was throwing rocks—his old method of liquid anesthetic was more self-destructive in the long run.

He thought about their dance—it seemed like days ago. Her strong, lithe body light in his arms. The elegant line of her neck, enticing his mouth to the hollow above her collar-bone. Her laughing up at him as he dipped her, the look of a startled fawn in her eyes. After tonight, he wanted her in his arms—safe.

He flipped off the headlights for the last mile—an almost full moon cast more than enough light to see. When her lights climbed the driveway's incline, he pulled over, parked and turned off the car. A hunting bird screeched overhead, and he heard the clunk of her car door closing. He lost her in the dark, until she climbed the porch steps and was caught in the lamplight spilling from the front window onto the porch. Her back was straight, her head up.

He smiled in the dark. Samantha Crozier was a looker, no doubt about that. But tonight, he'd discovered a lot more to admire, deeper in. She was a survivor.

She unlocked the door and opened it, bending to pet the dog. Then she was gone.

Nick crossed his arms over his chest and settled back.

He'd just hang around awhile and keep an eye out, just until the light went out, and she had time to fall asleep. She didn't need him standing guard.

But it made him feel good to do it.

CHAPTER TWELVE

AT THE CELLAR DOOR, Sam stepped forward, watching as her shaking fingers grasped the knob, turned it and pulled the door open. Her other hand fumbled on the side wall, feeling for the light switch.

The bulb came on, illuminating the stark space, the backless plank stairs and concrete floor below. She stopped, every sense straining for the source of the danger jangling in her mind.

What was that smell?

This basement was finished. She'd been down there several times.

Then why did it smell as dank as an old root cellar? And under that, there was the whiff of corrupt roadkill.

In spite of all that, she wanted to go down there. Needed to. The need pulled, even as instinct held her back. After teetering on the brink for seconds, Sam did the unimaginable. She took that first step down.

The dim light faded halfway down, swallowed by the basement's inky dark. Of course the lights were out.

At the bottom landing, she patted the wall to guide her forward. Five steps in, her boots scuffed dirt. The cinderblock wall ended in damp earth that crumbled away beneath her fingers.

A sliver of moonlight filtered in from a small, high window. When her eyes adjusted, she realized the darker shadow opposite was a cavelike opening in the dirt wall.

The fear she felt earlier had been a trickle compared to the dread that now leached into her soul. Somehow she knew, with every vibrating cell in her body, that even if she left this room alive, she'd no longer be the person who had walked into it.

A DOG'S BARK jerked Sam out of the dream in the exact same spot it had ended the night before. She fought the sound, wanting to reach the end—win, lose or die.

More barking. She opened her eyes to the darkness, and to Bugs, panting by the side of the bed. Not barking.

She'd forgotten; she'd recorded his bark as a ring tone. She glanced at the alarm clock. *Three. Three a.m.? Has to be. If it were p.m. it would be light outside.*

Heart hammering, she groped on the milk crate nightstand for her cell. "What?"

"Sam, it's Beau. Look, I'm really sorry to call. But I need help."

She bolted up. "What's wrong? What—"

"Look, it's no big deal, but I got picked up tonight. By the cops. I'm at the police station, and I really don't want to call my parents. They'd freak out, and I just can't deal with that right now. I don't know anyone else to call, and my mom will lose it when she finds out I'm not in bed in the morning, and—"

"Beau! Give me a second, here." When she got out of bed, she tripped over Bugs and almost went down, her collarbone punishing her for clumsiness. Fumbling for the light switch, she grabbed the pencil and pad from the floor beside the bed.

"I'm ready. Give me the address. I'll be there in a few minutes."

"Thank you. I'll make this up to you, I promise. I'll put in extra hours, I'll—"

"We'll talk when I get there. Just give me directions."

She tossed on some clothes and her leather motorcycle jacket, and within fifteen minutes, parked the Jeep in front of the Widow's Grove Police Department, the only fully lit building on the block. She pushed through the glass door, squinting in the fluorescent glare, shivering in the arctic air-conditioning.

Municipal-green linoleum led up to a faux-wood front desk. A massive officer sat behind it. His salt-and-pepper crew cut did little to disguise either his retreating hairline or his glistening scalp. His small, sharp eyes surveyed her while he shuffled papers with blunt, Vienna-sausage fingers.

"What can I do for you, little lady?" His tone intimated that the "lady" part was probably a stretch.

She clamped her jaw on her own attitude. "I understand you have Beau Tripp here? I'd like to know what the charges are, and if I could see him."

His lips pursed. "Mr. Tripp is our guest due to curfew violations. Are you family?" He looked over his cheaters with a steady stare that made her want to confess to something.

"I'm his employer. Can I post bail?"

"He will be cited. We only release minors to parents. I left a message for them two hours ago."

Sam pasted on what she hoped was a sincere smile and used her very rusty charm. "Can't you cut the kid a break? I'll see that he gets home. Doesn't everyone deserve a second chance?"

"As a repeat violator, the term 'second chance' doesn't apply. And the rule dictates that I release him to a parent or guardian."

I'm sure the rules dictate that you shouldn't be fifty pounds overweight, but that's obviously not an important one. God, she wanted to say it. "Could I at least see him?"

"I'll get him." The swivel chair squealed in relief when he stood and lumbered through a door behind the desk.

Ten minutes later, the cop returned, Beau slouching behind him. He looked more disheveled than usual, his hair hanging limp on his shoulders. His usual uniform of black appeared slept in, and probably had been.

"Sam, thanks for coming. I—"

She cut him off with a raised hand. "Just tell me what happened. And if you value your job, it had better be the truth."

He stuck out his jaw and tucked his hands into his back pockets. "Some friends and I were hanging out. That's it. We weren't drinking, we weren't causing any trouble. We were walking home when a cop stopped us."

"So your friends are here, too?"

"Um, no."

"Why is that?"

"Perhaps his attitude had something to do with his dispensation," the officer offered.

She turned and glared. "You're not helping." She turned back to Beau. "Is that true?"

Beau stood, eyes defiant. "He just wanted to hassle us. They push us around, just cuz they can. They get off on it."

She raised her hand again. "Were you out after curfew?"

"Yeah, but—"

"Then you gave him a perfect reason to hassle you. I'm not saying the cop didn't have an attitude." She ignored the officer's snort. "But you put yourself in that position. Shifting blame is the last resort of irresponsible people."

Beau's shoulders slumped and his face crumpled. "I know."

"I don't waste my time on losers. There are too many talented kids out there who are responsible, and want to learn. Clear?"

"Yes'm."

The front door slammed open, admitting a woman who, at first glance, looked like a high-society matron. A soft pink sleeveless silk shell was tucked into expensively tailored buff linen slacks. Her well-cut hair, with perfect subtle tones of blond, screamed exclusive hairdresser. Her face suggested good breeding, with high cheekbones and a refined nose. She was tanning-bed brown and society thin.

And drunk. Not the falling-down variety, or even the speech slurring version, but Sam knew the subtle signs. Her linen slacks were rumpled, and a watermark stain darkened the silk blouse. Her hair pressed flat on one side, and her makeup was smeared. All these could be attributable to the late hour, but Sam knew better.

At Beau's sharply indrawn breath, she glanced at him. His face showed lightning flashes of emotion: anger, embarrassment and a small boy's disappointment, before a stony mask of disgust fell into place.

"What is it now?" the woman asked in a reedy, high-pitched voice. "Have you graduated to shoplifting? Doing drugs? How many times do I have to be called down to *this* place?" The woman moved within inches of Beau's face. "Look at you. You're slovenly, sullen—"

"Mom, please. I only…" Beau sputtered and backed up.

Sam could tell he was mortified—for his mother, for himself.

"Excuse me. Mrs. Tripp, I'm Samantha Crozier."

For the first time, the woman seemed to notice she was not alone with her son.

"And what are you?" She looked down her perfect nose. "You're old to be with a high-schooler. And frankly, bikers aren't his style."

An ugly drunk. Poor Beau. "I am your son's employer."

"Mom, please, let's just go home," Beau soothed. "I didn't want to bother you, so I called Sam to take me home."

She reared back, nostrils flaring. "What are you saying? That I shouldn't be *bothered* when the police pick up my son? What are you insinuating, young man?"

"Mom. Please."

"Not another word. You will get out to the car. Now."

"Ma'am?" The desk cop used an official voice. "Have you been drinking this evening?"

The woman's eyes narrowed and her lips pulled to a thin, bloodless line. She tucked her chin and threw her shoulders back. She looked like a cobra about to strike. "How dare you?"

The front door opened again, and a man in a suit stepped in. He looked ready for a business meeting, except his thinning hair showed that he'd been running his hands through it, and the knot in his tie was pulled down, the top button of his shirt undone. "Carol, what's taking so long? How hard can it be to pick up one delinquent?" He didn't even look at his son. "I've got a plane to catch in—" he checked a gaudy Rolex "—five hours."

The cop gave Beau's dad an assessing look, then said, "I take it that you'll be doing the driving, sir?"

He let out a long-suffering sigh. "Yes, I'll be driving." He turned to his wife. "I'll be in the car. Can you move this along?" He stomped out.

"I'm sorry for bothering you, Sam," Beau said.

At the shame in Beau's eyes, her heart cracked open and let him in. He should be enjoying his teen years, not dealing with crap like this. "We'll talk later. It's going to be okay, Beau."

Carol Tripp stepped between them. In her twisted patrician features, Sam glimpsed the beast of Beau's home life.

"Are you supposed to be helping?" she screeched. "We pushed him to get a job to stop things like this from happening. Now he's calling you instead of me when he needs help. This job is not having the effect we anticipated." She looked Sam over, from the motorcycle boots on up. "Seeing his 'employer,' I understand why."

Sam fisted her hands and bit her tongue. Matching wits with the witless was hopeless. Even when you won, you lost.

Beau took his mother's arm and steered her to the door, murmuring in a quiet, conciliatory tone. He held the door open and his mother strutted through it. Beau threw a last worried glance over his shoulder, and was gone.

LATER THAT DAY, Sam sat on the hall stairs, making a list of supplies when Beau knocked on the screen door. Worry ground deep into the planes of his face. She put her clipboard down and motioned him in. "I didn't mean for you to take a trip out here on a Saturday. You could've waited til Monday, after school."

"I wanted to talk." He took a seat on the step below her and turned sideways, his back against the wall.

She waited.

Finally, he said, "Sam, about this morning." He took a breath.

She waited.

He stared at the wall, a muscle working in his jaw.

"Okay if I say something?"

He nodded.

"You have no control over what your mom is, or what she does. So you do things that will piss her off, just to make her feel the pain you do."

He frowned down at her.

"And then you look at other kids, who don't have to deal with any of this shit. That makes you madder still."

Red spread up from his T-shirt, staining his cheeks. "How would you know?"

She looked out the window to her unkempt yard. "I was sixteen. Our class put on the play, 'The Glass Menagerie,' and by some miracle, I earned a part. It wasn't a big role, but

I was so excited that I memorized lines until I knew every-one's parts."

She smiled. "I know you'll find it hard to believe, but I didn't quite fit in at my high school. This was my chance to be a part of something, not just watching from the outside."

Beau sat, elbows on his knees, and listened.

"The night of the performance, the show had sold out. Everyone was there. I was onstage, well into the second act, when the door at the back of the auditorium banged open. Everyone in the audience turned to look. My dad stood there, drunk."

Beau winced.

"He started down the aisle, muttering to himself, every eye on him. I tried to ignore it and just go on with the scene, but I was so embarrassed that my mind just went blank. I forgot my lines.

"My dad pointed to me and said, 'That's my Sam up there. Isn't she beautiful? Hey Sammie, I'm here. I told you I'd come!'" She shifted on the stair, still uncomfortable all these years later. "One of the teachers sitting in the front row got up, took my dad's arm and tried to lead him away.

"My dad was a happy drunk, but that night, he wouldn't go quietly. He got louder and more belligerent when they tried to walk him out. He stumbled, and a few other men got up to help. There was my little disheveled dad, surrounded by all those men in business suits. They led him away, him yelling at the top of his lungs about how he wanted to see his daughter act."

"I'm not going back there." The steel in his voice brought her head around.

"I'm not. I told her today. I'm quitting school, finding a full-time job, moving out."

His mind was made up. But she had to try. "Beau, that makes no sense. You have a month of school left until graduation. And you're not going to get a contractor's license without a high school diploma."

"Then I won't. Doesn't matter, anyway. They threw me out."

"Your parents?" Surely his father would have interjected some sanity? "Both of them?"

"Yeah. Tough love. They're big fans."

"Shit." She stood and stepped around him, pacing the hallway, trying to think past the red haze in her head. How could parents give up on their child that easily? He wasn't a drug addict, for Chrissake. "Hang on. Just let me think a minute."

"Sam, this isn't your problem. I've got it under control."

She stopped in front of him. "Oh, do you? Where are you sleeping tonight?" He looked away. "And you are not quitting school."

"Bullshit." His chin lifted. "You can't tell me what to do, either. If you don't want me to work here, fine." He stood. "Who needs this crap, anyway?"

She put her hand on his arm. "Beau, stop." A tremor ran through the corded muscles under her fingers. This kid was a bomb waiting to go off. "You're right. I have no hold on you. You can leave. If you want to."

The screen door hit the wall as he slammed through. Bugs barked in the backyard.

She rushed to the door but then forced herself to slow down, and lounge against the frame. She raised her voice. "Just one thing, before you go."

He took the porch steps in one leap.

"If you give up your dream to punish your parents, who wins?"

He stopped but didn't turn.

"Ever heard the saying that success is the best revenge?" She could almost hear him thinking.

"Beau, give me ten minutes. Then I'll let you go."

He looked at his car in the drive, then exhaled a grumbling sigh and sat on the last step of the porch.

Her heart pinched when his taut back slumped. She crossed the porch and leaned against the porch railing.

God, I know that pain.

She ached to sit down and hug him. She wanted to hug herself. Instead, her hand stole to touch his head. When he didn't shrink away, she petted his hair while she thought.

It wouldn't be appropriate for him to stay here, even though she had room.

But wait. She wasn't the only one with a spare room. "I've got an idea. Don't move." She jogged to the kitchen and picked up the phone to call in the cavalry.

Two hours later, it was solved. Tim had talked to Beau, and they'd worked out a deal. Beau could stay in one of Tim's cabins, rent-free, provided he stayed in school and graduated. One disaster averted.

WIDOW'S GROVE HAD changed with the times, but the old-fashioned post office remained, where patrons' mail nested in cubbyholes along the back wall. Nick reached the front of a long line and stepped up to the counter. "Hey, Harve, what's the news?"

The old man rolled his tall wheeled chair to the box the Pinellis had owned for forty years. "Well, let's see…the country's going to hell, the kids are a mess, and…" He rolled his chair back and placed one letter on the counter. "You have this."

Nick glanced from Harve's somber wrinkles to the official-looking envelope. The California State Seal on it smacked him like a thug's sap.

California didn't have a prison system. It was the "Department of Rehabilitation and Corrections." As if lipstick made *that* pig sexy.

"You okay, Nickie?"

Realizing he'd stood staring too long, Nick shook off his daze. "Yeah."

"Screw that, Nick. You can't pick your family. You do good things in this town. You have people who care about you."

"Yeah. I know." He slid the envelope off the counter, and into his back pocket. "Thanks, Harve." He turned away, held the door for a spandex mommy with a jogging stroller, then followed her out.

He walked hard and fast, dodging tourists, his past burning like a sheet of acid. Most people looked forward to April—the grass in the hills transitioning from green to gold, the cloudy mornings, the warm afternoons that hinted summer's heat.

Nick dreaded April. Mainly because it was the anniversary of his mother's death. The second reason rode in his back pocket. Inside the official envelope was a personal letter from his father. Nick knew, because every year on The Anniversary, his father sent a letter. Not that Nick had ever read them.

Just read it. How could he hurt you more than he has? The sun hammered his head, and his black T-shirt worked as a magnifier, intensifying the heat.

Yes. Open me, his father's deep, rumbly voice ordered.

The envelope crinkling taunts with every step, he turned off Hollister to get away from the crowds.

He winced. Shame rubbed flesh left already raw by the acid bath of guilt. He'd lulled himself with his new life. He could now go a day without seeing his father's swarthy face around every corner. He no longer saw his mother's willowy shape among women in a crowd. Forgetting was a good thing. Life became day-to-day simple. It allowed him to pretend he was like everyone else.

But it gave reminders like the one in his pocket.

Oh, hell, what's the use? He could pretend the rest of his life, and he still wouldn't fit in. His past made him separate—apart. Always.

His parents' love story was the stuff of local legend. His father's family moved to Widow's Grove midyear. When his parents slapped eyes on each other in high school, they became the talk of the town. The D.A.'s daughter and an immigrant from the bad side of the creek. A Cinderella story in reverse.

No "happily ever after" there.

Jesus, he was thirsty.

His feet stopped. To discover why, he looked down at them, then up. Conversation drifted through the open door of the Bar None. Squinting, he could see the hot pink Schlitz sign through the gloom. Pool balls clacked. The husky laugh of Rhonda, the bartender, was a "welcome home."

Nick didn't always want a drink. In fact, after the first year or so of AA, the physical need faded. And he didn't want a drink now. He *craved* it. When the bar blew a beery breeze into his face, the need grew teeth. And claws. Nick knew the crazed animal in his chest would lie down only before the comforting oblivion of booze. Need sang in his head.

The past lay always, coiled in the back of his brain. Days like today it struck, fast and hard.

Before he could give in to the need to medicate, he did an about-face and strode down the sidewalk, not sure where he was headed. Until the door of the Farm House Café came into view.

He walked in, the smell of onions and bacon grease washing over him, loosening the knot in his gut.

Jesse looked up from her math puzzle, her face lit with delight. "Nick! It's good to see you." Her eyebrows drew together. "What's the matter?"

He eased down onto "his" stool at the counter, pulled the

envelope out of his back pocket and slapped it on the speck-
led Formica.

Jesse chewed her lips a moment. "Damn, I hate him. You
want some pie, honey?"

SAM SAT WITH a cup of coffee at the card table that consti-
tuted her entire dining set, supposedly reviewing the blueprints spread before her. But she wasn't. The dream last night
was the worst yet. It had left her dragged down and hopeless
at the edge of dawn, frantic to get on her bike and travel—
anywhere.

She looked around the tired kitchen. What had she been
thinking? Settling in at Widow's Grove had been a bad idea.
Very bad. The past had been gaining ground, even when she
kept busy, every day. Now here she sat, in the middle of a
huge project.

The dreams were escalating—eating up the years between
her and—What Happened. She felt raw, as though her skin
was being peeled back. Exposed.

She'd *told*.

The mug thumped when she set it back on the table. How
do you take that back?

Nick, that was a story—I made it up. Oh, yeah, he'd probably buy that.

She'd learned to live with it, inside her. But how could she
handle it, now that it was outside? Weird, but the story, spoken from her lips, became real—something that really happened and wasn't just a bad time that existed in the shadowy
part of her mind. Like a roman candle, once lit, a chain reaction began; it couldn't be put back *in.* And it terrified her.

Her cell phone blatted the opening bars of "Highway to
Hell." She winced at the irony.

Jesse chirped, "Hi, sweetie. Get a move on, we're going
shopping."

"You must have dialed the wrong number. I don't shop. Besides, I have a ton of work to do."

"Oh, you can work anytime. I don't get much time off from the diner and I need to buy something to wear for my Fourth of July barbecue. It's physically impossible for me to go shopping by myself. Really, it's some kind of genetic deficiency, so you've *got* to go. Think of it as helping the handicapped."

Sam took the phone from her ear and stared at it. Distance blurred Jesse's words into a birdlike chirping. Talking with her was like jumping into a raging river: you didn't know where it began or ended—best to just let it pick you up and figure things out as you were carried along. She raised the phone, knowing that her friend wouldn't have noticed her absence.

"—besides, what are you going to wear? I swear if you show up at my house in jeans and a T-shirt, I'm not letting you in."

"If you'd let someone get a word in, you'd save a lot of time. What barbecue? I haven't heard a thing."

"Oh, honey, didn't I tell you?"

Sam raised a hand to her suddenly aching head. She didn't have a good feeling about this.

"Carl and I love to entertain, so when it gets warm, we plan parties. We invite everyone we know and they all bring something to eat. There'll be music and dancing."

Dancing? This was getting worse by the minute.

"Our parties are legendary. It gives all the women in town a reason to shop for summer clothes. The department stores should be giving me a kickback."

"So you have something against T-shirts?" Clothing was not at the top of Sam's list of priorities, and shopping for it even lower. "You cannot need something new to wear. I know for a fact that you haven't worn the same outfit twice since I've known you. Where do you put all your clothes?"

"Oh, that's why I married such a handy guy. Carl remodeled all our bedroom closets to be walk-ins, so I've got plenty of room." Jesse laughed. "Besides, it's impossible to have too many clothes. Every woman knows that— except for you. I bet all the clothes you own would fit into one closet."

"You say that like it's a bad thing. Can't I just stay home and hit myself in the head with a hammer instead?"

"If you don't like shopping, it's because you haven't shopped with me before. Be ready, grasshopper."

Two hours later, Sam threw herself into a garish orange plastic chair in the food court of the mall in Santa Maria.

"Have pity and just leave me here to die." She dropped an armload of colorful shopping bags, and they scattered at her feet. "You didn't tell me that you only brought me as a beast of burden." She slumped in the chair, and massaged her sore arches. "Couldn't you have just rented a burro?"

"Don't be silly. You know the only animals allowed in the mall are seeing-eye dogs."

Sam was pretty sure she hated Jesse, who looked fresh and cute in tight pink capris, a pink cotton shell and strappy, bejeweled sandals. "How can you look so disgustingly pert? Aren't you tired? You're wearing heels, for Chrissake!" She dropped her head on the table.

"I *told* you, I'm a professional. I'll go get you coffee. Then we'll go buy *you* something."

Sam doubted that even a double shot of espresso would help.

When Jesse returned, she set a grande and a Danish in front of Sam, and settled in. Sam had seen that look before. The hungry-crow-eyeing-roadkill look. "So. About Nick."

Sam was too tired, and knew she'd lose anyway, so she rolled over and showed her belly. "Okay, I had dinner at his house. He's a great cook." She sipped her black coffee. "And a better kisser."

She ignored her friend's squeal, but the people at the neighboring tables didn't.

"Settle, Yenta. I have questions. And if you're a friend, you'll tell me the truth. I deserve to know, in case…" She rolled the hot cup in her hands. "What happened with Nick's mom?"

"You're right. You deserve to know. It's not my place to tell you." Jess considered, tapping her nails on the table. "But you could just as easily find out from anyone in town, I guess.

"It's not like it's a huge secret, anyway. We're just protective of Nick." Jesse leaned in, lowering her voice. "Nick's father was a laborer. He worked odd jobs: road construction, fruit packing, janitor, for a while." She leaned her chin on her hand. "He was sexy. In the way Mediterranean men are sexy—dark skin, romantic eyes and huge biceps. Half the women in town would have left their husbands if he'd wagged his finger. But he didn't give any of them a look. He was mad for his wife." A line appeared between her perfectly penciled eyebrows. "Not, 'Awww, that's sweet' mad. I mean as in rabid-dog mad. He was that jealous.

"Even so, it might have been okay, but the economy went bad. Nick's dad couldn't find a job. Heck, no one around here could. But Nick's mom found one as a barmaid at a biker bar on the other side of the creek." She winced. "Everyone in town knew of the couple's fights. Heck, the walls of their old shack were so thin, it's amazing we couldn't hear them yelling from town. The cops were called almost every weekend."

"How old was Nick?"

She looked away. "He was fifteen when his father shot his mother dead in the parking lot of that bar."

Sam put a hand to her mouth. "Jesus."

"Jesus had nothing to do with it." Her blue eyes sparked. "There were twenty witnesses, and all of them testified at the trial—they were half in love with Traviata Pinelli. Open and shut case. The bastard got twenty to life."

Sam wasn't sure she wanted to hear more. So she whispered. "And Nick?"

Jess sat up, her jaw tight. "Well, we weren't going to let the county take him."

"Who is 'we?'"

"The town, of course. The poor kid had been through enough. He was a good boy, smart and well-mannered. Old Milt Haversham, on the city council, had pull with the county, and backed them off." Jesse got busy, throwing their trash into a bag in angry spurts. "We all took turns, cooking and leaving food on his doorstep. And money. And wood. It had to get damn cold in that shack in winter. If he caught us at it, he'd turn us away. He was a proud kid. When he applied for a job at Peterson's Auto Parts, he damned sure got it."

The coffee turned sour in Sam's stomach. She imagined a younger Nick, vulnerable and hurting. She wasn't the only one with heavy-duty baggage.

Jesse's hands stilled. "But I guess the weight of all that history dragged him down. By the time he graduated, he was hanging with the delinquents, running the back roads at night, drinking. He was on a tear. Two years later he blew out of town, and didn't come back for over a year."

She bent to gather her bags. "The guy who came back is pretty much the one you see today. End of story. And if you tell him I told you this, I'll make you go shopping every weekend between now and the end of the year. *Including* Black Friday."

Sam regarded her over the rim of her latte. "What's Black Friday?"

Jesse rolled her eyes. "I'm going to assume that was a joke, and if it's not, don't tell me—I can't take it. Now. You've distracted me enough. On to the important stuff."

"Why do I get the feeling I'm not going to like whatever's cooking under all that hair?"

Jesse cocked her head. "You're already gorgeous. All we need to do is glamorize the package a little. You've got good bones. The key to looking good is knowing what plays up your assets."

"Yeah, easy for you to say, Miss Priss."

"You've got to be kidding," Jesse leaned over the table and got in her face. "I'd kill for your height. I can't wear a skirt over my knees without looking like a squat toad, and I can forget ever wearing boots. They make my legs look like toothpicks with canapés at the end."

Sam had to smile at that.

"You are what you wear, sweetie. I know you subscribe to *Construction Weekly* for business, but you really shouldn't use it for fashion tips. Look, I'll show you." Jesse grabbed her hand, dragging her from the chair.

"Oh, no, not another store. I don't think I'm up to this, Jesse."

"Quit your whining, grasshopper. You are about to get a lesson from the master in the fine art of shopping. Just sit back, observe and hold your applause until we're done."

Jesse marched into the closest boutique and after ten minutes of rifling the racks, selected a blouse and skirt. "Now, try this on, and when you come out, do *not* look in the mirror. I want to pull this together before I unveil my masterpiece."

Sam thought Jesse was getting a little carried away with the drama, but donned the outfit, anyway.

Jesse stood back, squinting. "Okay, we're almost done. Come with me." Jesse grabbed her hand.

"Wait, Jesse!" Sam grabbed her leather jacket and shrugged into it. She wasn't leaving the store like this.

A teenage clerk accosted them as they walked into the crowded mall. "You can't leave the store wearing clothes you haven't paid for!" Jesse stopped, but didn't let go of Sam's hand.

"Cindy Boward, you know where I live. I babysat you when you were making messes in your diapers. Do you think I'm going to leave without paying?"

Passersby sniggered, and the poor girl flushed scarlet.

"That'll teach her to interrupt an artiste at work." Jesse dragged Sam into a shoe store a few doors down from the boutique and plopped her into a chair at the back of the store. She selected a pair of strappy espadrille sandals with tall cork soles from the display and got a sales clerk to dig in the back for a size ten.

"Jesse, look, I admit you may have something here, but heeled sandals? I'm going to look like an Amazon."

"With your long legs? Are you kidding? Every eye in the place will be on you. You've got to learn to flaunt what you've got, darlin'. And take off that biker jacket." The clerk returned with the shoes. Sam looked around, thankful that she didn't know anyone. When she finished tying on the sandals, Jesse pulled her up in front of the tri-fold mirror.

Sam just stared.

"You'd look better if you closed your mouth, hon."

"I didn't know…"

Jesse'd chosen a handkerchief skirt in a red-and-yellow print, with a hem that ended in points from midthigh on one side to midcalf on the other. Jesse pulled the elastic neckline of the white peasant blouse down, leaving her shoulders bare. It ended in a wide-smocked elastic band, mid–rib cage.

Jesse then looped dangling earrings through Sam's ears and lifted her hair, pushing it onto the top of her head. "Voilà!" Jesse looked far too smug.

I look like a magazine model!

Men will look at you. The little girl's warning rang in her head. *Their eyes will crawl all over you.* Sam wrapped her

arms around her waist. The thought of flaunting her body—
her skin—made her feel a bit queasy.

"Nick is going drop at your pretty feet."

Nick. She'd love to have Nick see her like this. Have *his*
eyes roaming over her. But could she do it?

Jesse took her hand. "Now. Let's talk makeup."

Just shoot me.

CHAPTER THIRTEEN

BRAKING FOR THE TURN into Widow Grove's nursery, Sam grabbed Bugs's collar to brace him. She couldn't get the image of a grape arbor, growing by the side of the carriage house, out of her head. Ana had told her over coffee on the porch that if Sam didn't plant soon, she'd have to wait until next year.

And she wouldn't be here next year.

It'll make a nice feature when I sell the property.

She parked the Jeep, then snapped the leash to Bugs's collar. After his excavation in her backyard, not to mention his performance in Ana's garden, she was convinced this dog was half mole. She wasn't taking her eye off him near this much loose dirt.

"Come on, mutt, let's go." She opened her arms and he scrambled into them. The Jeep was tall, and his legs were short. Close up, she noticed his skin was a healthy pink, and the bald patches were starting to sprout hair. She grunted, lifting him down. "Another month or so, and you'll be ready for your debut at the pound, dude."

He galloped the few steps to the end of the leash, and looked back, as if telling her to hurry. She'd miss the pain in the ass. It had only been three months, but she could hardly remember a time when he hadn't been underfoot.

Maybe she'd pick up some bulbs for Ana, if she could find something the woman didn't already own. Sam stopped by about once a week, but was no closer to learning why the old woman was so reclusive. She'd invited Ana to come, but wasn't surprised when she'd declined. But the fear that flashed across her face at the invitation had been very real.

She and Bugs wandered the outdoor aisles, Sam admiring the myriad choices, Bugs investigating the smells around every display. She had bent to read the label on a grapevine when she felt a touch on her shoulder.

"Excuse me." An East Indian accent flowed soft and melodious. "Are you Samantha Crozier?"

At first, Sam thought a young girl stood next to her. "I am."

The soft brown eyes held a woman's awareness, despite being set in doll-like features. Everything about her seemed soft, from her milk-rich coffee skin, the shiny black hair that fell straight to narrow shoulders, the relaxed linen of her blouse and slacks, to the expensive cordovan loafers on her tiny feet.

The woman held out a business card. "My name is Bina Rani."

Sam took the card, ignoring everything but the title, "Clinical Psychologist." She stiffened.

"Nick Pinelli asked me to speak to you."

"He did, did he?" Nick spoke with a total stranger about her problems? How *dare* he?

The woman backed up a step. "I have upset you. I beg your pardon. He recommended that I talk to you about my house."

Sam heard the words through a haze of anger, like the sound of buzzing bees in her head. "I'm sorry, what did you say?"

"My husband and I have bought a Victorian home. It needs a lot of work, and I am looking for a contractor. Nick is our mechanic. He told me about you, and that you own a bulldog. When I saw you with the dog…" Her worried eyes scanned Sam's face. "Are you all right?"

A potential client. And Nick had sent her. Embarrassment displaced the anger. Sam felt her heartbeat in her ears. Luckily, her red face could be the product of either. "I'm fine."

She slapped a smile on her face and put out her hand. "It's nice to meet you."

The woman's manicured hand disappeared in Sam's. Tiny women made her feel a bit like Gulliver in the land of the Lilliputians.

"Your dog is cute. May I pet him?"

"Sure. Though 'cute' is a bit of a stretch." She tightened the leash, so the woman wouldn't get slimed.

Mrs. Rani squatted to pet Bugs. "We own two dogs, a pug and a Pomeranian. Except they really own us." She smiled up at Sam. "I'd like to talk to you about my house sometime. We are new in the area. Nick couldn't say enough nice things about your work."

Guilt burned. She knew Nick wouldn't betray her confidence. Didn't she? She thought of the deep voice, on the phone at night. His eyes, over wine, at dinner. Yes. She did.

She forced herself to focus. A potential client, and here she stood, mooning like a girl. "I have some time now. Why don't you tell me about your house?"

They strolled the sandy paths between rows of potted plants and Bina explained the work her home needed. They shared stories of falling ceilings, outdated plumbing and problems that came with a century-old home.

When they reached the end of the last row, Sam stopped. "Are you busy for the next hour or so? I'd love to see your house. Maybe I could give you some quick suggestions on where to start." This woman was nice and easy to talk to, but Sam realized her offer had more to do with a guilty conscience.

"Oh, would you? I don't have any appointments until afternoon, so we'd have plenty of time." Bina gave Sam directions to her house and they agreed to meet there in a half hour.

Sam and Bugs returned to the aisles, in search of bulbs and grapevines.

THE RANI HOME perched on a small patch of lawn beside the main street of Widow's Grove. A Victorian in the Eastlake Cottage style, it was compact but tall, the first story set above a half floor with windows at ground level. Obviously, no renovations had yet been made to the outside—the siding was broken in places and paint peeled away in strips.

Sam lifted Bugs to the sidewalk, then studied the home. Rickety wooden steps led to the small covered porch, its gingerbread scrollwork missing in places. Small windows graced the square bay turret to the right of the porch, and she'd bet her best sharpening stone that the windows leaked.

Standing on the sidewalk, she squinted to blur the damage and see the facade as a whole, selecting and discarding ideas to repair it without altering the style or integrity of the period.

"Sad, isn't it?"

She jumped. Bugs leapt at Bina, who attempted to fend him off and pet him at the same time.

"Bugs, down! You know better than that. I apologize. His manners are a work in progress."

"Oh, that's all right. Wait till you meet my two. Bugs is a perfect gentleman in comparison."

"Bugs, sit." The dog obeyed, and looked up at her, the picture of canine comportment.

"Wow. I'm impressed," she told him.

"Do you think there's any hope?"

"No, lessons would be a waste of money. He'd flunk out."

"I meant the house." Bina shaded her eyes and looked up at Sam with a smile. "We moved in eight months ago, and have spent all our time and effort to make the interior habitable. Come in, I'll show you." She led the way up the steep stairs to the porch. "Watch yourself. Some of these steps aren't even."

The interior was in sharp contrast to the outside. Glowing plank wood floors led from the vestibule to the characteristic long hall. Creamy doorframes and cornices stood out against dark walls. Muted Turkish carpets showcased the antique furniture in each room.

The tour was interrupted by the sound of toenails scrabbling for purchase. Two small figures hurtled into the room. The dogs made a beeline for Bugs, frantically circling him in full cry.

"See what I mean?" Bina yelled over the barking. "You have little to fear of Bugs's behavior in this house. He could probably teach these ruffians a thing or two about manners. Hey, leave off, you monsters!" She grabbed the passing collar of the pug, and swung the Pomeranian into her arms. "This dust mop is Tassel, and the puggy one is Yoda."

Bugs strained at his leash, wriggling and whining to be free.

"Let's let them get acquainted out back where they can't tear up the place." Bina led the way to the kitchen and out the back door.

A waist-high picket fence enclosed the yard. Sam unsnapped Bugs's leash. The three dogs tore around the grass, chasing and sniffing each other, tails waving.

"I think they'll be okay out here." Bina dusted her hands. "Now, on to that coffee I promised." She led the way back to the warm, modern kitchen.

"I think I have kitchen envy." Sam admired the warm wood cabinets and new appliances.

"They completed the work last month. They repaired the roof, and the interior, but I've left the exterior cosmetics for last, because I'm just not sure what to do."

"Your house poses some interesting challenges. I've got to devote most of my time to my project, but I think I can come up with some ideas that should enhance the Victorian facade, and make it more livable at the same time."

Bina's soft brown eyes lit up. "That's *just* what I want to do. Nick was right, you're very perceptive." She poured the coffee and brought the cups to the table.

Perceptive? "Don't get too excited until you see what I come up with. One woman's prize is another's nightmare."

They sat. At Bina's question, Sam explained how she'd come to settle in Widow's Grove.

Sam sipped her coffee. "How did you and your husband end up here? This is somewhat off the beaten track for a psychologist, I would think."

"We immigrated five years ago. In India, the population is very dense—there is not enough opportunity for young people. My husband, Shiv, being the second son, would not be taking over his family's import business." She crossed the room to refill their cups at the trendy coffeemaker.

"Luckily, his family is well-off, so when he completed university, they offered to send him to the United States to finish his medical degree. Shiv took a position at the hospital in Santa Maria, and I set up a private practice here in Widow's Grove."

"I thought I was brave moving across the United States. I can't imagine taking on a new country. It must have been hard for you, trying to adapt to a new culture. How do you like it here?"

"Well, it has not been without its challenges. This is a small town and we are foreigners. We love the area, but have found making friends is more difficult than we expected." She stirred cream into her coffee. "I've also had challenges in building my practice. I suspect that people are more comfortable with someone of similar culture to talk to about their problems. I'm developing relationships at the hospital, though, and I'm getting busier."

"What type of counseling do you do?"

"Oh, I especially enjoy treating children, but my practice

is not large enough to specialize yet." Bina hesitated, but then seemed to come to a decision.

"Sam, I do not know you well, but I hope you don't mind if I ask you something. If it makes you uncomfortable, please tell me. Is that all right?"

She straightened, on alert. "Okay."

"When I met you at the nursery, you were obviously upset. I could tell you thought that Nick had betrayed a confidence."

"A confidence. How did you know that?" Why had she relaxed around a psychologist, for cripes's sake?

"Well, it really wasn't much of a stretch." She leaned in. "Am I making you uncomfortable? I tend to be direct—too much so, according to my husband. I don't want to offend you."

"Being direct is something I've been accused of a time or two in my life." Sam managed a weak smile. "I don't want to offend you, either, but I have to be honest. I don't think much of psychology in general."

"Oh, I'm sorry. Did you have a bad experience with a therapist?"

"I've never been to one."

"Did you know someone who had problems with one? There can be personality differences, just like you find with any person you meet."

Sam spied the dead-end alley this conversation was leading to. But no way out. "Um, no. I've never known anyone who went to one. I mean, I might know them, but never knew they went…you know what I mean."

"Then where did you get that opinion? That's not a judgment. I'm just curious."

"*Oprah, Doctor Phil, The View,* stuff like that." Sam ducked her head, sure her face must be tomato-red. But she refused to lie, even if it made her look like ignorant trailer-trash. "It's not like I watch much, but seems like they have more of the type of people on those shows that need that kind of professional…" She focused on the empty coffee cup in her hands. "Let's just say I'm an idiot, and let it go at that, okay?"

Bina threw her head back and laughed, a bellowing belly laugh. Sam blinked in surprise. She would have expected a lilting tinkling from a woman like this. Bina laughed loud, like a barfly cutting loose on a Friday night. For some twisted reason, that made Sam feel better.

"I'm sorry. I'm not laughing at you. I promise, I'm not. It's just that getting your opinion of psychologists from Oprah is like getting your building experience from a magazine you picked up on a newsstand." She wiped her eyes. "Oh, God. Oprah. You really slay me." She got up and walked to the counter.

Sam stared after her. *I could like this woman.*

Bina reached into a jar on the counter and put a handful of cookies on a plate, then brought them to the table. "I'm not going to try to change your mind, either about psychologists, or the people who visit them. Just let me say that there's no big mystery in what goes on behind a therapist's door. Really, it's just like having a friend to talk to only better, because with a friend you have to watch what you say and consider their feelings. With a therapist, you don't have to worry about that.

"Now, on to important subjects, like my house!" She laughed again, and Sam relaxed.

But she couldn't quite dismiss the promise in Bina's words—the lure of having a nonjudgmental expert to talk to. Maybe she'd even know something about dreams.

Yes, but. This would be telling *another* person about her past—and she hadn't even meant to tell the first. She already felt like she was walking around with her guts hanging out, for any passerby to see. Was she ready for this?

No. But a tornado doesn't care what you're ready for—it just catches up to you and rolls you along.

Sam tucked the option away, to consider later.

FIVE DAYS AND seven AA meetings after his almost slip, Nick felt more himself—his sober self. He turned off the kitchen lights and padded in stocking feet to the bathroom, to brush his teeth before bed.

In the grip of his past, that day, walking into the bar had seemed so natural. It wasn't until he got home that the fear hit him. He reeled back, like an agoraphobe on the crumbling lip of a high place. The days following were worse. If he'd almost slipped without even realizing it, how solid was his sobriety? How could he relax, knowing he was *that* close to falling into his old life?

"Conscious living. That's how." Finished, he put up his toothbrush, clicked off the light and stepped into the bedroom.

He dropped onto the bed, pulled off his shoes and checked the alarm clock. The light of an almost-full moon shone in, turning his bedroom into a foreign landscape: flat, colorless, solitary. Lying back on the pillow, he speed-dialed Sam's number.

He'd debated with himself the past week, but hadn't called since the night he'd cooked for her. He wanted to give her space, to ease into the fact that someone else knew her secret. But he also needed to know she was all right.

She picked up on the first ring, almost as if she'd been waiting.

"Buona sera, signora giovane."

"How do I know you're not talking dirty to me in Italian?"

If she were covering awkwardness, she was doing a good job. "Hmm. That hadn't occurred to me, but it can certainly be arranged. Just give me a few days to brush up on the terminology—"

"No, really, I'm good."

Her husky chuckle did something good to his insides. "So? How've you been?"

"Busy. Crazy busy. The students are really working well together. I hired them only to help with the grunt work, but I have to tell you, I'm enjoying them. It's so satisfying to see them learn, and grow, in their skills and maturity."

His spine relaxed into the mattress. He hadn't realized how these phone calls had changed his nights. Until they'd stopped. Who was he kidding? They'd changed his days, too, giving him something to look forward to—something to hope for.

"I'm glad you're getting help. And that you're helping the kids. A win-win." Well, if she was ignoring her elephant, he could ignore his, too.

He knew he owed her the story of his past, especially since he now knew hers. But it felt so damn good, having someone know him for who he was now—not who he was then, or from gossip about his infamous family. It made him feel—clean, somehow. As if he really *was* Sober Nick. He put an arm under his head and crossed his ankles.

"Oh, and I meant to thank you. I met Bina Rani at the nursery the other day. What a sweet woman. And her house! She accepted my bid, and I'm working up the plans now. The money from that is going in my business account to help fund my next project, wherever that may be."

Oh, great. He'd just made it even easier for her to leave. Disappointment bit, like the taste of vinegar. But why should it? She'd never hidden the fact that she was a come-and-go biker chick.

Yes, he'd known from the beginning that she was leaving. The weeks were flying toward December, when the renovations would be complete. But he also thought that the house, the town and the people were starting to anchor her to the dark earth of central California. And he could only hope there was enough time left to forge a relationship that would add weight to that anchor.

He imagined her throwing a leg over the Vulcan and riding away. He ignored the pinch in his chest. *She is worth taking a chance.*

"No, seriously Nick, thank you."

"*Non è niente.* It's nothing."

AFTER AN EARLY-MORNING run on Independence Day Saturday, Sam straightened the kitchen, cleaned the old leftovers out of the refrigerator and wiped down the counters. She stood in the middle of the worn but clean room, looking for something else to do.

"Oh, just admit it, Samantha. You're procrastinating." She thought of herself as brave, but imagining being on display before a townful of people she didn't know made her itch for the Vulcan and the open road.

Bugs lay, head on paws, glancing at her out of the corner of his eye.

"Oh, don't you give me the hairy eyeball. You think this is going to be easy? Thanks to Jesse, I have a blouse that feels like a bikini, and I'm wearing heeled sandals on uneven ground, which means I'm a pratfall waiting to happen."

She ticked worries off on her fingers. "Nick will be there. I haven't actually seen him since…" Her stomach did a lurch off a high dive. "He *knows.*" She stopped staring into space and got back to counting.

"Jesse's already told me that anyone who is *anyone* in town will be there. There's going to be country-western music and dancing, which I know nothing about. Other than that, it should be a really kicked-back affair."

Bugs cocked his head. *"Grrrrine?"*

"No, you can't go. Sorry, bud. I could use the moral support, but I'm afraid your manners aren't quite up to polite company." She'd been working with Bugs, and in addition to sitting on command, he now lay down. When it suited him. She could just see him, drooling on people, tearing through the backyard scattering guests, plates and drinks.

Gritting her teeth, she walked upstairs to her shower.

Two hours later, Sam parked the Jeep in front of the Jurgens' home outside of town. In spite of lingering over her dishabille, she was apparently still early; the street stood empty in front of the typical, brick-clad ranch from the '70s. A covered porch graced the front, the strip of garden before it overflowing with colorful perennials. A broad swath of emerald lawn looked as if a weed wouldn't have the audacity to put down roots anywhere near the place.

She shut down the engine and sat a moment, her stomach awash in butterflies, brushing the sides, looking for a way out. She inhaled a few deep breaths. "It's just a party, for God's sake! I know several people that will be there. I am going to let go and have a good time. I deserve it."

And sitting in a car talking to yourself is just strange.

She retrieved her bowl of potato salad from the back of the Jeep and tottered to the front door as purposefully as high-heeled sandals would allow. *Why do women like these silly things?* The screen door opened before she could knock.

She was engulfed by Jesse and her perfume. Her friend pulled her in the door. "Oh, honey, you look like a million bucks. I love how you did your hair. Simple, but elegant."

Sam touched the back of the French twist. "You wouldn't say that if you'd seen me fighting it for forty-five minutes. I needed three hands to copy the picture in the magazine. I have this vision of the whole thing letting go in the middle of dinner."

Carl stopped in the hallway. And stared.

"Well, what do you think, Carl?" Jesse waved her hand in front of her husband's blank stare. "Hello, Carl?"

Sam crossed her arms over the bare skin of her waist and wondered why she hadn't thought to bring her motorcycle jacket.

"I didn't recognize you, Sam. I don't think I've ever seen you in a skirt. You look great."

His quiet voice held a bit of…awe?

"Thanks." Sam forced the words around her locked jaw.

"You are going to knock Nick's eyes out of his head, sweetie. You just wait and see if you don't."

The butterflies preened. Sam looked away.

Jesse grabbed her arm. "Come on in and help me, will you? I'm behind, and there are still a million things to do."

Jesse led the way to a large kitchen. Painted a warm yellow, it seemed to pull the sunshine in through the window over the sink. Vegetables in various stages of preparation littered the counter, and bags of groceries covered the butcher-block island in the center.

Jesse put her to work, filling her arms with condiments, paper plates and plastic utensils to deliver to the backyard. She walked to the front hall and turned right, winding her way through the overstuffed living room furniture to a sliding door standing open to the backyard.

She stepped onto the large redwood deck, dropped her armload onto a glass-topped table and looked around. Lawn chairs crowded the space, and a row of unmatched grills lined up in military precision along the left railing. Surrounding the patio, the green, rolling yard stretched behind the house, ending at the slope of a tawny hill. The deck formed a semicircle, its broad steps curving around the outside edge. Picnic tables dressed in gaily colored plastic tablecloths circled a hardwood dance floor in the center of the yard. Trees shaded the tables, and white cloth lanterns hung from the lowest branches.

"Wow, Carl, you guys are serious about your parties. Where did you get the dance floor?" She addressed Carl's broad back as he bent over one of the grills, firing the coals.

He glanced out at the yard. "Some friends and I built it one summer after talking at one of these parties. A few of them play instruments and they started jamming. The women wanted to dance, so we built the floor in sections to haul it out here for parties."

Her butterflies began a polka. "Great idea."

She'd just returned to the kitchen when the doorbell buzzed. Sam shooed Jesse out to greet her guests and continued filling baskets with potato chips and spooning dip into brightly colored Mexican pottery. Jesse diverted everyone into the kitchen to meet her.

They came bearing dishes. The women stayed to unwrap their offerings and complete last-minute preparations, tossing salads and warming dishes in the microwave. Sam gave up trying to remember names. The women asked questions when they heard she was the newcomer who'd bought the old Sutton house. They asked about her occupation, her motorcycle and where she'd gotten her outfit.

At first she was reticent, afraid to be seen as the local freak, but after some friendly grilling she realized the women weren't judging, just curious. A few even sounded envious. Chattering away, she carried the last armload of baskets to the backyard, put them on the food table and grabbed a soda from the cadre of coolers lined up against the window. She dropped into a chaise and took a few solitary moments to survey the yard.

A couple dozen people in summer clothes, drinks in hand, lounged in scattered groups. A herd of kids ran across the grass chasing a Frisbee, ignoring the adults' admonitions to move to the side yard.

It looked like an avian sanctuary she'd visited once, where

colorful exotic birds flitted from branch to branch, their
voices combining into a jangle of sound. She chuckled to
herself, certain that the mayor's wife, with her high-pitched
voice and large, flower-splashed muumuu would not appreciate the analogy.

Her pulse took a happy skip when her attention snagged on
a pair of broad shoulders. Nick squatted in the yard, having
a serious conversation with a little girl holding a huge beach
ball. Sam took her time checking him out, his soft eyes, lips
and olive skin, set against his strong chin and cheekbones. A
lethal combination. He wore stonewashed jeans and an ivory
muslin shirt, the sleeves rolled snug against serious biceps.

Sam glanced back to his face and realized with a jolt that
he stared at her.

Her face burned, but like an animal caught in a spotlight,
she couldn't look away. Her heart thudded, heavy in her chest.
But her stomach felt weightless. His eyes held her, compel-
ling her to—what?

Time drowsed in the warm sun. Nick smiled and stood.
When the cool air brushed the backs of her hot knees, Sam
realized she'd stood as well. Her skin ached for touch, with a
strength that seemed to pull him across the lawn by the simple
force of the wanting. He came in a slow, loose-hipped walk,
scanning her from hair to pink-polished toes. He climbed the
patio stairs, releasing his breath in a long, low whistle that
she felt in the floor of her pelvis. The muscles of her thighs
and belly tightened.

Nick stepped up to her. Still holding her gaze, his arms
took her in. His head dipped, hovering over the fragile junc-
ture at the base of her throat. She swallowed. He inhaled.
When his lips lightly brushed the intimate spot, she shivered,
intensely aware of the points he touched—his hands, on the
bare skin of her back, his legs, pressing heat through the thin
material of her skirt.

He growled, *"Bella serata. Bella donna."*

Apparently everyone within earshot had been eavesdropping, because they burst into applause.

Snatched from the safe cocoon of Nick's regard, Sam glanced around, face flaming. She buried her head in his shoulder. He threw his head back and laughed. Lifting her off her feet, he spun her in a circle.

"Don't be shy, Sam. These old people just don't remember what it's like to be young in the spring." When he set her down, a man tending the grill handed him a soda. She beat a hasty and, she hoped, dignified retreat to the house.

Just inside the sliding glass door, a matronly woman in tight Bermuda shorts sighed. "My husband hasn't looked at me like that in years."

"I haven't felt that hot since our air conditioner died in the heat wave last August," giggled another, fanning herself with a cocktail napkin.

Jesse bustled over and put her arm around Sam. "Oh, Carmen, it's probably just a hot flash. You old biddies are jealous."

"Damn straight, we are!" A young blonde raised a margarita glass in a toast.

A man in an "I kiss better than I cook" apron yelled that the meat was ready and everyone headed for the patio.

Sam soon found herself with a plate of food, squeezed between Nick and Dan Porter on one side of a picnic table. Dan wore a loud Hawaiian shirt, khaki shorts, with flip-flops on his broad feet. He'd brought a date, an English teacher he worked with at the high school. Edith wore glasses, a Hawaiian shift and large tropical fish earrings that swung just above her shoulders.

Easy banter continued through dinner. The balm of everyday things in everyday lives flowed over Sam, soothing her unease. This wasn't so bad.

Not so bad? When had she ever mingled? Felt lulled by a feeling of belonging? Being seen by a crowd as part of a *couple?*

Exactly never. Conflicting emotions pulled at her: worry, trepidation and jittery nerves laid over a core of—rightness. She felt like an imposter, as if she'd stepped into someone else's skin. These people related to the smooth exterior, not glimpsing the seething mess underneath.

She glanced at Nick, relaxed and talking to Dan Porter between bites. *But he knows.* And he hadn't run yet.

He just wants your body, the little girl whispered.

Maybe. That didn't feel right, but the little girl had been right before. Damn that faulty compass of hers—she'd paid more than once for trusting the wrong person.

Be careful. Sighing, Sam rose to help clean up.

As the sun edged over the hill, everyone sat chatting, listening to a young man playing classical guitar. A slight breeze stirred the tree branches, keeping away the heat and the bugs. Sam reclined in a chaise lounge, half listening to Nick who sat at the foot, discussing the last city council meeting with one of Jesse's neighbors.

Full and content, she closed her eyes and inhaled the cloying scent of night blooming jasmine. Snippets of conversations wove through her wandering thoughts. She had no idea she'd drifted off until a voice in her ear wakened her.

"Hey, Sam, wake up. It's time to boogie!"

She opened her eyes to Nick, just inches away. She smiled and stretched, surprised to see night had fallen. Small fairy lights winked in the tree branches bordering the dance floor. Sodium spotlights surrounded it, as well, highlighting the soft gold of the wood.

"Oh, it's magical!"

He chuckled, then took her hand and pulled her out of the lounge chair. A small group of musicians began a western tune. She and Nick joined the other couples heading for the dance floor.

"Whoa up, cowboy!" She planted her feet, pulling against his hand. "I don't know how to dance to this. I'm a Midwest girl, remember? Rock and roll I can handle. I can even disco in my kitchen, but this stuff…"

The couples danced in a loose circle, women twirling under the men's arms in moves that appeared choreographed.

Nick looked into her face and smiled. "No time like the present to learn. The only recommendation I have is that you lose those pretty shoes. I don't think they're made for dancing." Still she held back, watching the dancers.

"Don't worry, Sam. I'm not going to let you look foolish."

He'd captured her thoughts so perfectly that it brought her head up with a start, expecting to see him laughing at her. Instead, his eyes held a patient waiting.

The acceptance convinced her. Maybe butterflies could learn to country dance, too. Their polka was getting old.

She sat on the chaise, untied her sandals and tucked them underneath. She took his hand, and a steadying breath. "Okay, big guy, lead on, but don't say I didn't warn you. At least I can't hurt your feet stomping on them barefoot."

The glossy wood of the dance floor was cool under her feet when he led her to the center, couples revolving clockwise around them. No one seemed to notice the couple at their center.

"This is simpler than it looks. It's called a two-step, because you take two steps, then turn, two steps and turn. Watch their feet. Everyone does different things from the waist up, but the steps are the same."

He was right. "It's pretty. All the colors going around like a kaleidoscope. Is that why they do it?"

Her hands clasped loosely in his warm ones. He smiled at her. "Leave it to a woman to notice the ambiance. They circle so they don't crash into each other. You cover ground, and if everyone were going in different directions, it would look like a pileup on the freeway. Now, let me show you."

She shivered when Nick's hand slid over the sensitive skin of her lower back exposed by her short peasant blouse. He enfolded her other hand in his and laid it against his shoulder, then drew her close, their thighs brushing.

She touched her forehead to his shoulder, inhaling his comforting metallic spicy scent. When she relaxed, they slid together like puzzle pieces. A perfect fit.

He put his fingers under her chin, lifting her head. "Don't look down. It'll distract you and make it harder to follow. You'll be able to feel my next move."

"Mmm-hmm." He stood so close she could feel lots of things. And she was beginning to enjoy this way too much.

"Here we go." He backed up two steps, did a quarter turn, and advanced two steps.

He held her loose but close—so close that her feet did know which way to move. He turned again and took two steps. After the first full circle, she anticipated his moves. The song's swinging one-two cadence beat inside her chest and her body responded.

"See, I told you this wasn't hard." Nick moved with the same fluid grace he had that night in his kitchen.

She was done thinking. Sam closed her eyes and felt: The cool air on the nape of her neck, his hips, lightly brushing her skirt, the tiny movements of his warm fingers on the bare skin of her back.

Nick pushed her out, raised his arm and spun her in a circle. She was ready the second time he spun her, faster.

She laughed as her skirt flared and the scenery went around in a blur.

"Tinker Bell."

She cocked her head at him, not wanting to break the spell with words.

"That's who you look like under the lights. I feel like I'm holding a woodland fairy in my arms."

Her next step wobbled.

"Sam, do you know how stunningly beautiful you are?"

It wasn't his words; it must have been the lights. With the shadow that fell over Nick's face, the world shifted. His warm smile became a leer. Glistening blubbery lips revealed flat, yellowing teeth. Her butterflies lost their rhythm and crashed into each other. She stepped back, shrugging out of that suddenly straitjacket embrace.

"What?" He stepped from the shadow and became Nick once more.

Of course. He'd always been Nick. Was she losing her mind?

"What is it, Samantha? Are you all right?"

The concern pierced her. For some stupid reason, tears pricked her eyes. She fought the urge to take his shirt in her fists and sob into it—to give in, to let go. To be vulnerable. Before she could, she turned and escaped the dance floor, stumbling a bit at the edge.

She ran, the grass cool on the soles of her feet.

You should have known this wouldn't work.

She *had* known. But there was something about this man. She couldn't hold the wall of indifference that she'd built between herself and every other male. The wall that kept things light. Safe.

She'd known the storm was coming. Hell, he'd even *seen* it.

Dammit, she knew better than to want. It always got snatched away. Always.

Skirting the lights, she ran up the hill on the dark side of the house. Halfway up, she felt a hand on her shoulder.

She stopped, breathing hard.

His voice came from the dark behind her. "Why are you running? I only told you how pretty—"

She whipped around. He stood outlined against the light, her sandals dangling from his hand.

Better shoved away than snatched away.

"So I'm obligated, right? I need to be polite while men stare. Because I'm *pretty.*" She spit the words at him. "Everyone assumes it's a blessing. It's not. I feel like some kind of genetically defective chameleon. All I want is to blend into the background, but it's green, and I'm hot pink." She put her palms on either side of her face, as if she could rip it off. "This is a magnet that draws men. I didn't ask for it—I don't want it!"

She couldn't see him, but knew she'd revealed too much. Again. What was it about *this* man that made the truth come out of her mouth when she meant to lie?

In his eyes she'd seen the reflection a beautiful woman. And it scared the bejesus out of her.

Time to finish this. "This is not going to work. Go away, Nick." Without touching his fingers, she snatched the laces of her sandals and walked away.

CHAPTER FOURTEEN

YELLOW LIGHT SPILLED from the screen door and kitchen windows, but shadows ruled the corner of the porch where Nick sat in the swing. Somewhere between the dance floor and the porch, his feelings solidified from nebulous to stone. He wanted Sam. Not just the gorgeous outside—but the sweet, vulnerable, damaged woman beneath the skin. He had no intention of getting chased off like a stray hound. If she wanted to get rid of him, it was going to take more than what she'd shown him so far.

He saw just when Sam realized she didn't have car keys; she stopped halfway to the Jeep and patted her skirt, as if feeling for her jean pockets. She trotted up the sidewalk and into Jesse's house.

He scrubbed his palms on his jeans, forcing his body still, waiting. His foot bounced on the boards of the porch, waiting. Two minutes later she slammed out the screen door, and moving fast, started down the porch steps.

"Does that usually work?"

She froze like a kid caught sneaking cookies, then turned, squinting into the shadows. "Does what work?" Her words sounded more resigned than angry.

"Driving men away. Does it usually work?"

"I don't know. I never let one close enough before." She blew out a breath. "But apparently it doesn't."

He chuckled and patted the wooden seat next to him.

"Come, sit down. Talk to me for a few minutes. I promise I won't keep you long."

She hesitated a lengthy moment, then with a resigned sigh, took the step up to the porch, crossed the shadows and leaned against the porch rail, facing him.

Convincing arguments crowded his mind. Good arguments. *Useless arguments.* He pushed them aside and closed his eyes, imagining himself lying in the dark, talking to her on the phone. "Though my imagination bludgeons me with it, I can't know what you went through, Sam. Not really. I do understand that you're afraid of men—"

"I'm *not* afraid of men."

He hadn't known a wail could be a whisper.

She looked at her feet. "Only you."

Bubbles of hope hit his brain like the fizz of fine champagne. *There's a chance.*

She continued, "I have a lot of thinking to do. The other night. You saw. I'm standing on the edge of something…big. I'm wobbly, and I don't have the luxury of a safety net." She crossed her arms over her chest. "I can't take a chance on a relationship, Nick. You can't make me." Her words trailed off in a little-girl voice.

He smiled, grateful she couldn't see it. "Hon, I'm not trying to make you do anything. But sometime, when you're doing all that thinking, you may want to look at what is."

She spun away to stare out at the shrouded yard. The murmur of the crowd was only a pleasant backdrop to the music of the neighborhood. A screen door slapped down the street. Crickets rubbed out their mating songs in the grass. The subtext of traffic drifted from far away.

He stood and crossed the porch to stand a step farther from her than he wanted to be. Using their physical attraction to nudge her decision wouldn't be fair. "Sam, I know about loss, and pain. I also know that life is a cold place all alone."

Right here. He should tell her about his past, right here.

But he'd already taken a chance when he told her he was an alcoholic. Load on top of that the fact that his mom was murdered by—uh-uh. Not going there. Not right now. She'd be in the wind in a heartbeat. Assign him to hell for being a coward, but he could live with that easier than losing her.

He needed to touch her. To smooth the lock of hair that had fallen out of the fancy twist held together with bobby pins and magic.

"Look, you're back on the road when the house is finished. I know that. We're both fragile people, Sam. But maybe we have a chance to step into a place for little awhile, out of the wind." He leaned over the rail to catch her gaze. "We're friends, and from what you've told me, I may know more about you than anyone still alive." He forced the edges of his mouth up, as if her answer weren't a fork in his future. "Relationships have been founded on less. What do you think?"

She faced him, her eyes flashing liquid in the light from the windows.

He dangled in the seconds that ticked by.

"I think a windbreak would be nice for a little while." She tipped her head to the side. "What the hell. I survived a tangle with a car. Maybe I can survive a tangle with you." He didn't hear a smile in her words.

When the tension drained, relief poured in. It was a chance. A chance to show her that all men don't hurt. That a relationship could sustain her—sustain them both. He stood, savoring the fullness of the moment when Samantha let him in. He felt like Indiana Jones, after he negotiated the booby traps in the temple. Before the spiders.

Don't get carried away, dude. She said "a little while."

He'd take that. He'd take whatever she offered willingly. He wanted to kiss her senseless and mess up that prissy hairdo.

This glamorous creature was amazing, but he missed the biker chick. *My biker chick.*

For a little while.

He stepped into the empty space and took her in his arms.

SAM NESTLED SAFE against Nick's chest, well aware that safety was, like a heat shimmer at the horizon, a mirage. But for right now, she'd take it and pretend. The storm that began a few months ago—hell, who was she kidding—years ago, had eaten away at her tough facade, finding cracks she hadn't known were there, eroding her resolve. She was weary. Soul weary. She doubted she could run now, even if she'd wanted to. And for the first time in her life, she didn't really want to. Was it wrong to grab at the solace Nick offered? Just for a while?

You know it is.

A blank place in her chest ached like a sore tooth. It was dangerous, this wanting. Sam knew from experience that driving a flag in the ground at the top of a hill and saying out loud, "I want this," was asking fate to drop a bomb.

She searched inside to see how she felt about that.

Nick waited, the moon lighting the blatant hope on his face.

I don't care.

The rain would come. But until then, she decided to make the most of this respite from the wind. She brushed the backs of her fingers over his cheek, noting the unexpected softness of his skin against the slight beard stubble. His unique scent, mingling with the cloying smell of jasmine should have clashed. *Hmm.* She inhaled and held it, storing it in her memory.

His breath hitched. His face hovered, so close that the skin of her cheek tingled. When he slid his hands through her hair, bobby pins pinged off wood, and the whole heavy mess fell to her shoulders. He made a sound, a cross between a purr and a growl, deep in his chest. His fingers ran along her scalp, combing through her hair, over and over.

The intimacy of it shot a bolt of lust to her crotch. She hadn't known that in a man's hands, hair could be an erogenous zone. She became suddenly aware of the frilly scrap of material between her legs when her moisture touched it.

Restless, she put her hands on his shoulders, to anchor her to the porch. Closing her eyes, she let her head fall back and pushed away cautious thoughts. They'd be there, waiting, later. For now, feeling was enough.

He touched his lips to the curve of her jaw, and trailed whisper kisses down her throat. His hands moved over her back, brushing the naked flesh exposed by her peasant blouse. A delicious shiver slid down her spine. His mouth moved lower, dancing along her collarbone. Then lower, to the top of her breasts, edged by her scoop-neck blouse. A bowstring of want tightened her nipples. *Me. Touch me.*

She leaned into him, hoping he couldn't feel her blazing heat through their clothes, aware of the muscles of his thighs and the thrust of his erection. His hands slid lower, cupping her buttocks. He lifted her, slow and close. Her damp crotch felt every inch of him on the way up, and she squirmed in a spasm of pleasure. He sat her on the porch rail, and stepped into the open space between her legs.

She cupped his face in her hands, raising it until her lips barely touched his. "I don't care what happens later, Nick. I want you now."

The bass vibrations of his moan touched the skin of her lips. Nick kissed her with a focus she'd never experienced, as if his body was only a conduit for the force of his spirit. She recognized that spirit from their late-night phone calls, now given physical form. He greeted her with his mouth, as if she were from his past—an old love. As if he *knew* her.

As he made tender love to her mouth, her mind tipped, falling into him. She clutched the lapels of his shirt in her fists and clung, his hard body her only anchor in a sea of feeling.

Voices—discussing cupcakes? Sound and light burst into her consciousness, waking her like a splash of cold water. She realized that a light had come on, the screen door had opened and people were stepping onto the porch.

She jerked away. Nick's slow hands gentled her, smoothing her hair. She hopped from the rail, face blazing.

The mayor and his wife didn't seem aware of them. They waved their goodbyes to the Jurgens. But Jesse's sly glance missed nothing.

Sam said, "I'd better be getting home, too." She smoothed her skirt, tucked her hair behind her ear then faced Jesse's smirk. "I had a wonderful time. You two really know how to throw a party."

"It looks like we weren't the only ones throwing a party." Jesse smiled. "Okay, hon, I'll let you go. But if you don't stop by the café tomorrow, I'll hunt you down like a cur dog."

Sam knew the threat wasn't idle. Jesse would have her spilling her guts sooner rather than later. "Okay, I'll talk to you tomorrow. And Jesse?" She tucked her hand in the crook of Nick's elbow. "Thanks."

"You're very welcome, sweetie. That's what friends are for."

A small thrill fluttered through her when Nick took her hand. They walked across the lawn to the door of the Jeep, where he turned her to face him. "We have a deal, right? You're done running for the next couple of months."

"Sealed deal, Pinelli." She held up her hand, with last finger out. "Do you want to pinkie swear?"

"Nah, I trust you." He leaned down and brushed a featherlight kiss on her lips. It had none of the earlier heat, but its sweetness touched her in another way entirely. It brought to

center the big step she'd taken tonight. And at this moment ,
at least, she was glad.

"Besides, after that kiss on the porch, I don't think you
could chase me away with a claw hammer."

"You're the one with the hammers, Sam. A mechanic uses
different tools." He waggled his eyebrows and winked at her,
then headed off down the hill, whistling.

"Hey, Pinelli." She tossed after him, "Did I mention tools
are my favorite thing, ever?"

"BINGO!" NICK CLICKED ON the photo ad for full chrome turn-
signal lenses on bikeboneyard.com. His fingers flew over
the keyboard, entering his credit card and shipping info, then
clicked Buy, holding his breath until the site acknowledged
his purchase. "Score!" He punched one fist in the air. The
phone on the counter rang. "Pinelli's, this is Nick."

"Well, you sound happy." Sam's sexy alto voice came over
the line. "Did the Dodgers win a double-header?"

"No. Better. I just bought the prettiest Vulcan turn signal
lenses you ever saw. I was about to call you."

"Good job!"

"Now if I could just find a gas tank. I could make do with
your tank, but it's sacrilege to Bondo a classic bike. That, and
decent rims are proving to be the hardest. And your rims are
cracked. There's no fixing that."

"You are a mighty hunter, Pinelli. You'll find them eventually, I have no doubt. But in the meantime, let's celebrate
you bagging the lenses. You want to come to dinner tonight?"

"*Well,* I don't know. I have standards. What are you cooking?"

"I thought I'd just—oh, shut up, Nick. Are you saying that
if I cook Spam, you won't come?"

"Spam?" He gulped. "I'm sure the way you fix it, it's really good."

Her chuckle let him know he'd been had. "Gotcha. Come on over around six, okay?"

"Even Spam couldn't keep me away."

He hung up, more elated with the call than the turn signal lenses. He knew this was more than dinner. This was Sam, letting him in. He didn't know if she was aware of it, but he sure was. He'd worried that after last week on Jesse's porch, Sam would be shoring up her walls.

Tonight, he hoped to explore the unchartered territory behind them. And he couldn't wait.

AFTER WORK, SHE took a quick shower, threw on stonewashed jeans, a light blue oversize T-shirt with a slouch belt and ran downstairs to clean up the kitchen.

Maybe tonight Nick would trust her enough to talk about *his* past.

She kicked off her shoes, tied a large dish towel around her waist and tuned the radio to an oldies station out of Santa Maria. The radio blared out "Walkin' in the Sand" by The Shangri-Las, and she sang along while she washed dishes, hips swaying to the beat.

A featherlight touch fell on the back of her neck. She let out a squeal and whipped around, holding a wooden spoon out as a weapon.

Nick put his hands up and stepped back, smiling.

"Christ in a sidecar—you scared the crap out of me!" She put her hand over her racing heart.

"I tried knocking but you couldn't hear me for the music. A woman living alone shouldn't leave her front door unlocked, you know."

"And what could I have to fear when I have a ferocious watchdog?" Bugs sat on the porch, nose against the screen door, stumpy tail ticking. She walked over and let him in.

Toenails scrabbling, Bugs tore over to Nick and threw himself on his side for a good belly scratch.

Squatting, Nick obliged. "His hair is growing in nicely, I see."

Nick looked good. An ivory dress shirt with the sleeves rolled up on his tanned forearms, slim cut jeans stretched tight over his thighs and butt. He looked better than good. A warm spot heated her chest, spreading outward. She wanted to walk over, to trace the line of his long, workman's bicep. She wanted to smell the vulnerable hollow at his throat. To lick it, to see what he would taste like.

Yeah, Crozier, and then what? A cold sheet of reality doused the warm spot.

He stood. "You looked so cute when I came in. Bare feet, dish towel and all, singing into that slotted spoon."

Tucking her hair behind her ear, she stepped into her loafers. "Hey, when I hit the road on my next concert tour, you'll eat your words, Bucko." She turned and wiped the sink, for something to do.

Nick's arms came around her waist, and pulled her snug against his chest. "I got no work done today, thinking about spending the evening with you."

She felt the rumble through her back, and his breath tickled her ear. She inhaled the becoming-wonderfully-familiar smell of Nick. "I had a pretty interesting day, myself." She slipped out of his arms and pulled off her dish-towel apron. "Hey, I've got iced tea in the fridge." She opened the refrigerator door and retrieved the pitcher and a plate of fruit and cheese she'd cut up earlier. "Do you want to have this on the porch?"

"Sounds good. Remind me later, I've got dessert in the truck." He lifted the pitcher of tea and two glasses and side-stepped Bugs, who danced a jig around his feet.

They sat on the front steps, watching the dog chase grasshoppers in the front yard and talking about their day. Nick told of the latest scandal—a member of the city council had been caught in a compromising position in council chambers with a married constituent. "He told everyone that she'd come to him for zoning advice."

"Advice she obviously took!" Sam chuckled. "Hey, I understand. Easements and setbacks always make me hot."

Nick raised a grape to her mouth, holding it an inch away, his attention riveted on her lips. "I can't wait to find out what else makes you hot."

At his breathy whisper, her smile melted in a flush of heat. She leaned in to take the fruit, watching him watch her. When her teeth grazed his fingers, his clipped groan had desire braided in it. He tilted his head and captured her mouth.

His lips held the sweetness of the fruit. When he deepened the kiss, something flowed between them—electric, but not electricity—more a jolt of molten power. Startled, she sat back and raised her fingers to her tingling lips. "Did you feel that?"

Nick appeared a bit startled himself. "Better try it again to see if it's a fluke." He slid his hands under her hair, tilted her head and kissed her. The power began again, a flow coursing between them. By the time he lightened the kiss, they were both breathing heavy. He nibbled her bottom lip, then reluctantly released her.

Her guts felt like heated candle wax: warm, soft, pliable. "That has to be you—it sure isn't me."

His green eyes had darkened to a deep jade. He cocked his head and studied her face. "I think it's us, babe."

The endearment shot through her like a sparkler, white-hot bits of fire falling on her tight heart. She'd never been anyone's "babe."

When Nick held out his hand, hers settled into it, pulled by the need for touch. She twined her fingers in his, feeling the roughness of working man's hands. She wondered what they'd feel like touching the tender skin under her breasts.

The sparkler's white-hot bits of desire fell to the floor of her pelvis, starting a fire. She wanted to know. Soon.

She whistled for Bugs and when she stood, Nick followed. Her limbs weighed heavy, as if she'd drunk wine rather than tea. She let the dog in, then led Nick into the parlor, to the edge of her bed. But once there, she hesitated. She hadn't planned this; only followed her body's strident demand—Nick, in her bed. When had her body ever taken control of her mind? *Never, that's when.*

He must have sensed her reserve, because he took both her hands in his. "Are you okay?" At her nod, he said, "Sam. I need you to know. Nothing will happen between us, if you're not all-in. Ever."

His jaw and lips were set tight, but the softness in his eyes drew her. This was Nick, the savior of her nights, the keeper of her secrets. "Oh, you're wrong. This bothers me, but not the way you think. I'm not afraid, Nick. I've never been afraid. Well, not since—" She untangled her fingers and allowed her hands free rein. Her thumbs slid up, tracing the shallow depression along the pale skin on the inside edge of his bicep. "Do we need to talk about that now? I'd rather just…" She went up on her toes to kiss him.

The surge of power hit again, coursing through her, firing her nerve endings, leaving her hyperaware of every touch. His arms came around her to rest at the hollow of her back. Her nipples sliding against his chest hardened, sending a bolt to her crotch so strong she moaned.

She ached to explore his skin. Would it be as smooth as she'd imagined, lying in her bed, listening to his voice on the phone? She reached up and unbuttoned his shirt, exposing a muscular chest with a light line of hair between his nipples, trailing to the waist of his jeans. *Hmm, nice.* She closed her eyes to concentrate on the feel of him under her hands.

His hands were busy. She felt a tug and heard her belt hit

the floor. Then his roughened hands were on her at last, awakening the sensitive skin of her stomach. Yes. This is what she'd imagined. Whorls of sensation spread, like ripples on water, to the vortex between her legs. She leaned into him, hearing their breath laboring. Her mind, now only a conduit for sensation, threw out random thoughts. *Maybe Nick is the key to the lock.*

His strong hands cupped her breasts through her bra, and she shuddered as his long fingers found their tips. "Sam."

He touched her as if she were ancient porcelain. Something about his gentleness brought out the opposite in her—making her want to tear at him, to scratch his back with her nails, and pull him into the center of the fire he'd ignited. "We're wearing way too many clothes, Pinelli."

"I wanted to go slow, but…"

She bit his neck.

His fingers dug into the skin at her waist. "Maybe later." He groaned.

They fumbled at each other's zipper, but soon realized it was much faster to strip their own. Shoes and jeans flew into a crumpled heap.

They stood, finally naked, breathing heavy, taking each other in. God, he was gorgeous. His muscles weren't a bulging weight lifter's. They were long, work-made muscles. Sleek. She followed the line of hair to the sexy indentation of his hips that drew her eye down. Evidence that his need matched hers bounced against his stomach.

"Wow." Oh, God, had she said that out loud?

One side of his mouth lifted in that killer grin. He growled and reached for her. They tumbled onto the bed, laughing.

But when their skin touched, laughter died. Sam lay on her side, eyes closed, feeling the hair of his chest against her nipples, his hand, sliding down the skin over her ribs, the arch of his foot, sliding over the muscles of her calf.

He kissed along the underside of her jaw. "God, Sam, you're perfect." His hands cupped her breasts, his fingers moved as if imprinting the feel, the heft of them.

When he rolled her stiff nipples between his fingers, her hips spasmed and she moaned. Her need was a wild animal, ripping and tearing. She pulled his hips to her, grinding into him.

"Jesus," he breathed. "Sam, I want you so badly—have wanted you so badly—"

She took his lips—she tasted the wildness in him. She guided him to the beginning of her, just touching. He didn't move—except for the trembling. He stroked the hair at her temples and looked down at her, his eyes dark, his jaw tight.

She realized he'd left this to her—it would be her choice. She took him into her quickly and deeply, not wanting him to have any doubt. He moaned then, and began to move slowly. So slowly.

Sam stared up at the silly ornate cornice on the ceiling. Separate. Alone. *Please, God, not now.* One moment she'd been enmeshed in Nick, body and mind. The next, the slap of a cold wave of reality brought her back. Nick moved in her, and she struggled to get back to that warm, wild place, but the wave had passed, leaving only a stark feeling of clinical detachment. She tucked her chin over his shoulder and moved with him, so he wouldn't know.

NICK KNEW. ONE minute they were wrapped together, bodies and minds. Then she was gone. Not physically, but every other way that mattered. He pushed himself up on his elbows, holding her head cradled in his hands, to look into her face. What he saw there made him frown, and he held himself still. "Am I hurting you?"

Her features collapsed. She covered her face with her hands.

He slid out of her but didn't go far, settling beside her, holding her. Given what he knew of her past, he shouldn't be surprised. But the lightning shift from lusty to broken woman left him flat-footed.

"I'm s-sorry, Nick. I th-thought it would be different this time." Her breath hitched.

"Shh, it's okay, babe. Really, it is." He brushed a damp curl from her cheek.

"It's not. I know it's hard for you to stop. I'm not afraid. We can—"

"No. We can't. You think that I'd just go there, without you?" Ignoring his aching gonads, he reached for a tissue on the milk-crate nightstand and handed it to her. "Who would do that?"

"Only every other guy." She blew her nose. "I'm a basket case. I swear, I almost *never* cry." She looked away.

He touched her cheek. "Sam. Look at me. Please don't shut me out. Not now."

She gazed up at him, her damp eyes huge with sadness. "This is how it is for me. If I were afraid, it would be easier." Her hands fisted in the sheets. "At least it would be something I could work on. That's what makes this so goddamn frustrating!

"It was amazing, with you. I thought, this time... But then it's like a switch flips and I'm lying there, staring up at the ceiling." Red spread from her chest, up her neck, to her cheeks. "No one ever noticed before."

"Never?" He shook his head. "You've been hanging with the wrong people." He took her chin in his hand. "I'm here because I want *you*. Yeah, I want sex. But if I can't have you there, sharing it, then I don't want what's left."

"But you can't just keep going to a certain point and stopping—isn't it bad for you or something?"

He laughed, pulled his arm up and rested his head on his

fist so he could see the emotions play across her face. "That's just what teenage guys tell girls to get into their pants. I'm a grown man, Sam."

She looked at him, hopeful but guarded, as if she were afraid to believe.

"Don't think this is some kind of sacrifice I'm making, either. This trip we take together, babe. If I can't have it all, I'm not settling for less. When this happens for us—and it *will* happen—it's going to be worth waiting for."

He leaned in, and dropped a chaste kiss on her lips, and on the end of her red nose. "Now, how would you feel about skipping dinner and going straight to the strawberry pie?"

CHAPTER FIFTEEN

By MIDWEEK, SAM's nerves were ragged from the sandpaper of regret they'd rubbed on for two days. Sure, Nick had said everything was good. He'd kissed her good-night on Saturday. He'd even called before she fell asleep on Sunday. She hustled him off the phone. When he called the next night, she'd done the same. And the night after that.

He said all was good. But for how long? No matter how beautifully crafted, a man wouldn't stay long with an ice sculpture in his bed. She knew she was going to have to face Nick again. But right now, she felt more than naked. As if she'd stripped more than clothes that night; she'd stripped her pretty skin, exposing the squirming mess underneath. She was beyond embarrassed.

And at the same time, she missed him. Missed his chuckle on the phone, in the dark. Missed the special look in his eye; the one that told her that, for whatever twisted reason, he'd chosen her.

But hope was something she didn't do. So she didn't hope. But she *so* wanted to.

That night with Nick had tipped the scales. She had forced her shaking fingers to dial Bina's number and schedule an appointment for tomorrow. Maybe Bina would have some answers—Sam was fresh out.

You're not going to be here long enough for it to matter, anyway. Here it was, almost August. She estimated the house would be complete by late November. Four more months.

Then she'd put the house up for sale, ship her stuff to the next town, get on her bike and put Widow's Grove in her rearview mirror. She pictured the road running under her front tire, the wind and a road song blowing thoughts out of her head.

Her total world encompassed in the view from her face shield.

Without raising his head from his paws, Bugs blinked at her with his sad eyes.

"Never said it would be any different. You knew that coming in." She bent to pet his head, listening to the kids talking in the other room over the sound of hammering.

Pete stuck his head in. "Sam, Tim hasn't showed up yet. We're supposed to be working on the sink in the kitchen, but I can't do more until I talk to him."

Tim usually arrived first, anxious to get started each day. Worry, like a rivulet of ice water, trickled into her mind. She hadn't talked to Tim since he'd left work last Friday.

"Okay, Pete, do me a favor while we're waiting, will you? The yard is getting out of control again. I lost Bugs in the grass twice the other day. Would you mind cutting it?"

He groaned, but then held up his hands. "I know, I know. I'm going."

Sunny came in and asked a question. Sam turned her attention to the matter at hand, but a part of her mind still worried about Tim. She got Sunny started on measuring the space, and then walked out onto the porch.

Tim's decrepit truck labored up the hill.

When he pulled up, she stood tapping her foot on the drive.

"Sorry I'm late, Sam. I just stopped—"

"Raven, why don't you have a cell phone like everyone else on the planet over the age of four? I just realized I don't have any way of getting hold of you if you're not home."

"Now hang on a minute, missy. I've been taking care of myself longer than you've been alive. I don't need a keeper to change my diapers yet, but when I do, I'll call you." He crossed his arms and thrust out his chin.

God, will this day never end? Here she was, taking her frustrations out on a little old man. "You're right. I apologize. I get a little excited when I'm worried."

"That's okay. I'm not used to having people worry about me." He uncrossed his arms. "I was on my way, but I passed Ana's house and saw her in the yard lugging hoses, so I stopped to help. Do you know that feisty little thing tried to throw me off the property? Held me at bay with a garden rake! It took me a while to calm her down."

Sam chuckled. "I had pretty much the same experience the first time I visited. Her bark is worse than her bite, though. I'm trying to develop a friendship, but it's been a tough sell." When he would have walked away, she touched Tim on the sleeve. "I know you're protective of her past, Tim, but I would like to help her if I can. It would help if I understood more about how she got to where she is now."

His gaze raked her, deciding. "What do you want to know?"

"How long have you known Ana?"

"Nigh on to forty years." Tim's gaze strayed to the cottage at the bottom of the hill. "My wife, Nellie, and I went to school with Ana's husband, Glenn. He went off to war right out of high school. My parents were old, and since I was an only child, I stayed to help with the farm. I married my Nellie a year later." His voice softened. "Childhood sweethearts, we were."

He shook his head as if to clear it. "Anyway, we had dances. Once a month, young folks would gather at someone's barn. One of us would bring a phonograph and everyone else would bring records. How we danced. Those were some good times, let me tell you." He smiled a bittersweet, faraway smile.

"That's where we met Ana for the first time. She was a tiny thing, shy about her English. But there was a glow about her. You know how some young women are, just so fresh and pure that the life just shines from their faces?" Tim's face flamed, as if realizing he was talking to a woman. "Yes. Well. Anyway, that's how I met her."

"How long has she lived alone in that house?"

"Glenn's been gone ten years, now. Sad thing, that. We called it 'getting senile' back then. Ana refused to send him away—said that he'd been raised on this land and, by God, he'd die on it. She saw that he did, too.

"Did it all by herself. Got so she didn't want anyone seeing Glenn like that, so she wouldn't allow visitors. We didn't want to intrude, or make her uncomfortable, so we all gave them space. Took him years to die, and I guess Ana just got used to being alone. Maybe now she doesn't know how to do anything different." Tim sighed, and the truck door groaned when he opened it. He reached in and pulled out a pipe wrench.

"I'm off to work. No telling what my assistant's gotten himself into."

Sam watched Tim walk away, considering his words. She now understood what her niggle of curiosity had been—why her feet had so often made the trip down the hill, in spite of Ana's rebuff.

We're not so different, she and I. Left alone, could she end up a recluse, chasing people off her porch with a claw hammer? At the bleak picture, a shiver of unease shot through her.

She walked up the drive, relieved that she'd had the guts to call Bina.

What a great room. Floor-to-ceiling bookcases were saved from being oppressive by the filtered light through a large bay window. A padded window seat overlooked the backyard. The flowered chintz pillows would've called Sam to curl up with a book if she'd been in Bina's office for a different reason. Instead, she fidgeted in an overstuffed wing chair opposite a delicate French provincial working desk.

She'd set up an appointment a few days ago and regretted it since. *This is so not me. Why am I here?*

She knew why. The nightmares. They now bled into her days, staining them with shame. With all her previous projects, she'd pulled off the road, completed them then jumped back on the bike and kept moving.

This time when she'd stopped, the past caught her. Memories landed and enfolded her with leathery wings until she couldn't get a free breath.

This place was changing her. The town, the people, the dog. Nick. Something had shifted in her. Her need for connection, like a massive snake, awakened. It wrapped around her guts and commenced squeezing, tighter than her memories.

She felt as though she were watching a family from the outside of their house, the warm light spilling from a living room. She was no longer content to observe from the sidewalk. She wanted to walk up, knock on the door and be welcomed. She wanted a real relationship with a man. She wanted…so much.

And she *hated* wanting.

She stood and smoothed the creases in her jeans. Bina would think she was strange, but she had to get out of here.

Bina walked in the doorway, carrying a modern silver coffee service. "Have a seat, Sam. The mutts are busy tearing up the backyard, so we shouldn't be interrupted."

Sam glanced at the door. She thought about the dreams. She sat.

Bina poured their coffee and took hers to the window seat. Slipping off her shoes, she tucked her feet under her and settled into a pillow-lined corner. "You seem a little apprehensive, Sam. Why don't we just chat? No agenda."

Sam picked up her mug, then set it down. "Apprehensive. That's one way to put it." Before the silence could stretch out, she shoved the words from her mouth. "Do you know anything about dreams? What they mean?"

Bina blew on her coffee. "Do you have recurring dreams?"

Sam stared at the cup in her lap, steeling herself to open the door guarded for so long. She took a deep breath and turned the knob.

"I'm working in a house. It's a different house every time, could be a mansion or a cottage, old or brand new. Sometimes I'm alone, or there could be a party going on.

"At some point I become aware—in the back of my mind, somehow I know—there's something horrible in the basement. Once I know about it, I can't avoid it. It's like those scary movies, where the girl is walking down the cellar stairs, and you're yelling, 'Don't do it!'"

Bina nodded.

"The closer I get to the stairs, the more terrified I become. I know there's something down there. I don't know if it's a monster, or a demon or what, but in my dream I know there are worse things than dying. Even knowing that, I go. I'm *lured* to it." She shuddered. "I can't convey the impulse. Or the terror.

"When I get to the bottom of the stairs, the floor goes to dirt. There is an opening in the earthen wall opposite me. I perceive that there's a labyrinth of tunnels beyond where *it* lives. All I want to do is run, but I can't make my legs obey.

"I can hear it getting closer. I can even *smell* it moving down the tunnel toward me. Musty, with the scent of old things. Dead things. It's so real. I know that once I see it, I'm never going to be the same." She put up her hand, as if that would ward off the memory. "It's just on the other side of the wall," she whispered, afraid the words could summon it. "Then I wake up."

A chill spilled down the back of her neck, and bumped down her spine. Just recounting the dream brought back the emotions. "I know it sounds like a kid's nightmare. But it feels like my soul is withering the closer the demon gets."

Bina's threaded eyebrows creased. "I'll need to know more about the difficulties you're having. But generally, dreams are our connection to our subconscious mind. Imagine your mind as a computer. The grunt work is done in code by the processor, the subconscious. Dreams are the interface to your awareness, see?"

Sam wanted the answers. She really did. But she also knew that if her damn bike was intact, she'd be on it right now, letting the wind and a road song drown them out.

No, you wouldn't. You've committed to doing this—you're not a victim any longer. I want to be someone brave. Someone to be proud of.

"Do you want to tell me about your past, Sam?"

She took a deep breath, sat on her hands to quell their shaking and nodded.

NICK USED THE WALK from his shop to the Farm House Café to decide.

Jesse knows Sam better than anyone. She can tell you what's up.

Yeah, but what, are you still in junior high? "Does she like me?" God, how embarrassing.

But if Sam's not talking, how else am I going to find out if she's trying to dump me? If she is, it's going to take me some time to decide what I'm going to do about it—to get my game face on.

Jesus. Men just aren't wired for this shit. Why can't women just say what's on their minds? He ran his hand through his hair. *This coming from a guy who's going to the girlfriend of his girlfriend for advice.*

Since the night she'd invited him to dinner, Sam would hardly speak to him. The walls were up, but now they were topped with razor wire. Her voice was cool and detached on the phone, as if he were a stranger. He'd tried to broach the subject of what happened, and she'd practically hung up on him. So they talked, but it was all B.S. chitchat.

And it was making him crazy.

After hesitating a few heartbeats, he pulled open the door of the café. He looked around at the almost deserted booths. *Good timing.*

"Hey, Nick, what are you doing here this time of day?" Jesse looked up from the Widow's Grove *Guardian,* spread on the bar. "Aren't there any broken-down cars littering the roadside hereabouts?"

"Nary a one, last I checked."

"Well, then, I'm glad you stopped by. It's downright dead in here."

A fact he'd counted on. He sat on a stool at the deserted bar.

"You want some coffee?"

"That's the best offer I've had all day. Thanks."

"All day?" Her eyebrows disappeared in her bangs. "I guess Sam has been working, huh?" She winked, pulled a cup from beneath the bar and set it in front of him.

"Don't you bust my chops, lady."

She lifted the coffeepot from the hot plate and brought it over. "Not me, Nick. I can't tell you how happy I was to see you two getting cozy on my front porch." She filled his cup. "She's super, isn't she?"

"Honestly?" He ran his fingers through his hair. "Yes. And no."

"Uh-oh. That tone calls for sugar." Jesse slid the glass back on the refrigerated display case on the wall, pulled out two dishes of pudding and set them on the counter. She dragged over a tall stool and settled on it. "Banana pudding helps in these situations. Trust me. I'm a professional." She retrieved two spoons from beneath the counter and gave one to him. "Now, talk, Nick."

No reason to play coy; he'd come here to talk. Even if he didn't want to flat out say it. "You don't really know me, Jesse. Sure, you knew me as a kid, but—"

"Oh, please, Nick." She rolled her eyes. "Let's see if I get this right." She held up fingers.

He hated when she did that.

She touched the first finger with her thumb. "You had tragedy, young. You had to face stuff as a teen that breaks down adults. You went a bit wild. You made mistakes." She touched the second finger. "But you've worked your ass off the past eight years, building back your reputation, as well as a business. It's firmly established now. You can stop working hundred-hour weeks." She touched her next finger. "In that time, you've managed to get your feet under you, too. You've given back to the community, assuring the Pinelli name will be known for something other than what happened fifteen years ago." She dropped her hand and picked up her spoon. "How am I doing so far?"

He nodded to keep her talking. Maybe she could tell him what would happen next, and he wouldn't have to say a thing.

"So now you're starting to lift your head up and look around. You're looking for someone to share your life with. Someone to give you the grandkids your mom would have so loved." Her eyes went all soft.

He shifted on the chair. If she was going to cry, he was out of here.

"You've done well, Nick. The whole town is proud—"

"But I also know I have limits."

Jesse paused, spoon halfway to her mouth. "Uh-oh."

"You're dead on, Jess. I'm settled. Right where I want to be." He rubbed his hands over his face. "So what kind of cosmic joke is it, when I find someone that could be those kids' mom, it's a come-and-go biker chick?"

Jesse put her spoon down. "You mean, wedding-shower, happily-ever-after in love with someone? With Sam?" Her smile started slow, but was blinding by the end.

"Jesus." He put up a hand. "Focus, Jess—don't go all girly on me now."

She dialed back the smile wattage, but it looked like it hurt her to do it. "Sorry." She cleared her throat.

"It's my own fault. I met her when she was passing right on through town, for cripes's sake. I should have kept it on a business level."

"Oh, Nick, you're such a guy. Do you really think you can control who you're attracted to? Dream on, buddy."

He didn't have much experience with this. Booze had chosen his girlfriends back in the bad old days. At least he now knew that didn't work. "I came here for *help,* you know."

"You're right. Go on."

"The other night we had an…issue." He shook his head. "Anyway, she won't talk to me. Not really." He stirred the pudding with his spoon. God, he'd rather clean out the grease well with his bare hands than do this. But he had to know. "You're her best friend. She talks to you. Is she looking to get rid of me?"

The corners of Jesse's mouth lifted, but two lines appeared between her eyebrows. "I don't think Sam has let herself realize yet that she wants the same things you do. I don't know what's going to happen when she does." Jesse relaxed, her face going dreamy. "But Sam is special. Isn't she worth taking a chance on?"

"I already have." He looked down at his coffee. "That's what scares me."

"ANA, I NEED HELP choosing bulbs for my yard. I have no idea what to buy. Won't you come to town with me?" Sam sat on Ana's porch, at her feet.

"I will not."

"Well, I'm going to keep asking. Maybe one day you'll say yes."

"You are a stubborn, pigheaded girl."

"Takes one to know one, Ana." She smiled. "I don't suppose you know anything about making jelly, do you?"

"Of course I do. Where did you grow up that you never learned this?" She frowned over her glasses.

"Hey, I'm a suburban girl. My idea of plant maintenance is pushing a mower in my yard."

"You need to grow the grapes first. You won't even have enough grapes for jelly for a few years, anyway. You get grapes, you come see me. I'll tell you then."

At the sound of a dysfunctional engine laboring up the hill, Sam looked up from her notes. Tim Raven's dilapidated truck pulled up, sputtered, wheezed then died in front of the cottage.

"Good morning, Ana," he yelled through the open passenger window. "Hey, Sammie. How are you ladies this fine day?" The truck door squealed open.

Ana snapped to attention like a junkyard dog on patrol. Her bony fingers went white on the rocker's arms, her mouth a thin, disapproving line. Tim slammed the truck door and stepped to Ana's picket fence.

"You have no business here. What do you want?" She growled the warning.

"Just thought I'd stop." Sam had never before heard wheedling in Tim's voice. "I have an idea for your garden. I see you watering your yard every day. I got to thinking. I could lay in an automatic sprinkler system for you. You could even have a drip line set—" He opened the gate, gesturing toward the delicate new seedlings set closest to the fence.

"I did not ask for your help. I do not want it. Go away." Ana stood and stomped into the house. The wooden door closed with a heavy thump.

Sam stood looking at the closed door for a moment, then ambled down the path to Tim's truck.

Tim squinted at the porch. "I only want to help."

"I know, Tim. I'm trying to get her to agree to come to town with me, but so far it's a standoff. For whatever good it will do, I'll put in a good word for you. Maybe if we tag team her, she'll come around."

"We can try." Tim shook his head. "Come on, I'll give you a lift up the hill."

In two minutes, Tim pulled up the drive and turned off the truck. "Having the parquet inlay in front of the fireplace match the fleur-de-lis in the stairwell window was brilliant."

"Hey, don't look at me. That was all Beau. That kid is an artist with wood."

"Well, that kind of detail will up the resale value of the house." He chuckled. "Or, you could keep it, seeing how it's about the perfect size for a couple."

"You do know that discussing my love life makes yours fair game, right?" She got out, slammed the door and rounded the back of the truck.

Tim stepped out of the truck, lifted the driver's door and pushed it until the catch clicked. He glanced down the hill at the cottage, then cleared his throat. "Let's go over the plans for the bathroom under the stairs again. I think the inspector is going to have a problem with the sink placement."

"You're a coward, Tim Raven, you surely are."

"You just worry about your love life, missy, and let me worry about mine."

She winced. *I don't have a love life.* "Touché, my friend."

CHAPTER SIXTEEN

SAM PARKED IN FRONT of Coast Lumber, got out and lifted Bugs from the Jeep. The sidewalk was crowded; the cute Danish village of Solvang was as much a tourist magnet as Widow's Grove. She waited for a break in the flow of people, then crossed the sidewalk, Bugs straining at the leash.

She stopped at a bike rack and tied the leash to it. Hand on the door, she heard Bugs whine. She looked over her shoulder. He sat, drooling on the pavement. Head cocked, he whined again. He lifted a paw, stretching it to her.

Man, he was cute.

She glanced at the people passing by within a foot of him. Her heartbeat stumbled for a few syncopated beats, then sped up. What was to keep one of them from untying the leash and walking off with him? Bugs was a friendly sort; he'd go willingly. She'd tied him up outside stores dozens of times. Why had this never occurred to her?

Bugs sat grinning.

She snorted a laugh. *You're losing it, Crozier.* Here she stood, worried about someone stealing a dog that she planned to take to the pound.

She called out to Bugs, "If you be good, maybe we'll stop and get ice cream before we go home." She pulled the door open and walked in, still uneasy with leaving him there. After all, at least the pound would see to it that he got a good home. Probably. Well, she'd just shop fast.

She waved to Oscar, the manager, on her way to the hardware aisle. She stood sorting through boxes of pipe fittings, looking for the size Tim needed. A feeling of being watched crawled over her skin, and the hair on the back of her neck lifted. She jerked her head up.

The pervert, Brad Sexton stood at the end of the aisle, watching her. He held a can of paint in one hand, the other in the pocket of his expensive slacks.

The singsong voice of her childhood whispered. *You didn't think he was just going to go away, did you?* The edge of the brass fitting sliced into her hand.

He broke into a broad smile and winked. He pulled his hand out of his pocket, raised it to his lips and blew her a kiss.

It hit her with the force of a slap, that kiss. But it broke her inertia. Anger exploded like boiling water in a microwave. How *dare* he gloat, seeing her fear? Just mad enough to hurl the fitting in her hand, she forced her fingers to relax. The fitting clunked to the floor and rolled.

They just know. The little girl's voice trembled.

Well, screw you, mutant. She straightened her arm. Lifting it slowly, she mimed a handgun, holding her thumb and forefinger out. She sighted down her thumb, squinted and dropped the hammer.

That wiped the smirk off his face.

She lifted her index finger to her lips and blew. She bared her teeth and dropped him a wink.

He frowned and, looking down, scuttled away.

"Not so fun when a cornered animal bites back, huh, ass-hole?" she muttered under her breath as she bent to pick up the fitting.

He's going to catch us. When you relax. You know what happens.

She dropped the fitting back into the box and left the aisle, heading for the exit door. Brad was nowhere to be seen.

What had she been thinking? Something about Widow's Grove had made her forget what she knew.

Stopping too long led to wanting.

And wanting led to hope.

And hope was the only thing that could blast through every wall she'd ever built to protect her soft core. Even bricks made from memories and her own blood, fired in the blast furnace of her fear, had never been any match for hope.

Hope was more dangerous than Brad Sexton, or any of that brotherhood.

Hope was the enemy.

She pushed the door open, walking fast. Seeing her, Bugs barked, and lunged against the leash. She untied him, fumbling in her haste. "You and I are overdue for an appointment, dog." She led him to the Jeep, and lifted him into the open window on the passenger side.

When she got to her side and hopped in, she crammed the keys in the ignition and started it, already checking the mirror for traffic. Bugs must have sensed her mood, because he sat quiet in the foot well, not looking at her.

"Nothing personal, mutt. Your hair has grown in. That was the deal. It's time."

Bugs glanced at her out of the corner of his eye.

She slammed her heart closed and drove to the animal shelter on the outskirts of Widow's Grove.

The place was a zoo. Dogs barked, bayed or yipped in frantic, staccato bursts. Cats yowled as if they were being pulled to pieces. She stepped up, third in line at the window of a dingy adobe building. A teenage girl walked out of the chain link gate, a fuzz-ball kitten clasped to her chest.

Sam looked down at Bugs. "See? Someone will adopt you right away. I'm sure of it."

Bugs wouldn't look at her.

You're out of here in four months, anyway. She had to salt the roots that were trying to dig into the soil of this damned town. She *had* to.

A man walked by, hand on the shoulder of a boy of around ten, who was trying hard not to cry. "He'll turn up, son. We'll check back in a few days."

A breeze carried the tang of desperation and urine. She wrinkled her nose.

Jesse, Ana, Tim, the kids—Nick. It felt like she'd been sleeping the past months. A good dream but one that ended in the aisle of Coast Lumber. She shook her head. She'd been acting as if she were living in a Disney movie. *What a fool.*

The old lady ahead of her stood at the window, an ancient Chihuahua in her arms. Its muzzle was gray and its claws had on a death grip on the woman's shoulder. "I'm moving in with my daughter, and she won't have an animal. You have to promise me that you won't put Pepe to sleep." Her lips quivered.

The county worker in a forest green uniform patted her shoulder. "Ma'am, I'm sorry. We can't promise."

Sam looked at Bugs. He sat so close she could feel him shaking against her leg. Shaking like he had that first night she saw him. The cut was now just a squiggly pink scar, running the length of his back.

He looked up at her. His stump tail ticked a couple of times, then stopped.

"Grrrrine?"

"Shit."

The man ahead of her in line turned, lips pursed, nostrils flaring.

Who would take a scarred-up bulldog who drooled like a waterfall, and farted like cannon fire?

"Son of a bitch," she said, just to see the man's distaste. Eyebrows raised, he took a step away.

She stomped back to the Jeep, Bugs bounding ahead at the end of the leash.

A HALF HOUR LATER, she slammed into the house, Bugs on her heels. She unhooked the leash, then walked to her bedroom and dug through her junk box. When she found her sewing kit, she snatched her leathers out of the closet and sank onto the bed.

The leather was supple, like skin under her hands. She raised them to her nose and inhaled the smell of sunshine and wind. And freedom.

She opened the sewing kit.

An hour later, she dropped the mess into her lap, not able to see through the film covering her eyes. Drops of blood from her fingers smeared the leather. The needle wasn't made for heavy fabrics, and she poked herself almost every stitch.

Her leathers and her helmet were her cloak of invisibility. People saw an anonymous biker, and their eyes just slid over them, and away. Without them she was naked—exposed.

She rubbed the patch of messy stitches, a wad of something big and tight blocking her throat. The road pulled her. The haunting cadence of Springsteen's "I'm On Fire" echoed through her mind. A strong wind of emotion swirled in the deep pit in her chest, moaning around the ragged edges.

Dropping her head in her leather-filled hands, she wailed, "I don't even *have* my motorcycle!"

She wanted too much. She'd been fooling herself, the past months. She'd gotten wrapped up in this life, and a stray dog was only part of it.

Nick was the biggest part. She *wanted* him. And not just for now. If she couldn't leave an ugly drooling dog, how was she ever going to ride away from the only man who'd ever cared to look beneath her pretty face to want who she really was?

She had to get out of here, before she couldn't.

The wad in her throat let go. The bed jiggled, and a wet dog nose touched her hand. She wrapped her arms around Bugs and sobbed into his shoulder.

"I'm so tired."

He whined.

"I'm so tired of being afraid."

A WEEK LATER, Sam sat at her kitchen card table, reviewing plans for Bina's house. When her phone blatted the opening to the Stones' "Satisfaction," she pulled it from her pocket and hit the button to answer, without taking her eyes from the paper in front of her. "Crozier Construction."

"Sam, you'd better get here and pick up your 'project.' I'm done with this kid." Tim's gruff voice shouted in her ear.

"Do you mean Beau? What's going on?"

"Just get your behind down here, before I kill him."

Click. A dial tone buzzed.

What the hell now? Beau had managed to graduate and stay out of trouble for two months. Since his parents had taken their car back when he moved out, Tim brought him to the site every day. She'd sensed a bond growing between the two, and had been glad of it. Beau needed a mentor, and Tim needed the companionship.

She was in the Jeep in less than five. If a black-and-white had been on the road to town, she'd have been hauled in rather than ticketed. The local cops held a dim view of forty miles over the limit.

She barely slowed at the turn in to Raven's Rest. Tim and Beau stood outside the office, angry faces inches apart. She could hear them yelling at each other from the road.

Gravel spit from the tires as she hit the gas in the turn, and the Jeep's rear slid, looking for traction. Tim's broad hand shot out and slapped Beau, hard enough to whip his head back. She slammed on the brakes, shut down the engine and was out and running.

She threw herself between them before the boy could use his shaking fists.

"What in holy hell is going on here?" She faced Tim, her arms outstretched to keep them separated. Tim's face was purple. *Jesus, I may need to call the paramedics.*

"Goddamn kid. I should have known not to take in a wild animal. It'll bite you every time." He glared over her shoulder. "I come back from fetching groceries and spy a car, almost out of sight behind *his* cabin." Tim poked a finger in Beau's direction. "He knew I don't allow women. I told him that the first day!"

"He's just sticking his nose in—"

Beau quit when she held up a hand, thank God. "How do you know he had a girl here?"

"Cuz I went up and knocked on the door, that's how!" He refocused on her face. "He comes to the door, and behind him there's a naked girl, sitting up in bed, holding a sheet around her! Go on. Ask your rich boy."

Sam spun to face Beau. His eyes were wild, the angry red handprint shocking against his pallid cheek. She'd seen Beau's "fuck you" look before, and knew that nothing would be resolved until she pulled the old and young bulls apart.

"Beau, let's talk for a minute." She looked over her shoulder. "Tim, it's hot out here. Why don't you go in and have an iced tea. I'll be in to see you in just a bit."

Tim made a disgusted sound in the back of his throat and stalked to the office, grumbling the whole way. She looked to Beau. "Let's go." She walked toward the road, hoping he'd follow. When he did, she threw silent thanks skyward.

"I'm so done with this shit." He spit on the ground. "I

thought when I left my parents' house, I'd be treated like an adult. Instead, I just traded one prison for another." He kept his eyes on his holey tennis shoes and motored on. "I owe you, Sam, but when we're done talking, I'm outta here. Just so you know."

She knew lecturing would just drive him away faster. She searched her knowledge base for some bit of wisdom to help her handle this.

Why do you care? You're out of here in like four months.

She stopped still. This wasn't her problem. This wasn't even like her. She was the observer—not the negotiator. At Beau's sound of annoyance, she raised a hand. "Give me a minute here, will you? I'm trying to absorb all this."

Why are you making this your problem?

The answer followed right on the heels of the question. Because Beau's situation reminded her of her own. She understood being thrust too soon into adulthood, and not having the skills to deal with it.

She couldn't go back to make different decisions in her own past. Why did she think that helping Beau with his would solve hers?

They won't. But it feels good to try to help someone else not fall into the holes that I did.

Except, by doing so, she again launched herself into a situation where she had no skills. She had no idea what to tell the teen. She started walking again, keeping her voice neutral. "I thought you and Tim got along. That you liked living here."

"I didn't know Jazz was coming. I swear, I didn't." He threw his hands in the air. "She just showed up at my door with a bottle of wine, crying. What was I supposed to do, slam the door in her face? Just because that old man lives in the nineteenth century…" His voice trailed off to an indistinct mumbling.

"Damn, Beau, can you slow down a minute?" Sam huffed out. "You're killing me, here."

He slowed his pace a bit. "We're just friends. That's all. She's going with a friend of mine, for Christ's sake." He raked a hand through his hair.

She looked up into eyes as wild as his hair. "Hang on, you're losing me. Jazz is your friend, right?" He nodded. "And she's going with a friend of yours." He nodded again. "And you *slept* with her?"

Beau rolled his eyes and blew out an exasperated breath. "She's a lesbian, okay?"

Sam stopped, putting an arm out to stop him from walking on. "What the hell does that have to do with anything?" She was starting to feel like she'd fallen down the rabbit hole. When had she gotten so old that the lives of teenagers had become an alien landscape?

"I told you it wasn't a big deal. It didn't mean anything. We were talking, and she was upset."

"And you were drinking." She hoped it had sounded like fact, not judgment.

"Yeah, and somehow we just ended up in bed. It wasn't like I planned it." He pointed back at Tim's place, now just a dot on the horizon. "Then the old man barges in, screaming. Shit, I thought the place was on fire. Scared the crap out of me."

"Look, Beau, I can see where something like this can happen. But you've got to understand Tim's reaction. You knew the rules."

"I'm done with everybody's rules. That's why I left my parents' to begin with."

"Oh, bull. That isn't why you left home. Forget who you're talking to? You left because of your mother."

"Yeah, but—"

"I've got news, Beau." She tempered her voice. Another screaming match would gain nothing. "You have less rules in your life now than you'll ever have." She ignored his snort of derision. "Don't believe me? What happens if I don't pay the electric bill? Or I don't have another job lined up after we finish the house?"

"You'll get on the motorcycle and ride. I could live with *those* rules."

She almost winced. "This isn't about me. Look at Tim. He lives under more rules than I do."

"I could live with those rules, too. He's all alone. He can do whatever he wants." Beau stopped and planted his feet, arms crossed.

"Yeah, he's alone. He's also old, and fragile. And he's trying to take care of those run-down cabins all by himself. If he had an accident, he could lie there a day or more before someone found him." Beau looked away. "He has almost no income. He's worked for himself all his life, so he gets almost no Social Security. Did you know that? I'm glad he comes out to the house, because at least I know he's getting a little extra income and one decent meal a day."

Ana's face appeared in her mind. "You think you have rules? How about living in fear? Of being old and not having anyone to take care of you? Of being proud and worrying about having to ask for handouts to eat? Those are the kinds of rules Tim lives under."

She waved a hand in front of his face to force him to look at her. "Who cares though, right? Just one more dinosaur, getting in the way. But that dinosaur took you in. He has almost nothing, but he shared what he has with you, because you needed a place to stay."

She turned on her heel to walk back to check on Tim, leaving Beau standing at the side of the road, alone.

TWO WEEKS LATER, Sam sat once more in Bina's home office, spilling her guts.

"Then suddenly, I'm staring up at the ceiling, feeling nothing." Sam sat perched on the dainty French provincial chair, her foot bouncing to give it something to do besides walking her out the door. "It's not a choice I make. It just happens." She picked at a hangnail and it tore off in a stinging strip. "No man ever noticed before Nick, and I'm not even sure if I'm happy about that."

Problems bubbled from the cauldron of her stomach. She stood and paced the length of blue-gray carpet before the window seat where Bina sat watching her, Zen-like. Inscrutable.

"But that's only part of it. It's this town. I've got to get out of here. It's changing me." She picked up a glass paperweight from the desk and tossed it from hand to hand.

"How is it changing you?"

"Bugs is a perfect example. I tried to take him back to the pound. That was the deal. When he healed, off he'd go. He knew it, I knew it." She bobbled the paperweight, almost dropping it.

Bina stood, took it and set it gently on the edge of the desk. "Antique crystal, sorry." She handed Sam a fuzzy dog toy to toss, instead. "Go on." She sat back on the cushion, one foot tucked under her.

"I got there and couldn't do it. The place was just so sad, I *couldn't* do it. That's what I'm talking about. The damn dog crawled under my skin. What am I going to do with a dog, on the road?" Her head felt as though ants were crawling on the inside of her scalp. She ran her fingers through her hair. "I'm going to *have* to get rid of him by December when I leave. But if I can't leave him now, how will I ever leave him after three months more of living with the smelly, drooling thing?"

Bina smiled like a Cheshire cat who just finished a bowl of cream.

"This is not funny, Bina. It's not just the damn dog, either. I don't let people close. I *can't* let people close. It doesn't work.

It just causes more pain. More *wanting*." She paced faster. "But I can't seem to stop it now. Don't you see?"

Sam threw up her hands. "Everything is out of control. My life has turned into this crazy runaway train. I'm pulling levers and brakes, but nothing's happening. Everything that worked before, doesn't now. I need to hit the road. Just ride, as far and as fast as I can. Any direction, it doesn't matter. Just. Away."

"Why do you work on houses?" Bina sipped from her delicate bone china cup.

"Because I'm a building contractor? Hello, Bina. My life is exploding here, and you want to talk about my career?"

"No." She set her cup in the saucer. "I want to know why you chose this to do. You don't just build houses. You take run-down wrecks and turn them into warm, cozy, beautiful homes. Why do you do that?"

"I told you the story. After Dad died, I looked around—"

"Why the wrecks? Why not just start from scratch, or build tract homes?"

"I don't know, I just started with our house—"

"You create a one-of-a-kind home. Something special. You said you could picture a mother in the kitchen—"

"So, what?" She stopped pacing. The damned woman just sat there, looking at her like a skinny female Buddha. "What the hell does this have to do with my life? Jesus, Bina, I thought you could help, here."

"Then you sell it. Dump it and move on, to the next state. To the next house."

Sam sighed. Fine, she'd handle her problems herself, same as she always did. *You know better than to rely on anyone else.* She was almost to the door when Bina's voice stopped her.

"Has it never occurred to you that in those homes, you create exactly what you long to have for yourself, only to walk away from it?"

Sam stopped.

"Over and over and over."

The words went off in her brain like flashes of lightning, illuminating what had been in shadows. As soon as Sam heard the words, perspective shifted. Six years of memories streamed through her mind; houses, before and after. The families she'd sold them to. Bina was right. Dead-on right.

Holy shit. She'd thought the storm would lessen when she started talking about her past. But apparently what happened so far was only a thunderstorm, and now she was watching Katrina bear down on her. Did she want to find out what would be next?

Did she have a choice?

"I'll let you go now, Sam. But you should know. You may experience a bit of…turmoil in the next few weeks, emotionally. Call me if you need me. Anytime."

Sam hesitated, hand on the doorframe. Silence. Buddha had spoken.

NICK TIGHTENED THE last screw and wiped his forehead on the sleeve of his T-shirt. Damn, this fall was a hot one. He walked down the steps of Sam's porch to survey his surprise. The cedar swing hung by a heavy chain from the porch roof, its splashy floral cushions cheerful against the backdrop of stark white.

Nice. He smiled. From this view, the house looked complete, pristine and perfect. Dressed in white with black accents, the stately Victorian could grace the cover of *Architectural Digest*.

Wiping his hands on a rag, he tucked it into his back pocket and climbed the steps to test the swing. He eased into it. The chains creaked, held. He relaxed, resting his arms across the back, setting it rocking with a push of his foot.

Grasshoppers buzzed in the yard and the sound of a tractor growling across an unseen field floated on the breeze. He breathed it in, relishing the smell of hot sage and the scent of freshly cut cedar.

He'd taken Jesse's advice, to make it harder for Sam to leave. He knew arguments wouldn't work. Sam had too many walls, too many excuses and way too much stubborn. Instead, he'd opted for the subliminal route. The swing made the house look like a home. An inviting place to snuggle and watch the sun go down. At least that's how he saw it. Hopefully Sam would see it the same.

But there was nothing covert about his plan for tonight; if she wanted to dump him, she'd have to tell him to his face.

He sat back to wait.

CHAPTER SEVENTEEN

THE JEEP'S RADIO blared Springsteen's "Tunnel of Love" as Sam navigated the sweeps in the road that led home.

Home, ha. This place wasn't home. It was purgatory—the resting spot between heaven and hell. She'd left hell behind, back in Ohio. Heaven? Well, it would be whatever showed up in the windshield of her Vulcan. She sang out loud, trying to drown her own thoughts. Coming out of the trees, into another bend, the craving to feel her Vulcan vibrating against her thighs was almost a physical pain. Instinctively, she leaned into the curves.

Unsettled and antsy, she gave up and snapped off the radio. Her fears queued up, vying for first spot. But always, the largest loomed over all, its shadow eclipsing even the warmth of the sun on her shoulders.

What if? She was afraid to even think it. As if the simple consideration could unleash the actual *possibility* of it happening.

The road had been her solace. Her comfort. Her religion. The one constant in her life since her dad died. What if in December, when she was done here, she threw her leg over the bike and hit the road, only to find the road was no longer there for her?

A crisis of faith. That's all this was.

But what if? The little girl's voice wailed.

What if this purgatory was permanent, with nothing that she could crawl back to? Nothing ahead to look forward to.

The rest of her life, hung between two nothings. Surely there was more?

A few miles farther, she emerged from the trees and saw it. Her house. The haughty old lady, frivolous gingerbread trim showing like lace on her bloomers. The facade looked as she'd imagined it: the shaded portico, flowery cushions on a porch swing…

Porch swing? She did a double take. Apparently this new addition came with an accessory: a hunky man in jeans and a denim mechanic's shirt lounging on it, rocking.

Her heart literally fluttered in her chest. *He bought me a porch swing!* Her face stretched to accommodate her goofy grin.

Then she remembered. Being naked with this man. Her failure exposed. Only her pride kept her from pulling a U-turn. She breathed bravery into her lungs and prepared to behave *as if.*

As if that damn house didn't look like home. As if Nick didn't look like he belonged on that porch. As if wanting a future like that didn't tear her apart.

Pulling in alongside the Love Machine, she shut down the engine. She took a deep breath and then another, until her butt cheeks loosened their death grip on the seat. *Oh, God. I'm so not ready for this.*

But at the same time, joy shimmered over her skin. *He didn't let me chase him away.*

She climbed the porch steps, aware that he watched her. She let a grin slip out. "How did you know? This is exactly as I pictured it, right down to the cushions."

"Because I know *you*." He patted the cushion beside him. "Come try it out."

Hearing snuffling behind the front door, she said, "Hang on just a second." She fumbled with her keys, unlocked the door and stepped back as Bugs barreled through. He circled her legs at a gallop, sniffing, then beelined for Nick. He slid into Nick's feet like he was home plate, belly in the air, panting a smile.

She shook her head. "The animal has no pride."

Nick chuckled, and bent to scratch him. "Glad to see you, too, Bugs."

She crossed the porch to sit beside Nick.

He leaned back, stretching his arms along the back of the swing. As if his body were a magnet, she nestled in the crook of his arm, head on his shoulder, feet bare and tucked under her.

Apparently, she had no more pride than her dog.

Nick set the swing rocking with his foot.

The sun kissed the hills to the west, softening them in a wash of gold. A flock of swallows swooped past, their night calls high and lonely. The rhythmic squeak of the swing's chains slowed the restless thrum at her core. Her mind quieted. She inhaled the rusty smell of autumn. And Nick. "Thank you."

She felt his chuckle on the sensitive skin of her cheek. "I'm not responsible for this part. God is."

It seemed so easy, sitting quiet with him. She was so weary of standing in the wind of the storm. All she wanted to do was put it all down, and for a little while, pretend that she could step into this alternative future—one she might have been living if her past had been different. For just a little while, believe the soap bubble dream. That this home was hers. That this man was hers.

It felt so natural when she turned her head to taste the warm skin of his throat. He dipped his head and they were kissing. Long, lazy, all-the-time-in-the-world kisses, reminiscent of their late-night conversations. Kisses of greeting. Kisses that promised more. Peace eased over her, loosening her knots.

She sighed. "I wish I could stay just like this. For about twenty years."

He twined his fingers in hers. "That would suit me."

They rocked until the sky went indigo, and all that remained of the sun was a lighter band of blue crowning the westernmost hill. When the crickets began the night's overture, she straightened. "I think Romano's will deliver. You want pizza?" She couldn't see his expression; there were no streetlights this far out of town. But he held tight to her hand when she would have stood.

"I hope I never find parts for that damned Vulcan." He almost whispered the words as if he wasn't sure he wanted her to hear.

But she had heard. Her hand spasmed in his.

"You gonna run again, Sam?" In spite of the hard words, they came out of his mouth soft. "Come a few months from now, when all the loose ends are tied up, are you going to hit the road?"

She'd been relaxed. She wasn't prepared. His words stung, down deep, where fear had rubbed her soul raw. Her anger flared, hot and fast. "You're calling *me* a coward, Pinelli?" The words snapped out. She didn't care to stop them, even if she could. "When were you planning to tell me about your parents?" She ripped her hand from his and stood.

She heard his soft exhalation, as if her accusation had hit his soft parts.

"I mean, really. You know my past. I bared my secrets to you—quite literally—in that room right there." She pointed to the windows at his back. "Yet you haven't told me what any local walking down Hollister knows."

He stood. "You're right." He walked to the edge of the porch and down the steps.

But she wasn't done. He hadn't paid near enough. "Who's

running now, Pinelli?" Sam used the singsong voice of the little girl who lived in her head.

He turned. "You want the bloody details?" He strode back to the edge of the stairs and stared up at her, anger stark on his face. "My father always had a mean temper. He made me and my mother's life hell, but it was worse after he lost his job.

"I was fifteen when he walked down the road to the bar with a gun in his hand. My mother worked there to keep food in the house, and a leaky roof over our heads. She was going home, to *him*." His voice escalated in volume and speed.

"It was closing time and she was leaving with the last of the customers, laughing at something a man said, when my father walked up. She wasn't flirting; she was going home to *him*. He never said a word. Just shot the man in the balls. When my mother screamed, he turned and shot her. In the heart." He took panting breaths in between yelling. "Before he could put a bullet in his own head, the men wrestled the gun away."

She didn't have to see his face. His voice dripped ice.

"Now we're even. Because that was just as willingly given as your secrets. Are you happy?"

"No, I'm not," she said through clenched teeth.

"Then why the hell did you bring it up?" He kicked the stair riser. The hollow thump echoed back from the hill across the street.

"I wasn't looking for the 'bloody details.'" She shook her head to clear the grisly picture. "I only wanted to know why you didn't care enough to tell me."

He let out a snort of derision. She wasn't sure if it was aimed at him or her. "I wanted just one part of my life that was clean, untainted—someone who liked me for me. Not Poor Nick Pinelli, the town 'project.' But for the man I am now.

"I didn't tell you, not because I didn't care enough. I didn't tell you because I cared too much."

She stepped down one step and reached to touch his face. Through her fingers she felt the truth of his words. He stepped forward, slipped his arms around her waist and rested his forehead between her breasts.

She combed through his thick hair, her fingernails grazing the scalp, around to the back, where the silky hairs at his nape grew upward instead of down. "Shh." His head rose and fell with her breath, and a fierce protectiveness burned beneath the bone where his head lay. "Of course I know how it feels to want no history." She stopped, realizing she'd spoken her thought.

Well, she couldn't undo the past, or save his mother. But she could give him this. "When I ride into a town, I always think, who will I become here? Who will these people think they met, after I'm gone?"

He lifted his head. She sensed his regard in the dark.

"Whoever they imagined, it wasn't me." She made herself let him go. "Until you."

He made a strangled sound in the back of throat. His hands tightened on her back. He seized her lips, and kissing her, released emotion into her mouth: frustration, pain, the aching loneliness of that orphaned kid. His tongue captured hers. His arms were iron bands, trapping her waist.

She should have been afraid—even claustrophobic in his tight embrace, but she wasn't. She absorbed it all, and tried to pass back some kind of comfort.

With a groan that ended in a ragged sob, Nick tore his lips away. "I'm sorry." His arms loosened their crushing grip. His hands came up to cradle her jaw. He ran a thumb over her swollen lips. "I hurt you."

"Your story hurt me, Nick. You didn't." She took his hand. Turning, she led him back onto the porch, opened the door and pulled him in behind her. The mingled scent of old and new wood brushed against her face. Bugs scooted between their legs.

Nick reached for the foyer light, but she pulled him away, into her arms. "Dark is good. I sometimes see things better in the dark. Don't you?"

Her kiss said, "Hurry, hurry." Electricity passed between them, and tinder caught, flaring hot. Her hands slid across his work-muscled back, testing the long tensile strength of the taut muscle. She yanked the back of his shirt free. Her hands made love to his skin as her lips loved his mouth. He reached for the hem of her T-shirt, but she caught his wrists. "No. My turn."

His hands relaxed to his sides. She exposed the skin of his chest one button at a time, kissing every inch she bared, breathing in his heady essence. After she released the last button, she pulled it off and led him to the stairs.

After rising two steps, he turned to her. "Sam…"

"Shh." She caressed the soft skin of his ribs with a slow slide south, where low-slung jeans snagged on his hip bones, and a line of hair disappeared beneath the waistband. He shuddered. When she mapped the hard line of him under the placket of his Levi's, he groaned. She unbuttoned the fly and the length of him sprang into her hands. Finding him naked under the denim shot a bolt of heat between her legs, a rush of moisture.

She circled the head of him with her fingertip, then leaned down and did the same with her tongue. He tasted like he smelled; solid, safe. When she took him into her mouth, his hands tangled in her hair and he growled, deep in his chest. She felt restraint in the quiver of his thighs, and the gentleness of his hands in her hair. She made love to him, enjoying the contrast between the suede-soft skin sheathing the iron below it. She explored him, gently rolling his balls in her fingers.

He pulled away with a strangled cry. "Not like this." Taking the two steps down, he caught her hand. "I want you, too." He led her to the parlor, to the edge of her narrow bed.

He stole kisses as he undressed her. His teeth grazed the point of her shoulder, his open mouth at the top of her knee, a flick on his tongue at the tip of one nipple. Golden liquid heat pooled in her pelvis, and her hands wouldn't still. But he made her wait, placing her hands on the edge of the bed and covering them with his own, while his mouth explored.

She wanted him. All the way, wanted him. Surely the miserly jailer in her head would allow—she jumped when his whiskers brushed the sensitive inside of her knee, and she twitched, deep inside. He leaned closer, his hot breath stirring her pubic hair. A dark, forbidden wildness zipped through her.

She grabbed his head, using her thumbs to lever his chin up. "I don't do that."

"But—"

"I don't. Ever."

He sat back on his heels, head cocked. "Okay." He climbed to his feet, scooted her over and lay down next to her. "Show me what you do like."

It was amazing. Right up to the second when she found herself staring once more at the ceiling, the cornice just a shadow in the gloom.

Of course, he knew. He stopped, looked into her face then rolled away onto his side.

She sat up and dropped her feet to the floor. "I'll see what I've got in the fridge to eat."

"What are you doing?" His breath was still ragged, his voice sharp.

"I know this is frustrating—"

"*This* does not make me frustrated." His hand fumbled in the sheets, then took hers. "Your pulling away frustrates me." He twined his fingers in hers, and tugged. "Will you come back?"

She let him pull her back into bed. He settled her in front of him and wrapped his arms around her. She snuggled in, knowing this was too good to be true—that Nick was too good to be true. Someone who knew *her*—not the pretty outside package, but her ugly seething inside, and still cared?

Even if she'd never have it all, she'd take all of this man she could get.

But how long would that be enough for *him?*

SAM OPENED THE refrigerator to get a glass of iced tea. It had to be ninety-five degrees inside the house, and the A/C wouldn't be delivered until next week. *Who knew that autumn could be so hot in California?*

The rush of chilled air bathed her sweaty face and she lingered a moment before closing the door. She gulped the entire glassful, wincing when brain freeze hit.

Her hair clung to her neck and sweat trickled between her breasts. The windows were open to catch any breeze, but there hadn't been any. She regretted her own rule of long pants on the job site.

Her mind strayed to Beau, as her tongue would to a sore tooth. He hadn't returned to Tim's after their talk a week ago. Where was he? Yesterday, she'd even called the police department to be sure he hadn't been picked up.

Pretty sad when you're hoping someone's been incarcerated.

In a last-ditch moment of desperation, she'd called the Tripp house. She knew Beau wouldn't have gone home, but felt they were at least owed a call to tell them their son had disappeared. Mrs. Tripp had informed her in a regal, if slightly slurred voice that since Beau was almost eighteen, he was on his own. It wasn't hard to see why the kid hadn't picked up the fine points of the whole respect thing.

This heat wave would break soon, bringing damp, cold nights. Did he have a roof over his head? Was he safe?

She raised the cold glass, listening as she rolled it on her forehead. Conversation and laughter echoed through the rooms. The crew had worked full time through the summer, making remarkable progress. The interior work was close to being finished, upstairs and down. The biggest remaining project was the creation of the under-the-stairs bathroom, and the carriage house build out.

The exterior work on the rear of the house had stalled. Beau had removed all the gingerbread trim. It sat abandoned next to the floor saw in the carriage house, waiting to be used as a template to cut replacement pieces.

She looked around the kitchen. The bay window over the sink brought light to the formerly dark room, and golden oak cabinets lined the walls. The light granite counters lent a clean, modern look. She'd replaced the worn plank floors with unfinished terra-cotta tile. The kitchen was her favorite room—well, next to the great room. But the bedroom loft was pretty amazing, too.

She'd always been proud of her projects, but this time her heart swelled with pride for the people involved as well. Any one of her team would be a great addition to a contractor's staff. Tim was helping Pete obtain his journeyman's license as a plumber, and Sunny was studying for a general contractor's license, planning to sit for the exam next spring.

At the sound of scratching at the screen door, she crossed the room to let Bugs in. He flopped on the cool tile, sides heaving, tongue lolling. Damn, she was going to miss this mutt. A memory of Nick, in jeans, the moonlight on the muscles of his bare chest burned bright in her mind. Other memories followed: Jess, standing behind the counter, Carl smiling through the cook's window, Ana, rocking on her porch, Tim, in baggy pants and perfectly shiny shoes.

She was going to miss a lot more than this smelly dog.

"Well, if you weren't out chasing squirrels, you wouldn't be so hot, dude. Maybe you should hang it up—you've never come close to nabbing one, anyway."

She pressed the button on the fridge, and caught the ice cubes that tumbled out. She carried them to Bug's water dish and dropped them in. She straightened, and yelled down the hallway, "Hey! Where are you guys?"

"We're in here. Or at least as much of us as can fit." Tim's muffled voice drifted down the hall from the bathroom.

She rounded the corner to see Tim and Pete sprawled on the floor, looking up at the bottom of the toilet tank. Sunny straddled the closed seat, holding the hardware in place. Not a square inch of floor space remained. The room practically steamed, between the body heat and the blazing sunlight streaming in her octagonal window. She'd had the glass special made, with the frosted glass fleur-de-lis to match the one in the stairwell.

She smiled at the sweaty trio. The moment would have been perfect if a sloppy kid dressed in black were there.

"It's too damned hot to work. Why don't you all finish what you're doing and clean up? I'm taking you all to dinner at The Farm House. My treat."

Pete let out a whoop from under the toilet. "Oh, man, that's my *favorite!*"

Sunny groaned and poked him in the stomach, then rose from her perch. "Ice cream, too?"

"Especially ice cream. Now, let's go. We need some air conditioning."

A half hour later, Sam opened the Farm House door to a solid wall of chilled air. "Oh, this is worth the price of dinner all by itself." She sighed.

"Well, y'all look positively wilted." Jesse stepped out of

the kitchen doorway, cool and fresh in a white, form-fitted pantsuit, makeup perfect, every hair sprayed into place.

"Easy for you to say, Miss Priss. You've got A/C." Sam lifted damp bangs off her forehead.

"I don't sit around eating bonbons all day, you know." Jesse glared, fists on hips.

"Okay, don't go all rabid Chihuahua on me, Jess." She turned to the crew. "Why don't you guys grab a booth in the back? I've got to talk to Jesse for a minute."

They squeezed by, joking and jostling each other, Tim bringing up the rear.

"Jesse, I've got an idea I wanted to talk to you about." Sam perched on a stool at the bar. "I expect the house will be finished sometime late November, and I was thinking about a holiday party. Maybe between Thanksgiving and Christmas?"

Jesse's face lit up, as she'd known it would. "What a super idea! I must be rubbing off on you."

"Well, you told me the story about the Christmas party there when you were a kid, and the picture stuck in my head. But it has to be classy, and I totally suck at this kind of thing. Biker chicks aren't known for their classy parties, you know."

Her friend gave her a soft smile. "Oh, sweetie, I think you're all kinds of classy."

"Would you help me?"

Jesse looked as though she'd just gotten what she wanted for Christmas. "Are you kidding? You know I'm the Grove's Supreme Party Momma. I'd love to help." She crossed her arms and tapped her lips with a perfect pink-frosted fingernail. "It's good we'll be getting a head start on this. Guests will need lots of advance notice around the holidays. How many people are you thinking about?"

"Oh, I don't know…all of them?" At Jesse's jaw drop, Sam shrugged. "I want to show off the house, and maybe attract potential buyers. The word of mouth will make all the effort worthwhile."

How fun would it be to have that beautiful house full of people? She remembered Bina's point, about how Sam created homes, only to give them away. She cleared her throat. "Besides, I can write off the expense."

Jesse rubbed her palms together, and her blue eyes glinted. "Oh, this is going to be the party of the year. I can't wait to sink my teeth into this one."

"COME ON, ANA. We've known each other for months. Surely you can trust me by now?" Sam sat on Ana's porch, sharing iced tea. The cloying perfume of roses hung in the still air, and the morning sun hinted at the searing heat to come. "I'll watch to make sure no one bothers you, and I'm a very safe driver. It's just a trip to the nursery. We could be in and out in a half hour."

Ana's expression didn't sweeten.

Sam sighed, wondering how to penetrate the old woman's stubbornness. "I just wish you'd let me show you the world, outside your fence."

"Why does this matter so much?" Ana sat frowning at her, sparrow eyes sharp.

"The truth?" Sam looked away first. "I guess I'd like to know that it is possible for people to change—to make the brave choice to do that thing they're most afraid of."

Ana stared at her, lips pursed, for so long that Sam thought she wouldn't answer.

"Do you think this nursery of yours would have orange poppies?"

Sam sat a stunned moment, then leaned over her lap, whispering, "Yesssss!" and pumped her fist, just once.

Ana sniffed. "And if you still have that yellow nightmare, I'm not getting in it."

Sam jumped to her feet. "Oh, no. I have my Jeep. I'll even put the top up for you. I'll run up the hill and get it. You go get your purse, and I'll be back down in a jiff to pick you up. Okay?"

When Ana nodded, Sam jogged down the sidewalk and leapt the gate with a single bound. "I'll be right back!" She took off, up the hill, happiness making her feel light.

Halfway up, in occurred to her. If an eighty-year-old recluse could do this, what excuse did she have, whining about being afraid?

None, that's what. Her feet flew. The blood pounded in her ears. *I'm not holding back anymore. I'm going to push through—no matter what waits for me on the other side.*

SONOFABITCH. A BALLOON OF ACID broke in Nick's stomach. He dumped the rest of the mail on his dining room table and carried the DOC letter to his safe haven, the kitchen. He fingered the envelope. Too thin and light to contain an inmate's letter.

What now?

Only one way to find out. But instead of opening it, he walked to the window and looked out. Unexpected letters from the prison system were never good news. And this one gave off vibes. Bad vibes. He ran his hand through his hair, feeling the heavy portent of change in the air. Was he ready for change?

"'God grant me the serenity to accept the things I cannot change, courage to change the things I can and the wisdom to know the difference.'"

Even saying it aloud didn't help. He marshaled his scattered serenity, took a deep breath and with shaking fingers tore open the envelope.

A minute later, he dropped the letter and bent over, waiting for the dizziness to pass. *Fifteen years?* The bastard got twenty to life, and he's eligible for parole after only fifteen?

He slammed his fist into the cabinet. *My mother's life is worth only fifteen years of her murderer's?*

"Not if I have anything to say about it."

He read the addresses; where to appear in person, where to mail letters, protesting his father's parole. He pictured himself driving to Folsom. Attending the hearing. Seeing his father. Imagined the feel of his hands around the man's throat. Squeezing. And squeezing. The man had taken so much: Nick's mother, his childhood, his innocence.

The need for a drink roared in Nick's ears and his body craved in gut-clenching waves. Sure, he'd made mistakes along the way. But he'd worked hard since he'd come home to Widow's Grove, to be an asset to the town. Hopefully he'd have kids someday, and he wanted to give them a surname that they could be proud of—not an embarrassment. His father had ruined the Pinelli name, and if it took Nick the rest of his life, he'd undo the damage.

But he also knew his limits. He wasn't strong enough to make that trip without committing a felony or falling off the wagon. Or, most likely, both.

And the son of a bitch wasn't worth that. He ripped open a drawer, pulling out paper and a pen. A letter wouldn't be as satisfying as strangulation, but hopefully, it would be as effective.

SAM SAT ONCE MORE in Bina's office, terrified, but determined to do whatever it took to get better. She gritted her teeth and rolled the cable-taut muscles of her shoulders. "I don't get it, Bina. I'm there, with Nick, body and mind. Then, it's like I'm jerked away, outside my body, watching sex happen, feeling nothing."

"What does Nick think?" As usual, Bina's dark eyes gave no hint of her thoughts.

"He's wonderful. He tries to reassure me that it doesn't

bother him, that he's willing to wait. But he's also a red-blooded man who's at home in his own sexuality. This is going to cause problems.

"It's about trust." She scrubbed damp palms over her thighs. "Nick's right about one thing. I've been a coward, running away when things get hard. I don't want to do that anymore. When I leave Widow's Grove, I want to leave with some self-respect."

Bina sat on the carpeted floor of her office, arms clasped around her knees. "Well, it's interesting you bring up trust. How does trust fit into sex?"

The question brought Sam up short. "What do you mean? I trust Nick."

"Picture that you and Nick are intimate. Put yourself there. Then ask yourself about trust."

Sam thought back to the night Nick had brought her the swing. She remembered him moving over her, in her. Remembering the orchestra of sensations his body played on hers. She felt a coil, winding tighter. Then...

"I'm afraid to let go of the emotion. No, that's not right." She looked at the floor to avoid facing Bina's regard. "I'd have to drop my guard. To be totally open. Defenseless. Exposed. If Nick saw what's really inside me, he'd leave." She put her face in her hands. "And seeing the knowledge in his eyes would destroy me."

"And what is this 'thing' that you can't let Nick see?"

The question was like a rock falling into a dark pool of water, ripples spreading outward. She hated dark water.

"Sam, look at me."

It took her a while, but she just managed it.

"You're ready to talk about this. You wouldn't be here, otherwise." She leaned forward. "You have to say it. Out loud."

The chair felt like a hot plate. But her legs wouldn't hold

her. She squirmed in the seat and pushed the words up. "Part of what happened with Mr. Collins is my fault."

She held up her hand when Bina would have spoken. "Do not tell me that I was just a kid, and I'm not responsible. I've heard that on Oprah. And it's bullshit."

Bina raised one eyebrow. "Really?"

"Oh, he forced me into the situation. That's a fact. But I'm not a total victim. I had choices. I could have told someone. I didn't." Her throat clicked when she swallowed. "I had excuses why I didn't tell. But what it all boils down to is that I didn't have the guts."

The ripples advanced through the dark pool, gathering force. She fisted her shaking hands. Telling Nick had been scary. Coming here was frightening. But this? She gritted her teeth and pushed the deepest truth past her locked jaw.

"Mr. Collins *knew* I wouldn't tell. The fact that we never spoke of it somehow made it worse. It made us partners, in a twisted way. Coconspirators in our own ugly secret." A shudder rattled from the back of her neck, down her spine. "And that secret is like a wasting disease. Over time, it's ruined everything."

Her lips pulled away from her teeth. "There's something seriously wrong with a person who can do that. How could you ever trust yourself after making decisions like that?"

"Don't you think he knew?" Bina touched Sam's arm and she jumped. "It's the abuser's secret weapon. They make the child feel they have responsibility for their own molestation. And that causes more lasting damage than the sexual abuse itself."

Sam shook her head.

"I could sit here for days and explain the psychology to you, but it wouldn't make any difference. You have to know it in your heart." Bina thought a moment. "You say that you had choices. What were they?"

"I could have told someone, obviously."

"Let's assume you had. What would have happened next?"

"I don't know, because I didn't *do* it!" She leaned over and crossed her arms over her stomach, rocking in the chair.

"But what do you *think* would have happened, if you had?"

"They would have stopped it. But this was my dad's boss. They'd have looked at my bleary, alcoholic dad, and wondered why he didn't protect me." The words sped up. "The social workers had already been to the house once, and filed a report. They would have taken me away."

"What would have happened then?"

"They would have put me into foster care."

"Then what?"

"Things might have been okay for me, but my dad—" Her voice cracked. "He would have lost his job. With Mr. Collins in jail, the whole crew would have. Dad drank his way through every construction company in the county. He wouldn't have been hired. He probably would have ended up homeless." The dark water of emotion rose, filling her. It breached the levee, to track down her face.

"What else could you have done?"

"I could have killed him." That cold, high voice didn't sound like hers. It sounded like the little girl's. Sam stopped rocking. "I fantasized about it in my bed at night. I would grab a screwdriver, and stab the SOB." She shook her head. "At the time, I thought they'd put me in jail. I know now that they wouldn't have, but I'm glad I don't have to live with the guilt of that on top of everything else."

"Okay. What else could you have done?"

"I could have run away. But the cops were bound to notice a kid that young on the streets. They'd have brought me home, so the only thing I would have accomplished was scaring and hurting my dad. And bringing the social workers down on our heads."

Bina put down her coffee cup. "Okay. You've come up with four legitimate solutions to the problem that nine-year-old was faced with. Looking at it now, as an adult, which is the best choice?"

All those choices would have hurt others. Mr. Collins she didn't care about, but the men who worked for him didn't deserve to lose their jobs. But that paled compared to what it would have done to her father. She'd let it go on, because to do anything else would have destroyed her father.

Could it be that simple? Maybe not, but she couldn't deny the truth, either. "The only option I had was the one I chose." She took a shaky breath. "Better I lived with the guilt than my dad. *I* could handle it." And *that* was the real truth.

"Do you know any young girls, about the age you were then?"

"The youngest girl I know is Sunny, one of the teenagers on my work crew."

"Okay. Close your eyes. Picture Sunny at the age you were then. Can you do that?"

Sam visualized a towhead in pigtails, with sun-browned summer skin and skinned knees.

"If Mr. Collins had taken Sunny into the back bedroom—"

"Oh, God, please don't make me go there."

"Would what happened in that room have been Sunny's fault?"

The answer exploded from her. "Good God, no!"

"Then why is it yours?"

She rolled her eyes. "Bina, I'm not stupid. I know it isn't my fault."

"I know you do. The adult. Who lives in here." She tapped her temple. "But that's not where that little girl lives. She lives here." She put her hand over her heart "And she doesn't believe it. Not a bit of it."

"Why would I care what she thinks? She's a whiner, a

wimp, who's afraid of everything." She should have known better than to tell Bina about the voice.

"Ah, but you should care," Bina said. "She's a part of you, Sam."

"Well, I'd rather she just go away."

Bina's perfectly arched eyebrows lifted farther. "And how's that working for you, so far?"

"What do you mean? I don't hear her voice often, and when I do, I just ignore it."

"Oh, really? Why do you think she keeps you traveling from place to place, no friendships, no ties?" With one graceful motion, Bina stood. "Is that what you see adults around you doing?"

Sam sat back, feeling like she'd walked into a wall she hadn't seen.

"So, if you're not in charge of all your decisions, who is?" Bina dusted dog hair from the seat of her pants.

The little girl, making decisions? That's ridiculous. Her mind wanted to skitter away from even contemplating it. *You committed to seeing this through. Just do it.*

Adults had roots. Homes. Families. They weren't afraid of ties—they sought them. They didn't create everything they wanted, only to give it away. They had compasses that steered them in the right direction. They weren't afraid all the time.

Damaged children did all those things.

"Holy shit. That's mutiny."

Bina threw her head back and brayed. Sam only just resisted putting her hands over her ears. Through the window, she saw the dogs stop chasing each other, and look toward the house.

Another logic grenade went off in Sam's brain. *Oh, please. There's only so much truth I can handle in one day.* "Are you telling me I have multiple personalities?"

"No, Sam. That little girl is really just an unacknowledged

piece of your psyche. It's your past, influencing your present." She put her hands on her hips. "The question is, are you willing to do what it takes to put the past behind you? Are you willing to let the adult in you step up and make the tough decisions?"

Here it was. The line in the sand. Her past was hell, her present was purgatory. What was beyond the line? Did she have the guts to find out?

Hell, she didn't have the guts not to. "I'm ready."

"Good girl. I'm proud of you. Come on around the desk. I want you to sit here." Bina pulled out the desk chair.

"You mean now? I thought maybe next time I come—"

"This will only take about fifteen minutes." She patted the back of the cushy office chair.

Sam crossed the room, feet dragging.

"It's not electrified, and I'm not going to tie you in it. I promise." Bina walked across the room to a closet, opened it and rooted around.

Sam sensed that she was close—so close to getting to the bottom of the steaming mess of the past inside her. She should have been excited about that. But instead, it felt like she was back in the nightmare, her mind screaming, *Run!*

Forcing her knees to unlock, she sat, hands on the desk. Seeing that they shook like a cold-turkey addict, she hid them in her lap. The sound of paper tearing came from the closet. Bina backed out, a huge piece of white butcher paper in her hands. She walked over and laid it on the desk.

"Here." She extended a huge, thick carpenter's pencil, but when Sam reached for it, Bina pulled it away. "Nope. Left hand."

"Bina, I can't write with my left hand."

"I know you can't." She patted her on the shoulder. "But the little girl can."

Sam lifted a hand to her aching head. "I knew you'd get

all woo-woo on me eventually." She squinted at Bina. "Are you sure you've never been on *Oprah?*"

Bina laughed. "All you have to do is ask the little girl what she wants you to know. That's it." She walked to the door. "I'll be back in ten minutes."

Sam stared at the paper. The pencil felt like a foreign body in her hand. "This is stupid." She didn't even like that kid. She sat, pencil hovering over the ridiculously huge piece of paper.

The clock on the wall ticked. Loud.

Putting her right hand to her neck, she massaged the steel ropes alongside her spine. God, this was embarrassing. She pushed back against the chair.

Well, she wasn't saying it out loud. *Okay, what do you have to say? What do you want me to know?*

Her hand began writing.

SOME TIME LATER, Sam lifted her head to see Bina seated across from her, watching. She looked at the paper. It was filled with downward sloping lines of scrawling cursive. It looked like a third-grader wrote it.

And she had no clear memory of writing it, or what it contained.

"Read it, Sam. Not out loud. She wrote it to you."

Shaken by what had just happened, Sam wasn't about to argue.

I'm so alone.
No one knows. No one can know. I'm all alone.
Daddy needs me. I have to take care of him. But I'm only a kid.
And I'm all alone.

There was more, but she couldn't read it—her vision was filmy. She touched her forehead to the paper, arms wrapped around herself to hold her guts in. She remembered. Exactly what it felt like when she *was* that little girl. So afraid. So alone.

A strangled sound came, unleashing rattling sobs that, for the first time, didn't shred her throat.

Other than handing her tissues, Bina didn't move. Sam's tears poured through the breaches in her walls, toppling them, dissolving the bricks. When it was over, she expected a stinking mudflat of emotions to remain, but that's not how it felt. She felt scoured, gentled. Clean.

CHAPTER EIGHTEEN

DAYS LATER, IN the shade of the small cottage's porch, Sam listened to the creak of Ana's rocker, the birds' songs and the silence inside her head. In the months they'd known each other, Sam strove to get Ana to speak, but Ana had taught Sam of the joy of silence. She closed her eyes, relishing the calm.

Peace. So that's what it feels like.

The quiet was disturbed by the sound of an ancient engine, laboring. Tim pulled up in front of Ana's house, and cut the ignition. The door squealed as if in pain as he opened it and took the big step down.

He marched to the gate like Patton leading a charge, chin set, eyes steely.

Ana stood.

Uh-oh.

He stopped at the bottom of the steps, took off his battered bowler hat and looked up at her. The look in his eyes softened, and a side of his mouth lifted, just a bit.

"Why do you stand staring?" Ana barked.

"I was just thinking about the first time I saw you. The Christmas dance at Yeager's barn. Do you remember?" He smiled. "You wore a green dress with a white lace collar and sprigs of holly in your hair."

"That was too many years ago to think about now. What do you want here?" She tucked a stray wisp of hair back into her coiled braids.

"I want to be your friend, Ana. That's all. I have no hidden agenda. I don't want to frighten you or change you."

She lifted her chin and looked down her Aryan nose at him as if he were a cockroach on a wedding cake.

"You and I were friends once, Ana. We spent time in each other's homes, remember?" He twisted the hat in his hands. "All our friends are gone—passed on. I'd just like to be able to stop by to talk now and again."

Her scowl deepened. "I know what you would like, Timothy Raven." She shook a bony finger at him. "I took care of one man until the day he died. Changed diapers, fed him, tried to keep up his name and his reputation, long after his mind had gone." Her tone was as brittle as her words. "I will not spend the rest of my life taking care of another."

Tim dropped his arms to his sides, hands open to her. "I thought someone could take care of *you* for a change."

She lurched back as if he'd slapped her.

"You and me, we're alone in the world. I would like to make things easier for you. No strings. Just friends, if that's all you want." He looked away, and resumed worrying the brim of his hat. "My Betsy died five years ago. Every day, I've missed her. Her singing in the kitchen, her step on the stair.

"You know that loneliness. I don't want to spend the rest of the time God gives me, living like that. No one should have to." He looked into Ana's faded cornflower-blue eyes. "I don't want that for the sweet German lass I used to know."

Ana stood, looking down on him for the longest time.

"You, take care of me?" She made a scoffing sound. "Look at you, Tim Raven. You can't even take care of yourself. You are a mess. Betsy would have a fit if she could see you now."

He looked down. So did Sam.

He wore the usual outfit: baggy pants, yellowed white shirt, moth-eaten cardigan. But his brogans were shined, his cheeks were pink from a shave and he *had* put in his teeth.

"My sweater may have a hole or two, but it's my favorite. And Betsy always loved a man with nice shoes."

Sam's heart ached for him. She hoped they'd forgotten she was there.

Ana cleared her throat. "I will think on what you have said. More than that, I will not promise." Head up, she walked into the house, closing the door softly behind her.

THIS TIME, WHEN SAM trudged downstairs to get another arm-load of her belongings, Bugs flopped on the floor of the parlor. She'd decided to move to the upstairs bedroom. It made no sense to camp in the parlor when the bedroom loft was completed upstairs.

"Hey, Bugs, we're lucky it's just humid. We could have done this in that heat wave back in October." Sam lifted the junk box in the corner, dropped it on the stripped cot and looked around the bare room. Since she'd been bivouacked here, the parlor was the only room in the house not yet touched. The floor needed refinishing, and the wood window frames would have to be replaced. The crew could knock this out in a week.

There were details to be completed elsewhere in the house, too, but every day that the to-do list got smaller, the anxiety dancing along her nerves amped up. She finally had a completion date—November thirtieth. The party was set for the first week of December.

She plopped onto the mattress and looked out the side window at the dark clouds piling up in the north. The pounding beat of "Born to Be Wild" throbbed from the radio upstairs, and the call of the road pulled her insides, a hollow, restless ache.

She could head up the coast to San Francisco. Lots of Victorians there.

Wait a minute. Was this her want, or the little girl's? Was this her defective compass steering her in the wrong direction, yet again?

I don't know. How would I know?

She thought back to what Bina said. Would a grown-up do this? Well, maybe. There was nothing inherently wrong with being an itinerant building contractor.

But would you leave because you—the grown-up you— wants to? Or is it running?

Well, she felt better. More stable. The dreams were less frequent, now. Since the day in Bina's office, the little girl had been silent. Maybe it wouldn't be running.

But there was Nick. Their dates were wonderful, full of camaraderie, laughter and sexual tension...that ended in failure, every time. Her failure.

She stood, lifted the box and walked to climb the stairs one more time. Bina assured her that a satisfying physical relationship was not only possible, but inevitable. It was just a matter of her letting go.

Just.

She turned the corner at the landing and continued up. God knows, she was trying. But trying only made things worse. Every time she failed at sex, she put more pressure on herself, with expectations about the *next* time. Her nerves were starting to feel like overdone bacon.

And she'd invited Nick for dinner tomorrow. She felt like an athlete who trains for the games for years, then, in the most important competition, chokes. Nick may say that he was okay with it, but *she* wasn't. It was frustrating. She'd get right up to the edge of...something, yet another part of herself was always watching. Always judging.

She felt retarded, failing at something everyone else took for granted. Her last dirty secret.

As if that weren't enough, the thought of leaving Nick was getting harder to imagine. And that frightened her. Well, okay, so it frightened the old Sam. But the today Sam still felt the fear.

Guess there's more rows to hoe before I can rest.

"And more boxes." Rounding the corner at the landing she dropped the box in a chair, and snapped the radio off. The bedroom loft stretched before her, the length of the house. She'd broken up the long expanse by creating a sitting area closest to the stairs. Her bookshelf nested under the window, and with her overstuffed chairs, a floor lamp and a braided rug, it was a snug oasis that tempted her to drop everything, sit with feet tucked up and read.

She walked to her decadent purchase, the massive brass bed dominating the other end of the loft. It stood high enough off the floor to warrant the wooden steps she'd put beside it. An ivory quilt with an interlocking ring design covered it and creamy shag rugs lay scattered on the polished wood floors.

Bina was right when she said Sam had been denying herself a home. No more cots and card-table furniture for her—she decided she could take it all with her, and create a home wherever she found herself. She'd felt happy shopping for it, and she liked the sense of permanence the furniture gave her. A ridiculous extravagance, maybe, but it made her smile.

Downstairs, Bugs barked and she heard his nails scrabbling on the wood.

She shot a look out the window, but didn't see a car in the drive. Bugs's staccato barking moved off toward the front door.

What now?

She peeked through the curtain at the window, then ran down the stairs, stepped to the door and pulled it open, joy and relief mingling, rising in her. "Beau!"

He stood, hands in pockets, his face wary. Until he saw her smile, then the corner of his mouth lifted a bit. His usual uniform looked worse for wear. Grease smears and what appeared to be mud covered his jacket and jeans. A white tape bandage covered his left earlobe. "Hey, Sam."

She caught his sleeve, dragged him inside the door and enveloped him in a fierce hug as Bugs danced around their feet. He was safe. He was home.

A weight lifted. She'd tucked the subject of Beau in a cubby of her mind and had tried to ignore it the past three months. Only now could she realize how much she'd worried.

"Sam? I can't breathe here." She could feel tense muscles under the chilled denim of his lightweight jacket.

She backed up, but still held onto his jacket, her hands wanting to touch, as if it would make his presence real. *Beau's home!*

Anger followed on the heels of relief. She frowned. "Where the hell have you been? You scared all of us witless." She released him. "I should whup your ass." He looked as though the road had done her work for her. "How long has it been since you've eaten?" She touched the bandage and he flinched away. "What happened here?"

"Yesterday sometime, and it's a long story. I need to talk to you, Sam."

"Not before I get some food in you. Follow me." She led the way back to the kitchen.

He stood in the middle of the room, looking around slowly. "Wow."

She strode to the refrigerator, pulling out eggs, bacon and a pitcher of orange juice. "Wash your hands." She pulled an omelet pan from under the stove. He looked pained, like a toddler, needing to pee. "I know you want to talk, but give it a rest, Beau. First things first."

A few minutes later, she placed a loaded plate in front of him.

"What about yours?"

"Just eat." While he was distracted wolfing food, she examined him closely. He looked so—used. His hair was greasy and he was pale, except for the bruiselike shadows under his eyes. His knuckles were scraped, as were the knees that poked through his jeans. The gaping holes no longer appeared to be a fashion statement.

Seeing him like this hurt her heart.

She filled him in on the progress on the house, and what Sunny and Pete had been up to in the three months since he'd left. When nothing remained on his plate but a few egg smears, he sat back, holding his flat stomach.

"Oh, man, that was good. I didn't know how hungry I was."

She leaned forward, coffee cup cradled in her hands. "Where have you been, Beau?"

He took a deep breath, and looked at the ceiling. "I was so pissed off that day on the side of the road. I started to walk back, but then a truck came by. I just stuck out my thumb. I didn't set out to run away. It just kind of happened."

"Where were you going?"

"Didn't know, didn't care. I was just running. The guy in the pickup was going to Paso Robles, so that's where I ended up." He shrugged one shoulder. "It was okay at first. I cashed the last check you gave me, and I got a room at a crappy motel." The corner of his mouth lifted. "Did you know there are hotels that charge by the hour? That's only one of the million things I didn't know."

He didn't appear happy to have learned many of them. "Your check wasn't that big."

"I thought with what I'd learned here, I could get on with a contractor." He shook his head. "But once they got a look at me, and found out I was seventeen, the interview was over. They wouldn't listen. Wouldn't let me show them what I know."

"I'm sorry, Beau."

"Hey, that was the *good* part." He rubbed his forehead.

Little pills of dirt fell on the empty plate in front of him. "I didn't eat much, but even so, I ran out of money pretty fast. I wandered around town, looking for any kind of work. A guy who ran a redneck bar finally hired me to clean out the place when he closed."

She winced. *God, not this innocent kid, in a bar.* Thanks to her dad, she knew what the seamier ones were like.

"You wouldn't believe what a bathroom after a night full of drunks is like." He grimaced. "But it paid, at least enough to keep me in the whore motel, and the bartender fed me when I showed up for work."

"At first, I liked being on my own. No one to tell me where to go, or what to do." He raised his head to look her in the eye for the first time since coming through the door. "But you know, once I settled into the life, I realized that I wasn't living. I was just surviving. I kept interviewing with contractors, but eventually none of them would even talk to me." He glanced out the window. "I'd fall in that crappy bed at four every morning and see the days stretching in front of me—cleaning up barf and shit every night, getting no closer to what I really wanted to do."

"So you decided to come home."

"No, I'm not that smart. I still had hope, and too much stupid pride. I figured I'd screwed up my life, and it was up to me to straighten it out."

Sam knew from her own experience that no one could teach you a lesson like that—you had to learn it for yourself. But she wished she didn't have to hear how he learned it.

"Paso Robles isn't that far from here, but it's like a whole different state. It's redneck heaven." He touched the dirty bandage on his ear. "They'd give me a hard time at the bar, making fun of my piercings, my clothes, you know. The bartender would keep them off me most of the time, but one night, I locked up alone. Three Bubbas jumped me when I was walk-ing back to town. Beat me up, ripped out my earring."

"Oh, Beau—"

"That's what convinced me to come back. My situation here may not be the best, but at least I have a chance to earn my way to a career.

"You and Tim were right. I was a spoiled rich kid. Whether you take me back on or not, I just wanted you to know that I'm not that person anymore."

He slid his chair back, stood and walked to the back door. "Thanks for the food, Sam. Thanks for everything." He opened the door. "I'm going to go tell Tim the same thing."

Now that she knew the story, she worried retroactively. God, she should have tried harder to find him. Should have…

That's not your job, Crozier. If you wouldn't have gone through what you did, you wouldn't be the person—well, maybe not the person you are now, but the person you're going to be.

The latch clicked shut before she could move. She jumped up and moved to the door. Beau walked away, shoulders square, head high.

She opened the door. She'd give anything to be there when Beau talked to Tim, but knew she had way too much estro-gen to be invited. "Hey, Beau." He looked over his shoulder, but kept walking. "I've got to go see Jess. I'll give you a ride as far as town."

FRIDAY EVENING, SAM carried the large serving dish of hot stew to the table.

Sunny gave Pete a threatening glare. "Don't you dare say it, punk."

"But what if it *is* my favorite?"

Sam jumped in to avert bloodshed in her kitchen. "Sunny,

grab the basket of rolls for me, will you? Beau, pour the iced tea for me? Okay everybody, dig in."

After being loudly welcomed back by Sunny and Pete, Beau had settled in the past two weeks as if he'd never left. Tim had accepted Beau's apology, and allowed him to move back in to his cabin at the Rest. Sunny was even helping Beau study for his contractor's license.

Sam glanced around at her team. Their clothes were splattered with the carriage house's exterior color, blinding white. Beau was spotted with the interior apartment's French blue. The house was in the finishing stages, and lately the mood had been one of celebration.

Bugs barked, and ran for the front door. "Okay you guys, pipe down. We've got a few things to discuss." She heard the front door open, and footsteps on hardwood.

"Hey, where is everybody?" Tim rounded the corner into the kitchen. Conversation died. Everyone gawked.

Tim's thin, no longer grizzled eyebrows came together. "What?"

Sunny was first to find her voice, "Mr. Raven, you're positively stunning."

Tim's hair had been neatly trimmed. Comb tracks still showed in the sparse strands. His face shone clean-shaven and a blue-and-white striped shirt, still bearing package creases, was tucked into chino pants that didn't droop. His shiny wing tips were the only part of his attire that Sam had seen before.

A few weeks ago, replumbing complete, Tim had disappeared from the job site. Sam stopped worrying when she noticed his truck parked outside Ana's gate, most days.

Pete said, "Jeez, Tim, you look downright pretty."

The kitchen echoed with laughter and everyone talked at once.

"Let's give him a chance to tell us what's going on." Sam

patted the chair next to her. "Come on, Tim, pull up a seat. There's plenty of stew."

"I've been busy. This isn't my only project, you know." Tim sat, and the teens passed a plate around the table for him, filling it with stew and bread.

"Yeah, and that other project wouldn't involve a cute chick nearby, would it?" Pete asked.

Tim glared. "You keep a civil tongue in your head, son. Ana is a lady, and I expect you to speak of her as such."

"Yes, sir." Pete ducked his head and focused on his plate.

Sunny jumped in with a tactful change of subject. "Doesn't the house look great, Tim? Once we get the painting done, we're going to help Sam put up the Christmas decorations for the party."

"It's good. I can't believe how much you've gotten done since I've seen it last." The kids basked in the old man's rare praise.

"Tim, you are coming to the party, aren't you? I've been trying to call you to get an RSVP, but you're never home."

"I'll be here, as long as I can bring a date." His eyes twinkled with his smile.

"Ana's already invited. Do you think you can get her to come? I've been harping at her since I decided on the party, but she's still giving me excuses."

"I'll see what I can do. Now tell me what you kids have been up to."

Sam sat back and listened, enjoying the sound of a full house.

Whether I stay or go, at least I've had this.

Something Tim said caught her attention.

"The Hilton chain has offered me a ton of money for Raven's Rest. They want to tear it down to put up a Victorian hotel." He smacked his hand on the table. "Can you believe they think a newfangled hotel would be better than my cabins?"

The kids sat staring at each other, not sure if he was joking.

"I'd really hate to be the cause of one more eyesore in this darned town. The problem is, I probably won't be living there much longer, and I'm going to have to do something with it." A blush spread up his neck.

The table was silent. No one dared comment on his living arrangements.

"God knows, it's not like I'm making much. Seems most of the tourists hereabouts would rather pay two-fifty a night to sleep in one of those yuppie kennels." He shook his head.

Sam stood. "Let's think about it a bit, Tim. Maybe we can come up with some ideas."

She raised her hand to get everyone's attention. "Now, I want to talk to you all. I haven't mentioned it, because I just had the plans signed off, but I've got another house to work on, thanks to Bina Rani's recommendation."

"Hey, good for you, Sam," Beau said.

"Is it someone we know?" Sunny asked.

"Is it local? What do they want done?" Pete asked.

She put up a hand. "I'll tell you the details in a minute, but I wanted to know if you all were interested before I took the job."

"You mean you want us to help?" Beau sounded tentatively hopeful.

"How am I going to accept the job without my team? It won't take longer than a month or so, but I'll need all your skills to pull it off. Let me get the photos, and I'll show you." She walked to the great room to retrieve them, smiling at the excited babble that broke out behind her.

Who knew how long it would take to sell the house? January would be too cold to ride up the coast, anyway.

PETE AND SUNNY had pre-Christmas break exams the next day, so they left after dinner. Sam, Tim and Beau donned jackets and retired to the front porch to watch the sun go down. Sam and Tim settled on the porch swing, and Beau sat sprawled on the porch, his back propped against the railing.

Sam watched Beau, working a column of figures with a pad and pencil. "Okay, Beau, I know you. Your brain is smoking out of your ears. What's up?"

He worried at a hole in his jeans with a finger. "Um, I've got an idea, but I could be full of crap. I'm not sure."

Tim pushed the swing with his foot. "Well, son, you'll never know if you don't say it out loud, will you?"

"You're trying to decide what to do with Raven's Rest, right? I have an idea." He looked between Sam and Tim.

"Okay. Let's hear it."

"You know I want to start a woodworking business. And I need a place to live. So I was thinking. What if you turned the Rest into an artist's colony? You know, artists could rent the cottages from you and work out of them. They could sell their stuff to the tourists—it's just down the street from downtown, where they all hang out, anyway.

"Carrie Upton already makes a living, selling her willow chairs at the old garage downtown, and I know a bunch more people who'd love to rent workshop space. You probably wouldn't be able to charge much per cottage, but you'd make more than you make now with most of them empty, right?"

Tim rubbed his newly smooth chin. "Maybe."

"That way, you wouldn't have to tear them down and let them trash the place with another stupid hotel."

Sam spoke up. "'Raven's Artist Colony.' It's got a nice ring to it, don't you think, Tim?"

"Yeah, I kinda like the idea of sticking it to the Hiltons." He chuckled. "Now, I'm not promising anything, but I'm willing to consider the possibility."

Beau scribbled a few notes in the notebook.

"You might have come up with a pretty good crappy idea, kid." Tim smiled down at the top of Beau's head.

Sam was sure he didn't realize it was a proud father's smile.

WHEN HER FEET touched the bottom landing, she slid a hand along the wall to guide her steps. She knew better than to feel for a light switch. Stepping forward, her boots touched dirt. The point of no return.

Dread, like battery acid, trickled into her mind, eating away her resolve. She tasted her own fear at the back of her throat. She knew, somehow, that the thing also tasted her fear. She felt it in her mind.

Coming.

The walls of her protective inner dam burst. The trickle grew to a flood of dread, rising, rising. Her fingers clutched the wall. The damp earth crumbled away beneath her fingers.

Her eyes strained to open wider. To see through the black-on-black shadows of the cavelike opening in the dirt wall opposite her.

A clod of dirt hit and spattered, four feet away, in the tunnel. There! Forget hearing—she could smell its breath. The overripe scent of decomposing bodies. The smell of old grave dirt.

She strained to hear past her own labored breathing. Fear scrabbled like a mad rat in her brain, clawing to get out.

Get out! Get out! Get out!

She pushed down on the fear. Compacting made it more potent, but it took up less space in her chest. It made room for her heart to beat.

I'm not living like this anymore. She took a step. Better hell than purgatory. She took another. And another.

"I'm right here." She took the last step into the tunnel. "Come and get me, you son of a bitch."

Cold, damp cellar-smelling air brushed her face.
There was nothing there.

SAM WOKE SLOWLY on Saturday morning and lay staring up at her gorgeous wooden ceiling, running the dream over in her mind. Waiting to see how the conclusion affected her. A sweet rush of relief swept over her, banishing shivers like the warm sun breaking through on a cloudy day.

Was it over? Would that be the last time she had The Dream? She listened inside for the answer. *Yes.* She didn't know how she knew it, but it was as real as the peace that stilled her limbs and calmed her thrumming nerves.

Thank you, Bina Rani. And Nick Pinelli. Not only had he introduced them, she had to admit he was the catalyst of change. After all, if he wasn't waiting at the end of all this, she might not have had the guts to see this thr —

Nick, waiting at the end? That sounded like he was the goal. Emboldened by her newfound peace, she let herself imagine. Sitting on the porch of this house, their house, waiting to him to come home from work.

There's more kinds of freedom than riding a motorcycle.

For a little while, she lay in her big bed allowing herself to want.

Home.

CHAPTER NINETEEN

SUNDAY AFTERNOON, NICK walked behind the shop and lifted the heavy garage door of the old shed. Sun shone through the cracks in the walls and onto the Love Machine, giving it stripes like those safari vehicles at the Wild Animal Park.

He smiled, glad Sam's needing a ride back in April prompted him to drag it out of storage. After years of burying memories of his childhood to avoid the pain, the car reminded him of the good times—and letting Sam drive it, then driving it around town himself, in a weird way had given him his mother back.

And now the state was releasing the bastard that had taken her away. As vividly as if it was in front of him now, he recalled the official letter he'd received a few days ago, word for word.

Dear Crime Victim/Witness:
As per Victim/Witness notification procedures, we hereby inform you of the upcoming release of Donatello Pinelli, *on January thirtieth.*

Mr. Pinelli has been a model prisoner, and as such, is eligible for early release for good behavior. Since his crime was one "of passion," the Board finds he poses little threat to society at large.

He will, of course, be subject to rules of parole. Under separate cover, you will receive the contact information of Mr. Pinelli's *parole officer.*

Thank you for your input in this matter. The Board of Parole appreciates the views of the victims and their families.

A lancet of pain sliced into Nick's stomach. He grunted, breathing shallow until it quit. Old pain dug deepest.

He stepped between the car and the wall, opened the door a crack and squeezed through, settling in. He leaned back on the headrest, listening to the birds chirping in the crab apple tree. It didn't help. Even the smell of old leather and good memories didn't help. He wanted to kill the man. He wanted it with a need so strong his guts trembled with it.

He envied Sam, throwing a long leg over the Vulcan and hitting the road. He understood the call to take the future head-on, running to meet it. Leaving the old, screwed-up, ugly stuff behind.

But he also knew the world didn't work that way. Sam was learning that now, since the past had caught up with her in Widow's Grove.

When he turned the key, the old engine chugged to life.

He pictured Sam, head up, chin out, facing down the nightmares and the squirming worm-ball of her past. If she could do that, maybe there was hope that *he* could get through seeing his father again. Without drinking. Without committing patricide.

But first, he had to tell her about the letter. If he wanted to hold Sam's secrets, he couldn't keep any of his from her.

He took a deep breath. It would work out okay. They'd face this together. With her standing beside him, offering him quiet strength, there was nothing he couldn't face.

Even his father. Straightening, he shoved the car into gear.

A HALF HOUR LATER, he paused in the doorway of Sam's empty front parlor. "Let's see this wonderful furniture you've been telling me about."

Smiling, she closed the door. "Come tell me what you think." She led the way up the stairs. "I realized that I'm past the milk-crate-and-bedsheet décor, so I splurged."

He watched her slim hips roll as she took the stairs in her usual, no-nonsense stride. She looked good. More than good. Legendary. And the fact that she hated her own beauty hurt him in some inexplicable way—like seeing a cheetah, pacing the bars of a cage. It was unnatural.

They reached the top landing. The honey-toned wood floor of the loft stretched down the right half of the house. A huge brass bed sunbathed in the rays from the tall windows. It extended an invitation, one that pulsed heat to his crotch.

To distract himself, he stepped to the railing and looked down into the great room. The burnished floor shone, the inlaid mariner's compass in front of the hearth drew his eye.

"Hard to believe this is the wreck I toured seven months ago." He walked to the bathroom at the far end and stuck his head in. The claw-foot tub and black-and-white tile remained, but everything else had been replaced. A fixture with fluted glass shades overhung an ornately framed mirror. "This is amazing. Victorians are pretty, but I always feel like I'm going to break something. You kept the flavor, but it's still warm and homey. It doesn't seem like it should work, but it does." He turned to study the afternoon light playing over the planes of her perfect face.

Samantha Crozier was a study in opposites: artistic, pragmatic and, once you survived her punji-staked battlements, a tender, caring woman. He took a step closer. "You have a lot of talent, lady."

She looked down at her tennis shoes. "Thanks."

He lifted her chin and lightly brushed her lips with his, breathing in the smell of Sam: sunshine, sawdust and woman.

Hmm. She'd missed him this week. When his lips withdrew, she opened her eyes to a desperate look of longing in his. "What is it?"

"Is it possible you'll ever want me as much as I want you?" Emotion made his voice husky.

Scattered pleasure gathered—on the skin of her face, where his hand touched, fingers trailing down her neck. From his thighs, where they brushed against hers, sparking heat. From her nipples, hardening in an attempt to span the gap to rub against his chest. The stream of pleasure gathered, and then shot a bolt of desire deep between her legs.

This strong man knew all of her, and still wanted her.

And she wanted him.

But she hesitated. She didn't want to say it. But there would be no secrets between them. "I'm afraid," she whispered.

He smiled a soft-as-cotton smile. "Don't be, babe."

"I'm just so tired of failing at this." She worried her lip between her teeth.

His gaze warmed the skin of her face. Or maybe that was a blush.

"Sexuality's so much a part of you, Sam. All you need do is stop thinking. You know that I'm all-in—for as long as it takes."

His focused intensity made her nerves jump, but she forced herself to meet his gaze.

"Let me show you, Sam. Allow me the honor of being your first."

She frowned. "But you know you wouldn't—"

"Your entire experience consists of surviving abuse, then sex with men who thought only of themselves. That's not making love." He cupped her face in his hands. "In the only way that really matters, you're still a virgin. So I'm asking. Will you let me love you?"

Alarm bells clanged in her head. Let another in? All the way? She looked at his hand on hers.

That was then. The bells fell silent. *This is Nick.* A heavy wall inside her crashed down. But for the first time, it didn't come down between her and the world. It shifted, coming down between her and the past. At the solid *thunk* within her, muscles loosened between her shoulders, down her spine.

She felt disoriented, as if a huge magnetic shift had caused the earth's poles to swap. Would the result be the apocalypse or nirvana? It didn't matter, because she was all-in, too. For as long as it took. A delicate calm settled on her, with the fragile brush of silk.

She saw Nick for the first time, with nothing dark between them. His kind, dear face. His soft, patient eyes.

"I *know* what I'm asking." He wrapped his warm fingers around her cold ones. "But I'm asking."

Her chest expanded in a churning cloud of emotions. The past was there, gray and black. But so were the flashes of color: the cherry-red of the Vulcan's tank, the canary-yellow of the Love Machine. The gold sparks that were Nick. She hadn't known what cherished felt like, before. The emotions rose, filling her to overflowing.

Nick wouldn't hurt her. She trusted him; now it was time to trust herself. She leaned in and put her answer into her kiss. She opened her mouth to him, opened everything—her mind, her trust, her heart.

Nick heard. Pulling her close, he moaned into her mouth. Sensation swirled. His tongue, foreign, yet known. His arms, strong, yet yielding. He lifted her, carried her to the bed and set her on the quilt as if she were spun glass.

She lifted a hand to undo the first button of her cardigan.

"I've waited a long time to completely unwrap this package." He put his hand over hers, lowering it to the bed. "Let me, Sam."

He unbuttoned her sweater and slipped it over her shoulders, then unclasped the plain cotton bra beneath. He tugged it free, and it joined her sweater on the floor. His eyes roamed her breasts, his expression neither disguising nor apologizing for the wanting that burned in them.

He lowered her against the pillows and kissed her dizzy. "You are so beautiful." Cupping her breast, he leaned in, so close, they shared breath. "You might as well get used to my saying it. It's the truth." He lowered his head to taste her nipple.

The sight, as much as the sensation, made her moan. She ran her hands over his hair, needing the connection—needing to feel Nick. When he sucked hard, passion flashed and then receded, only to spike again when he nipped softly. She squirmed. His hand slipped between her legs and settled over her, solid, stationary, an invitation to move as she would. His lips released her, and she felt the shock of cool air on her nipple, even as the heat of his mouth closed over the other.

Nick was everywhere, his touch, outside, his essence, in her head. Some small part of her waited for the closing, for the fear. But it didn't come. She felt insulated from the outside, from the past. She was drunk with him.

His hair, thick and wavy, slid through her clenched fingers. He tasted the hollow between her breasts, then, as if knowing what she needed, he brought his mouth to hers in a deep kiss that held nothing back. His passion mingled with the foreign taste of her own skin on his tongue. It sparked the current between them that matched the vibration deep in her womb.

Then his mouth was gone, and her lips felt the abandonment her breast had, moments before. He peeled her jeans down her legs, revealing the new shell-pink, low-rise lace beneath. When his tongue danced at the edge of lace, the muscles in her belly quivered.

She realized that what she had felt in the past was only a pale shadow of this…thing that grew in her. *I want him.*

When his callused fingers traced the sensitive skin at the inside of her thigh, she filled her hands with cotton, clenching the quilt at her side to keep her from floating away.

She felt her own throbbing heartbeat at the junction of her thighs, then his mouth was there, hovering over the damp material, breathing a long exhalation over her. She jumped, both from the heat and the stark intimacy. She hadn't known it could be like this.

He made a sound like a growl in the back of his throat, then pulled the inconsequential scrap of material down, and away. Parting her legs, he stretched out between them. She looked down the length of her body to see him looking back at her.

Waiting.

She looked into his eyes. This was *Nick*—the only man who had looked past her beautiful mask, to the terrifying flaws beneath, without flinching. He didn't flinch now. He waited.

She heard no voices. Felt no fear. No hesitation. Only Nick—and the desire that coiled between them like a humming power line.

She smiled.

The heat in his eyes could have melted plastic. He held her gaze, even as he lowered his head. His fingers brushed her moist heat, coiling her insides tight as a watch spring.

When his lips delivered an intimate kiss, she caught fire. Raw need roared through her body and mind, burning away any thought beyond him. The watch spring tightened again, and her head thrashed on the pillow. Her legs quivered on the edge of…something.

His fingers plunged into her as his mouth closed over her mound. The earth fell away beneath her, as something rose in her. Something like anticipation, and fireworks, and clean, shameless freedom. It broke over her in a cascade of light and elation. Then she was falling.

Out of control.

She panicked, afraid she had shattered to pieces that could never be gathered. She screamed his name, and he was there. He held her close, rocking her, murmuring soft words that made no sense. She burrowed her head into the valley where his collarbone met his throat, and tried to breathe. Wishing she could climb into his skin, she clung, aftershocks rocking her.

His scent and hers mingled in the space between their heated bodies, pungent and musky. She lifted her mouth and kissed him, deeply, trying to convey what he'd made her feel.

Some of it must have gotten through, because he devoured her mouth, his breath quickened to match hers. She ended the kiss, pulling his shirt out of the back of his jeans. "One of us is way overdressed."

He chuckled. "I can fix that." He didn't bother with his buttons, just pulled his shirt over his head. He shucked out of his jeans, pulled a condom from his pocket and slid it on. Then he was back, arms around her, the skin of his chest sliding over hers.

She breathed against his lips. "No stopping this time, Nick."

HE WASN'T GOING TO give her time to think. Sam had finally taken that leap of faith, and he was going to do his damnedest to show her how amazing real loving could be. But it had been a long time for him, even before he met Sam, and this could be over way too soon if his body had its way. Sam deserved better, her first time. Her *real* first time.

Well, second. The smile on his face felt smug. Hell, *he* felt smug.

But he wasn't nearly done yet. He planned to love her into

a puddle of satisfaction. But she'd have to be almost there when he entered her—the way his body burned, he wouldn't last long.

He nuzzled her ear, and she rubbed against him like a cat, making a purring noise in her chest. When he nipped the delicate lobe, she moaned.

He'd known she'd be hot in bed, once she let herself go. The arch of her foot slid up his calf. He reached between her legs and found the hard bud he sought, and her hips bucked against his hand.

Raising on one elbow, he watched her. Eyes closed, with her mussed blond hair spread on the pillow, high color in her cheeks and swollen lips, she looked like a *Playboy* centerfold. His cock jumped, bumping her thigh. He allowed himself one long lunge of his hips.

Damn, keep your focus, man.

He kissed her deeply, miming with his tongue what he soon would be doing with something else. Delving into her with his fingers was almost both their undoing, and she thrashed beneath him.

She broke the kiss and pushed him back against the pillows and slid her leg over until she was on top, her hair falling to curtain her face.

"We've waited long enough, Nick," she panted.

He only had time to grasp her hips before she slid onto him. She was hot. And oh, so tight. *Sweet. Jesus.*

Then she started moving, gyrating against him. Eyes closed, the focused intensity on her face telegraphed something close to ecstasy. He slid his hand up her thigh, across the defined planes of her stomach until he was cupping the soft weight of her breasts. Sam tossed her head back and moved faster. He took her nipples between his thumb and index finger and pinched. She gasped and tensed, closing even tighter around him.

Her, not you. Focus, Pinelli. Her, not you.

He ran his thumb and forefinger lightly up her clit, then down, and felt the twitchy start of her coming.

Then he was gone, over the top. He grabbed her hips as he plunged into her, over and over. She screamed and collapsed on him, her nails biting into his shoulder as they bucked, together.

But that was all background to the roar in his ears, as he shot himself into her, deep, where she began. Finally, she was his. All his.

SHE LAY ON NICK like a blanket, both of them trying to get enough air to sustain life. Deep inside her, unknown muscles spasmed in sparkling aftershocks. Nick responded, twitching. Eventually, her breathing slowed. Her muscles lay slack, so relaxed she felt boneless.

Nick made a contented sound, a combination growl and purr.

She lay, head on his chest, adrift and becalmed, floating in a warm sea.

"I love you, Sam."

She felt the words in his chest, even as her ears heard them. But the warm sea rocked her. The sweet peace deep inside her answered, "And I love you."

Hearing her own words, her muscles tightened, inside, outside.

Have I lost my mind?

She wanted to slap a hand over her mouth, but she was so scattered, she wasn't even sure where her hands were. "I did not say that," she whispered as she slid off him, wanting to melt into the mattress, into the floor.

But Nick wouldn't let her go far. Arm draped across her rib cage, he pulled the disheveled sheet over them and settled, leaning his cheek on his fist. "It's okay, Sam. Even biker chicks are allowed to say it." He grinned, smug.

Maybe so, but I don't—er—didn't.

She felt stunned—her world had been suddenly and truly rocked. Love? Was this even possible? Bina's words whispered through her turmoil. Why couldn't she grab the good stuff for herself? Hadn't she earned it?

A home. Nick. Maybe sometime in the future, a wedding? A vision danced in her mind. Her and Nick, standing on the mariner's compass, in front of the fireplace, a man with a bible before them. A white dress, Jesse at her elbow, Nick in a suit, Carl standing beside him...

And while she was letting herself want, maybe kids, someday? A warm safe heat curled in her chest. God, she sounded like a high-schooler. Next she'd be practicing her signature.

Mrs. Nick Pinelli.

"We've got a lot to talk about." Nick's smile faltered, then fell. The muscles of his face tightened, forming furrows between his eyebrows and beside his mouth. This is what Nick would look like, old. Her happy bubble popped.

"But I need to tell you something first, Sam."

"Just tell me, Nick." She lay, bared in every way possible, waiting his next words, knowing they had the power to change her future.

"They're letting my father out of jail."

That was so not what she'd thought he'd say that her brain ground gears like a student driver on a steep hill. "What?"

"The end of January, he'll be set free. They say my father will have served his *debt*." He spit out the poisonous words.

Her brain caught the proper gear. Thoughts whirred, and after a few seconds, slipped into place. The answer lay before her, shiny and perfect.

NICK WATCHED. SAM'S SMILE didn't begin; it burst on her face, fully formed, lighting her from within. She looked like an angel. An angel with *the* answer. He caught his breath, await-ing the benediction her smile promised.

"He'll never find you, Nick." Her words were soft. She ex-tricated her hands from the covers to touch his jaw. "You can hire someone to manage the shop. Then, after the party, I'll put the house up for sale. We'll be gone before he gets out."

Leave? What? I'm looking for support, to help me stand and face him, and she's talking about running again? What, running is okay if two do it? How could she think I'd leave?

I've been living this little dream, all by myself. She doesn't know me at all.

Gathering steam, she barreled on. "How do you feel about San Francisco? They need towing and repair there, too. You could open a second shop.

"We could drive up the coast in the Jeep. Or in the Love Machine, if you'd rather." Beaming, she raised her hands in a ta-da gesture. "What do you think?"

Nick knew what it felt like, seeing light at the end of the tunnel, and a few seconds later, being flattened by the train. His brain felt bruised by its impact with reality.

You should have known. He rolled away to stare at the ceil-ing as the shiny future he'd held cupped in his hands sifted through his fingers.

"What, Nick?"

"I should have known." Bitter bile built at the back of his throat. He sat up. "You've never pretended to be anything other than the biker chick I met on the side of the road outside town that day." He ground the heels of his hands into his eyes, trying to rub out the vision of this outwardly perfect woman who, inside, was someone he'd never understand. "It's been me, trying to make you into something else."

When she grasped his forearm, he felt panic in her fingers, digging into his skin. Saw it, on her face.

"No, Nick, wait. We'd go *together*. Think about it—what I'm saying makes sense."

He scooted to the edge of the bed. "I let what I felt for you, and what I wanted, blind me."

"I don't understand."

He could see she didn't. "You're a cheetah, Sam. Running is what you're made to do. Cheetahs can't become house cats, even if they wanted to." He shook his head, devastated for them both.

"I'm not leaving Widow's Grove, Sam. Ever. If you understood anything about me, you would have known that." He looked down on her stricken expression. "I'd hoped you'd stand with me."

Her mouth opened, then closed. Her shoulders slumped.

Grief surged up from his gut into his throat. He had to get out of here. He snatched his jeans from the puddle of clothes on the floor, crammed his feet into them and then his shoes. He snatched his shirt but stood with it in his fist.

"Nick, don't. I can—"

"No, Sam, you can't." He shook his head. "You and me, we're too different—you always go, I always stay. It sucks, but that's just the way it is." He reached out to touch her, just once more. But he knew if he did, he wouldn't be able to leave. And then, he'd be lost.

He'd been lost once before. He couldn't risk his sobriety, too.

He dropped his hand to his side and strode for the door before he could do something to embarrass himself further—like throwing a chair through a window.

IT WAS MUCH LATER when Sam sat up in bed. Sinuses swollen, face bloated, it felt as if she'd spent the last hours floating facedown at the bottom of a pool.

When Nick walked away, she'd wanted to flop out of bed and grab his ankles to be dragged across the polished wood floor, all the while begging him not to go. Pride hadn't kept her from it. Not having a valid argument had.

She heard a moan, and at first thought it was coming from her. Sitting up, she listened. A violent wind howled around the eaves of the roof, and rain, hard as pebbles, rattled against the window.

That's not me whining, either. She looked over the edge of the bed. Bugs stared up at her, his entire body quivering. "Oh, Bugs, are you scared?" He whined again. She reached over and, grunting, lifted him. Her bed was normally off-limits to quadrupeds, but tonight, they both needed whatever comfort they could find. Bugs turned around twice and lay down beside her head. She put her arms around him and buried her face in his coat.

What the hell would she have told Nick, to get him to change his mind? That she was wrong? That she'd stay? Oh, sure, the past month or so she'd considered staying—in a daydream kind of way. Her and Nick, playing house. But as he told her why they wouldn't work, the reality of it smacked her in the face.

Her damned internal compass spun in lazy circles, one way, then the other. What should she believe? She now knew the old Sam, inside and out. She knew the little girl. But she didn't know this new Sam. She couldn't trust that she knew what she was doing.

But she trusted Nick's judgment. If he didn't believe she could change, maybe she couldn't. Maybe she *hadn't.*

She wasn't normal. She'd never be entirely whole. How could she have deluded herself into thinking her life would become a Disney movie? A happily-ever-after, complete with bounding squirrels and twittering bluebirds, trailing ribbons?

They'd have ended up sullen and hurt, neither knowing how to break the chain of disappointment, until she grabbed her leathers and helmet, fled to her motorcycle and the road.

But what if, after leaving, she still couldn't leave this place behind her?

What if she'd only swapped one inescapable past for another?

There'd be no getting this right. Ever.

But deep inside, that Disney movie still lived. She never would have admitted that before Widow's Grove.

So maybe she *did* have a small soft spot for happy-ever-afters. But she was also a realist. She was who she was. Bina was right; she was the one who built beautiful homes for other people, then rode away.

But wait, before that...I stayed, then. I took care of Dad.

Yes, she had. And look what that had cost her.

Bugs tried to lick the salt from her cheek. She turned her head, laid it on his warm, pudgy side and listened to the wind howl.

SUNDAY MORNING, SAM woke with a crying-jag hangover and the stench of dog breath in her face. She peeled open sticky eyelids to see Bugs's snoring mug on the pillow next to her.

"Ugh." She wrinkled her nose and rolled out of bed. The sky through the window was powder-blue, with only a few wind-torn clouds.

She patted Bugs's shiny coat. "Come on, dog. I feel a bout of frenzied distraction coming on. After a shower. And coffee."

Bugs closed his eyes.

"Do not get ideas about these sleeping arrangements becoming permanent, bub. Not happening." She dragged him, claws digging for purchase, to the edge of the bed, then lifted him down.

When she stood, an ache between her legs brought back the bittersweet memory of yesterday in high-def detail.

You did it!

Well, technically, Nick had "done" it, but she was right there with him the whole time. If it happened once, that made it possible. God, she hadn't known an orgasm could take the top of her head off. He'd played her body reverently, like an irreplaceable violin. Well, until the end. Her face heated with the memory of their frenzy. And she'd loved every bit of it.

Without her barriers in place, Nick had slid inside of more than her skin. She'd never snuggled up against someone else's soul.

Another ache blossomed. She put her hand to her chest as cold tentacles wrapped around her heart and squeezed.

Looking at the dirty, rumpled, dog-drooled sheets, her stomach turned over. She needed a shower. Bugs needed to go out. But she couldn't live with the evidence of yesterday's triumphant failure one more minute. Leaning over, she ripped the bottom sheet off, rolling the bedding into a giant wad.

The smell of sex and Nick billowed up, filling her head. She breathed in the sweet pain, knowing the memory would have to last a long time. It would be all she had of him. She could have cried—if her body wasn't a wizened shuck.

An hour later, clean and dressed, she stepped onto the back porch. The gale-force winds of last night had tapered to a chilly breeze.

"Whoa." At the edge of the property, the root-ball of a huge eucalyptus confronted her.

Bugs scooted around her legs, bounded down the stairs and across the yard, barking at the tree as if it were a burglar.

Coffee cup steaming, she crossed the yard to survey the damage. The tree stretched into the field a good forty feet, and yet the root ball wasn't much wider than the tree trunk itself. She shuddered, remembering Nick's explanation of how they got the name "widow-makers."

Guess a tree that tall can't survive with that small a root system. She snorted, and shot a look at the sky. "You know I get it, right? Blatant analogies are overkill, don't you think?"

Studying the huge trunk, she pictured a winter fire roaring in the fireplace. The wood would need to dry out and season first, but she could pile it on the back porch, out of the weather.

Not that she'd be here to enjoy it, but someone would.

Feet dragging, she headed for the garage, and her chain saw.

"Sonofabitch!" The wrench clanged to the floor, and Nick grabbed his barked knuckle. He knelt on the cold cement floor of the garage, rocking the pain away, glad there were no customers on Sunday to hear his outburst.

When the pain lessened, he surveyed the damage. Not too much blood, but the long bruise was going to ache for days. He glanced up at the dented gas tank of the Vulcan, and the damned frozen bolts that held it.

"You're as stubborn as your owner, and just as painful." He sucked his knuckle, then picked up the wrench and tried again. He'd located, purchased and installed new rims, but had no luck finding a tank that was less damaged. As much as the idea rankled, he was going to have to repair this one. He only had a couple of weeks.

It was only right that Sam leave town the same way she came in.

And it was his own stupid-ass fault if it left him wrecked.

He took his frustration out on the bolt, hauling on the wrench until he felt the blood pounding in his face. "Arrrgh!" The bolt broke loose with a high-pitched squeal that sounded like his pain. He unscrewed it the rest of the way and dropped it in the handleless coffee mug he'd brought for that purpose.

But she has changed.

The tough biker chick he'd met lying in the mud in Febru-

ary had morphed to someone softer. Someone who adopted a
repugnant stray, became best friends with the queen of Widow's Grove's social scene and helped out local kids. More
than all that, she'd faced the demons of her past and seemed
to be defeating them.

And yesterday, she'd let him in. In that massive bed, there
had been no barriers between them. They'd touched a lot
more than skin. In those few moments before he'd blurted
his hideous news, they'd been closer than he'd ever been to
another person.

He lay in awe of the power of that woman.

Realizing he was going about these bolts the hard way,
he stood and walked to the workbench that spread along the
back wall. He lifted a rubber mallet from its slot on the peg-
board. Pounding would be so much more satisfying. He returned and knelt beside the crippled bike.

If she's changed that much, she could—

Just stop.

That path would twist, back and forth, and end in a swamp
full of scotch.

Widow's Grove was an experiment for Sam—if it all went
bad she could bail, and start over at the next place. She was
like a beautiful wild mare that, the past months, had taken
shelter with a domestic herd. She'd even allowed him to throw
a saddle over her and ride. And that had been a watershed
moment for him.

But as much as he wished it—wanted it—he had no illu-
sions Samantha Crozier had been tamed. Even if she offered
to take him along, her first answer would always be to run.
Even if she agreed to stay, he'd always be waiting for the next
problem, the next disaster that would spook her and drive her
back to the road.

You can't tame a wild thing.

He pounded the wrench with the mallet, and was rewarded with the screech of the next bolt loosening.

He remembered her, looking down on him, wonder on her face as she came apart.

He pounded on the next bolt. It didn't move.

Would he really *want* that wild spirit tamed?

It was a moot point. And at the same time, he was glad that decision wasn't his to make. Because he knew what he'd choose—her by his side, in his bed. In his life. No matter if domestication diminished her. He was just that selfish.

He pounded the wrench, the vibrations making his bruised hand throb.

Finally the bolt let loose with a screech.

"Welcome to the club, you sonofabitch."

"OUCH, JESSE! MY HAIR may look great for the party, but if I've got burn marks on my forehead, it's going to ruin the look, don't you think?" Sam rubbed her singed hairline.

"Oh, quit your whining." Jesse continued wrapping Sam's hair around the steaming curling iron. "My aunt always told me, it hurts to be beautiful."

"In that case, can we just do it until I'm pretty? Beautiful is going to kill me." She'd managed to stay busy, and off Jesse's radar, the past week. But with the party a week away, Sam needed help—stylish female help. Jesse'd come over today to decorate the tree.

Somehow they'd ended up in the bathroom, drinking hot chocolate and demoing new hairstyles.

Jesse sat quiet for at least thirty seconds.

Having never experienced this in Jesse's presence, Sam looked up.

Jesse's expression oozed sadness, like those cheap prints of big-eyed stray cats. "Aren't we friends, Sam?"

The look lasered through Sam's brain to her guilt center.

Damn, she hated that. "What?" Maybe, somehow, the news that Nick dumped her hadn't gotten out in the nine days and fourteen hours since it happened.

"Well, I'm not sure I should say anything." Jesse grabbed another lock of hair and wound it around the curling iron.

Jesse, hesitant to talk? This was serious. "Just tell me."

"No, hon, you tell *me*."

Of course Jesse knew. She probably knew when Sunny's hamster farted. Sam fidgeted in the chair, thinking evisceration was looking like a better option than talking to Jesse about this.

In the mirror's reflection, Jesse's eyes held Sam's.

"Okay, you want to know?" Sam threw her hands up. "Nick dumped me. You happy now?"

Jesse's eyes got big. "That's not—"

"No, you're right. It's worse than that. He broke up with me after we'd just finished incredible, red-butt monkey sex, and I had the first orgasm of my life."

Jesse's mouth opened, and her eyes got bigger.

"Well, actually, the first and second of my life, but it doesn't matter, because I'm sure they'll be the last in my entire existence, and that's only the least of my problems, because his RSVP came back marked No, and I miss him so bad I can taste it, and I'm sleeping with a drooling dog with a case of bad breath, and am happy to, because then at least I'm not alone in that huge bed—" Her voice broke, so she stopped.

"Holy shit, girlfriend." Jesse dropped to her knees beside the chair. "You love him bad, don't you?"

At her nod, Jesse put her arms around Sam.

When the flood ebbed a bit, Jesse asked in a whisper, "You never had the Big O? As in *never?*"

Sam grabbed a tissue from the counter and blew her nose. "You caught me in a moment of weakness. We are *not* discussing that."

Jess sat on the edge of the toilet, elbows on her knees, hands dangling. "That's what girlfriends *do,* Sam."

"Well, this one doesn't." She mopped her face. "Jesus, Jesse, you have to admit I've come a long way. I'm sitting here with my girlfriend, trying out new hairstyles, crying over a man." She hiccupped a half laugh. "I've turned into a friggin' country-western song!" She dropped her face in her hands.

"He told me that you dumped *him.*" Jesse's voice was quiet.

Sam lifted her head. "He probably just did that to be gallant. I've never been dumped before, but I'm pretty sure I know the difference between dumper and dumpee. The dumper is the one who walks out."

"What happened?"

It came out. The whole sordid story. After, Sam sat deflated, worrying a damp tissue, but better. Just as Bina had said, talking to someone made it hurt a bit less.

"All right." Jesse crossed her arms under her ample chest. "You went down that pretty road with Nick, and now that you see where it leads, you're scared." She nodded, as if agreeing with herself. "Poop-your-pants scared."

"I thought you, of all people, would understand, Jess."

"Oh, I do. I understand that you've walked right up to the edge of wonderful, and you're too damn scared to take that last step." Jesse speared her with a look. "You're the biker chick. The toughest woman I know. What the hell are you afraid of?"

"A zillion things! What if we don't agree? What if we get bored? What if—"

"So what? If it happens, you make another decision." Jesse's features softened to something like pity. "No one has a crystal ball, Sam. I didn't when I left school with a duffel bag full of clothes and a huge heartache. For all I knew, Carl wouldn't want me back. Maybe the café couldn't support us.

Maybe," she threw up her hands, "a zillion things. You just do the best you can, and trust your gut."

"Yeah, but—"

"So the future's coming at you faster than you're comfortable with. Welcome to the human race, Sam. If you've learned anything since you got here, I'd have thought you'd learned that you can't run from yourself. Wherever you go, you're still there."

Sam knew that. Really, she did. But the clean, free, song of the road still pulled at her.

A crease appeared between Jesse's sculpted eyebrows. "And guess what? You're not the only one on the planet who's got a lot to lose. After all, if it goes bad, you get on your bike and leave. Nick stays. He faces his problems. Every day. One day at a time."

The reminder that Nick had fears and failings, too, made her feel about two inches tall—about cockroach height. God, was she *that* self-centered that she'd never considered Nick's insecurities?

She must have had a stricken look, because Jess reached out, patted her arm and smiled. "Honey, don't you see? Life's a crap shoot, and for once, you rolled eleven. You did the hard part. Now all you need to do is pick up your winnings."

Somehow, it didn't feel that easy. "You make it sound so simple."

"Simple? Maybe not. But stop thinking about it, Sam. Shut out all the facts and figures, and just *feel.* You'll know what to do." She dusted her hands on her perfect wool slacks. "Now, let's go downstairs, and add a little booze to this hot chocolate. I think we've earned it."

CHAPTER TWENTY

NICK STOPPED PACING. *Enough. Just man up and do it.*

He was sick of arguing with himself. Sick of not acknowledging what he had to do. Sick of his father in his life.

As long as he let those damn letters lie like land mines waiting to go off, his father would influence him, even if it were only by avoidance. He knew this was the next step to moving past what happened—and maybe it would strengthen him enough to deal, when the real man showed up in Widow's Grove. He strode to the kitchen, his guts writhing.

Sam did the work. You can, too.

He jerked open the drawer. Fifteen years—fifteen letters. He snatched up the oldest first, ripped it open, and began to read.

AN HOUR LATER, Nick sat at his desk in the shop, feeding the letters into the shredder. He enjoyed watching the noxious paper turn to harmless confetti at the bottom of the trash can. With every sheet, he felt lighter—cleaner.

He'd given those letters a bigger place in his brain than they'd deserved, all these years. They held no surprises. He'd been silly to think they would. How could they? Donatello Pinelli was always the center of his own universe. Everyone he knew orbited him. A handsome, charismatic man, with a massive ego and vicious temper when things didn't go his way.

The letters were full of excuses, rationalizations and arguments why Nick should forgive. This year's went so far as to suggest Nick should visit him. They'd have a good father-son talk.

Yeah, like that's going to happen.

Hatred still burned like battery acid in his blood, but at least the angst was gone. He felt better about himself. Maybe there was hope that Nick Pinelli was man enough to wipe clean the black marks on the Pinelli name.

BECAUSE OF THE crazy-busy days and restless nights, time advanced. The day of the party arrived. Sam ran shaky hands over her clothes, surveying herself in the soft bathroom lights. The claret velvet, full skirt brushed the floor, making her waist look tiny. The tightly fitted ivory blouse had a high collar that elongated her neck. The ecru lace sleeves were full at the top, but tightly fitted cuffs started at the elbow. Dozens of tiny pearl buttons trailed down the front, and from elbow to wrist. Sam turned to catch her profile. The outfit looked classy, in-period, feminine.

Maybe it was worth the time to button all the damn things after all.

Despite her misgivings, she'd attempted a period hairstyle. It looked simple when Jess did it. Just curl everything, pull it into a loose, twisted bun on the top of her head, and leave a few tendrils to trail down her neck. It looked good, too. No one would guess it took two hours and three burned fingers to get it that way.

The red crystal choker and tiered earrings flashed in the light, adding a touch of sexy to the buttoned-up outfit. She leaned in and carefully applied the ruby lipstick she'd bought to match the necklace, then stepped back.

If Nick could only see me.

She glared at herself in the mirror. *He chose not to be here. Remember?*

She walked downstairs, casting a critical eye to be sure no

detail had been missed. The caterer's voices echoed as they banged around the kitchen. She missed the sound of Bugs's nails on the hardwood floors, but knew it boded better for the party that he was having a sleepover with Bina's dogs.

Breathing in the heavenly scent of fresh evergreen, she crossed to the parlor and plugged in the lights on the massive Christmas tree in the front window. Transparent lights reflected in the dark windowpanes, and the frilly Victorian ornaments made the tree look as if it had time-traveled from the past.

Everything was in place. Perfect. She should be feeling festive. Celebratory. Smug, even.

"Get a grip, Crozier. You had a life before Nick Pinelli. You're going to have to pull on your biker-girl panties and make a life without him."

The doorbell interrupted her thoughts. She retraced her steps to the foyer and opened the door. Tim and Ana stood in the porch light, resplendent in holiday finery. Ana sported sprigs of holly pinned to the collar of her green dress, and twined in her silver braided coronet.

Tim wore a suit with a bright red vest and green-and-red plaid bow tie. He looked more like one of Santa's elves than the troll she'd met all those months ago.

"Oh, you two look wonderful!" She stepped back. "I'm honored to welcome you to my home."

Tim bustled his date across the threshold like a hen with her chick.

"The bar is set up in the great room, Tim. Why don't you get Ana a drink?" She turned to close the door, but saw Carl and Jesse climbing the porch steps. Several cars were pulling up out front.

It's showtime.

AN HOUR LATER, Sam added two more coats to the mound covering her bed. She walked to the railing of the loft, toed off her shoes and leaned her forearms on the evergreen-festooned banister, taking a quiet moment to watch the party, unobserved.

The scene looked like a modern-day Norman Rockwell painting. The great room was filled with brightly clad people, standing in scattered groups, drinking and talking. A fire burned in the massive fireplace, the mantel above dripped evergreen boughs and artfully arranged Christmas ornaments. The aromas of pine, cinnamon and turkey drifted to her, along with snatches of conversations and the carolers' harmony.

Jesse's cornflower-blue satin dress seemed to collect the light, perfectly suiting her blue eyes and porcelain complexion. The bodice was tightly fitted, but the skirt fell in lustrous folds, looking Hollywood-runway perfect. She and Carl were talking to Dan Porter, who had shed his suit coat to display a wide set of suspenders with surfing reindeer.

The mayor and his wife admired the mariner's compass in front of the blazing fireplace. Beau glowed, most likely more from praise than the heat of the fire. He looked very grown up in a suit and tie. She smiled, knowing that Tim had advised Beau what to wear. Beau's parents had been invited, but Sam felt relief when they declined. The thought of Mrs. Tripp celebrating around an open bar made her cringe.

Pete and his mother stood talking to Sunny and her parents. Several regulars from the diner had arrived, as well as quite a few couples she'd gotten acquainted with at the Jurgens'.

She'd invited everyone she knew in town, with the exception of Brad Sexton. Perverts weren't her idea of fun party guests.

Bina's saloon-girl laugh overrode the din. She stood out in black silk lounge pants and an electric blue sequined halter, her hair shining like molten onyx. Her husband, Shiv, sat in a chair nearby, balancing a plate of hors d'oeuvre on his knee.

Sam could just glimpse the edge of the snowy linen-covered buffet tables crowded with chafing dishes and platters of food.

Jesse was right. She'd gotten lucky, that rainy day she'd wrecked, outside of Widow's Grove. Her perfect career had led her to where she stood today, looking down on her beautiful Victorian filled with friends. It was so much more than she'd ever had—ever thought she could have.

And, for a few perfect moments last week, in the bed behind her, she'd had it all.

Too bad you realized that too late.

But Nick's news that day had come as a shock, and she'd blurted out the first answer that came to her brain. After that, it was too late. She'd ruined everything.

Sam fingered the garland on the rail under her hand. The dumb part was that she *knew* running wouldn't help. She'd learned the hard way that fear always caught up, even if she leaned over the Vulcan's tank and buried the throttle.

She snorted at the irony. Everyone thought Sam Crozier was so brave. Yet fear had ruled every decision she'd made. She'd wasted so much time looking back over her shoulder.

Maybe it was time she faced front, looking ahead to whatever came next.

Maybe bravery grew from living your life as if you weren't afraid.

No maybe about it. It was time.

It had taken losing Nick to jolt her from the past. For the first time in her life, she'd stumbled onto somewhere she actually fit. Damned if she'd squander any more time, focusing on what she didn't have, instead of all the wonderful things she did: devoted friends, a great group of teens to work with, a dog. And she actually owned the gorgeous house spread below her.

Joy rose, flooding her with well-being. Could this be contentment?

Decided, she marched downstairs. In the hall, she snatched a flute of champagne from a passing server's tray. She walked to stand in front of the fireplace, borrowed a fork from Shiv, and tapped her glass to get everyone's attention.

"Welcome, everyone, and thank you for coming tonight to help me celebrate the season, and the renovation of this beautiful house."

Pete's voice yelled from the back of the room, "Way to go, Sam!"

Laughing, several people applauded.

She smiled. "I told Jesse that I wanted to throw this party to thank you all for welcoming me to Widow's Grove. That was true, but I had other motives as well." She waved her glass at the room. "I thought dressing the old girl up in Christmas finery would tempt one of you to buy her." She lowered her glass, and her voice. "I also thought I'd drum up some interest in a new home for a bulldog I know."

She couldn't repress a huge smile. "But I want you to know. As of right now, both are off the market. I've decided to stay here, in Widow's Grove."

Jesse squealed. Everyone clapped.

Sam held up a hand. "Don't get me wrong. If anyone notices the superior workmanship of my team and has a project in mind, I'd be happy to give you my card."

Several people laughed, and everyone seemed to talk at once.

Ting, ting, ting. She had to tap her glass for attention.

"I'd like to propose a toast." She raised her glass, and waited for her friends to do the same.

"To the road. To Widow's Grove. To all my friends.

"And, as a friend of mine once said, *'Per cent'anni'*—for a hundred years."

WHEN JESSE FINALLY stopped hugging her, and after being congratulated by every guest, Sam retreated to the kitchen to regroup. She liked these people. Really. But large groups still overwhelmed her.

The kitchen wasn't any calmer. Caterers bustled, prepping trays for the buffet, and servers flitted in and out like nesting birds. Sam abandoned her barely touched champagne on the counter and headed for the back door.

She stepped onto the porch and released a held breath that came out in an icy cloud. The air was still, and as crisp as a fall apple. Her velvet skirt was warm but the cotton-and-lace blouse wasn't. She crossed her arms, tucking her hands in her armpits to preserve heat. The yard lay before her, wrapped in shadows cast by a flashlight moon. The stars glinted like hammered chips of silver on a black velvet sky.

For once, peace wasn't only external. Under her skin, anxiety lay down before a burgeoning *rightness*. She stood, relishing it. The thrum of disquiet had been a part of her for so long, she wasn't sure how to feel without it.

But I could get used to this pretty quickly. Smiling, she hugged herself tighter.

It was time to replace nightmares with good dreams; and for once, dreaming felt safe. She didn't need Bina to tell her that she'd turned a corner tonight. This time, she was staying.

"Staying." It even sounded right, said out loud.

"Born to be Wild," the road song that was every biker's anthem, drifted through her mind.

With an echoed ache of longing, guilt nipped her conscience.

But staying didn't mean she had to give up riding. After all, some of the most beautiful roads she'd ever ridden began at the bottom of her driveway. There would be weekends and vacations enough to slake her thirst for the road. And how much more fun would riding be looking forward, knowing she had the comfort of her own house waiting? Her sudden shiver was only partially due to the chill.

She became aware of a sound—a throbbing undertone that she now realized she'd been hearing awhile.

That's a diesel engine.

She stepped off the porch and walked around the side of the house.

The windows threw rectangles of yellow light on the concrete as she navigated a way between parked cars.

A flatbed idled on the road in front of the house. Her heart skipped at the sign: Pinelli's Repair and Tow.

She stumbled to a stop, afraid to move forward. But on the truck bed, chrome gleamed in the moonlight.

The Vulcan!

She stood, feelings roaring through her. The wind, singing its one-note song in her ears. The sun, warm through her leathers. Feeling the throttle, power, under her hand.

A shadow of a man reached for the handlebars, and she heard the kickstand snap up.

Nick. Her heart stumbled as her feet had seconds before. Her hopes and the confidence she'd felt, surrounded by her friends, went into free fall—ending in a splatter on the driveway at her feet.

He's only here to deliver the bike.

How could she face Nick with their breakup, reeking and bloated, between them? Her heart galloped, battering her ribs. She threw her shoulders back and sucked in her stomach. But that didn't matter, because she was staying. She'd have to get used to seeing him only as her mechanic.

Somehow.

Forcing her reluctant feet forward, she walked to the truck, arriving as the bike's back tire touched the tarmac. Her helmet swung from the handlebars. Coward that she was, she kept her focus on the bike.

Seeing it up close sent a fountain of joy shooting through her chest. The moonlight shone off polished chrome, and even in the dim light, she could see the candy-apple red of the gas tank. The leather of the seat was cold and hard under her fingers. So were the handlebars.

It was *perfect*.

She forced herself to stop stroking her bike, and look at the man who held it upright.

He looks awful.

Two days of stubble darkened his cheeks, and his hair looked like it hadn't been combed in at least as long. Even in the moonlight, she could see the bags under his eyes.

"Nick, what's wrong?"

He dropped the side stand and leaned the bike on it. Even his smile looked tired. "I just haven't slept in a while. I wanted to get this to you way before dark, but I just finished it an hour ago."

One recalcitrant curl hung on his forehead, and his soft dark eyes made her stomach ache. He wore the same clothes he had the first time she'd met him; a white shirt with a windbreaker thrown over it, a patch declaring his name on the breast.

He looks wonderful.

She allowed herself one last stroke of the tank. "You did a beautiful job. Thank you."

THE MOMENT STRETCHED out as he stood there, tongue-tied, not knowing how to start. His brain felt stale and sluggish, like his furry tongue after a night of drinking. He was so damned tired, he'd had to roll the windows down on the way out to stay awake. But he was determined to keep working until he completed his delivery.

Liar.

He'd wanted to see her, to watch her face light up when she saw the Vulcan. He wanted to feel what he felt right now— dorkishly delighted at having made Sam happy.

Then reality hit. He'd been so focused on the clock, he'd forgotten—he'd just made it possible for her to ride out of his life.

She looked fantastic. All prim and formal, with her hair swept on top of her head, looking like she'd stepped off a fashion plate from nineteen hundred. But her full lower lip and long, sexy neck reminded him of the woman beneath the proper clothes.

Jesus, she had to be freezing. *You have a jacket on, idiot.* He shrugged it off, and though she raised her hands in protest, settled it on her shoulders.

"Thank you. Again."

"Oh. I brought you something else." He unbuckled the black leather side bag with the dangling fringe and extracted his surprise; a candy-apple-red cruiser helmet, not much bigger than a yarmulke. He'd seen it in a catalog, and had imagined her riding in it, blond hair streaming. "I bought it months ago. Before..." Skirting quicksand, he started again. "I figured it would be fine for around town. It just seemed to belong with the bike." And with her.

Her smile wrenched his heart.

"It's perfect, Nick. I love it. Thank you." She stood for a time, looking down at the helmet. "I'm so sorry."

She said it so softly, he almost missed it.

"It was the wrong thing to say. Here you were worried about your father coming back. I wanted to save you, and I just blurted out the first answer that popped into my head."

When she looked up, the pain in her eyes hurt him. "I'll be all right, Sam. I've been working through it. If he has the guts to show his face in Widow's Grove, I'll be fine."

"I'm *so* glad." He heard her swallow. "I know you wouldn't leave, Nick. And I so admire that about you." She hung the clasped chin strap over her arm. "I just wanted you to know."

He caught movement at the corner of his vision and

glanced to the house to see Jesse, standing in the light of the open front door. Sam followed his line of sight. She tsked, and made shooing movements with her hands. Jesse put a hand on her hip in a pantomime of annoyance, but after a moment, went back inside.

"Jeez, that woman is like a momma hen." Sam stood facing away from him. "I wanted to tell you, if you need a friend to talk to when your father is released, I'm at the other end of a cell phone." She turned to him with a sad, crooked smile. "Especially late at night."

It tore at him, that sadness. Even before they'd been lovers, they'd been good friends. He so missed that. He wanted to reach out and wrap himself around her, to tell her they could make it work.

But he couldn't.

Long-distance relationships didn't work—especially when one party never planned to come back. He put his hands in his back pockets to take away the temptation. "Do you have any idea when you're leaving?"

SAM SWAYED, SUDDENLY dizzy. Realizing her knees were locked, she forced the muscles in her thighs to unclench. This was it. She'd know in a minute if she could still have Nick as a friend.

She couldn't dare hope for more.

"That's the thing, Nick. I just realized tonight that I'm not." She tried to halt her limbs shaking with a deep breath.

"You're not leaving." He frowned.

She nodded.

He cocked his head. "As in never?"

Didn't he care if she stayed? Had she ruined things so completely that they couldn't even be friends?

She made her feet be still, when they would have walked her back up the hill to hide in her house.

No, dammit. She was done running.

If she wanted it all, she'd have to risk it all.

She dug her nails into her palms, hoping the pain would grant her courage. "Why would I, when I've found everything I could ever want, right here in Widow's Grove?"

"Everything?" In the false daylight moon, she saw the hope on his face.

Hope balled in her throat so tight, the words wouldn't squeeze past. She nodded, instead.

"Whoop!" His shout echoed off the hills.

Then she was in his arms—Nick's strong, safe arms, with the smell of him filling her head. The world spun again, but this time, it felt perfectly right.

He leaned her back over his arm, watching her face. "It won't always be easy, you know. You could get scared again."

She put her hands around his neck, into the hair that curled at his nape, and brought her lips so close they tingled with the need to touch. "How could I leave? My mechanic is here." She brushed her lips across his, intending a kiss of welcome.

But he opened his mouth and took her in, his tongue taking and giving. His arms tightened, as if he'd never let her go. And that was just the way she wanted it. A blowtorch of heat drove the shivers from her body.

Oh, God, how did I ever think I was tough enough to leave him?

Suddenly, sound intruded. Nick lifted his head. "We have company."

She wasn't going to look. Embarrassed, she dropped her forehead to his chest. "Just Jesse, or all of them?"

Before Nick could speak, raucous cheering and applause gave her the answer. A long wolf whistle pierced the din. Sam knew that whistle. She turned, to the assemblage that filled the front porch.

Nick didn't let her go, just stood, arms around her waist.

"Way to go, Pinelli!" Jesse pumped her arm like a crazed football fan.

Nick inclined his head. Heart in her throat, Sam curtsied, then waved all her idiot guests back inside.

Jesse shot them a thumbs-up, then turned to herd everyone to the door.

Sam handed Nick the red helmet and lifted her old black one from the handlebars, then walked to the other side of the bike. Giggling, she hiked up her skirt and threw her leg over, gasping as the cold air hit her thighs.

Nick's eyes got big.

She straightened the bike and tried to release the kickstand.

"Damned girly shoes," she muttered, and tried again. When it retracted with a clunk, she settled the helmet on her head.

Nick held out the cherry-red helmet. "You don't want the new one?"

She snapped the closure. "Are you kidding?" She lifted her chin and tried for haughty. "It clashes with my skirt."

Looking poleaxed, Nick's gaze traced her long exposed legs, to her waist, and higher, coming to rest on her face. "Wow. You have changed."

She chuckled, turned the key, pulled in the clutch and fired up the bike. The engine caught with its deep, throaty rumble that settled in her chest.

Oh, man, she'd missed this. She closed her eyes, savoring.

She opened her eyes to Nick's smug smile. "Well? Slap that helmet on, Pinelli. If you're going to be a biker chick's dude, you'd better get used to it."

"Hey, I was born to be wild." He donned the helmet, fumbling with the buckle.

He reached down to drop the foot pegs, then threw his leg over the bike.

She watched over her shoulder. "Sorry about the butt-floss seat. Guess we're going to have to get a better one."

"Oh, I don't know." His arms came around her, warm, steady. "I could get used to this." His voice next to her ear overrode the growl of the engine. "Ready."

Heaven. I'm in Heaven.

With a flick of her toe, she dropped it into gear. Easing the clutch, she opened the throttle and inched the bike around the tow truck.

She goosed the throttle again, just to feel him tighten his grip on her.

Then they were flying. The bike's vibrations shooting sparkles of happiness through her. Laughter bubbled out, only to be snatched away by the wind.

"Hey, Pinelli," she shouted over her shoulder. "You know any good road songs?"

* * * * *